Threshold

Threshold

Stories

CAROL BRUNEAU

Vagrant Press is an imprint of
Nimbus Publishing Limited
3660 Strawberry Hill St, Halifax, NS, B3K 5A9
(902) 455-4286 nimbus.ca

Nimbus Publishing is based in Kjipuktuk, Mi'kma'ki, the traditional territory of the Mi'kmaq People.

Printed and bound in Canada

Editor: Paula Sarson
Editor for the press: Whitney Moran
Cover image: *Herring Cove, look-off trail* (2019) 36 x 36, acrylic on canvas
© Jeremy Vaughan
Cover design: Jenn Embree
Typesetting: Rudi Tusek
NB1686

This is a work of fiction. While certain characters are inspired by real persons, and certain events by events which may have happened, these stories are works of the imagination not to be taken as a literal or documentary representation of its subject.

Library and Archives Canada Cataloguing in Publication

Title: Threshold : stories / Carol Bruneau.
Names: Bruneau, Carol, 1956- author.
Identifiers: Canadiana (print) 20230586139 | Canadiana (ebook) 20230586155 | ISBN 9781774712719
(softcover) | ISBN 9781774712986 (EPUB)
Subjects: LCGFT: Short stories.
Classification: LCC PS8553.R854 T47 2024 | DDC C813/.54—dc23

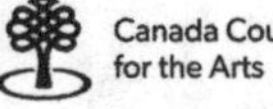

Nimbus Publishing acknowledges the financial support for its publishing activities from the Government of Canada, the Canada Council for the Arts, and from the Province of Nova Scotia. We are pleased to work in partnership with the Province of Nova Scotia to develop and promote our creative industries for the benefit of all Nova Scotians.

PRAISE FOR CAROL BRUNEAU

ADVANCE PRAISE FOR *THRESHOLD*

"Carol Bruneau brings you to the threshold of life in every one of her stories. She seeks out the breaking point of our hearts and minds; our internal landscape, against the vibrant panorama of the world and our place in it. This is personal. Halifax is her city, good and bad, and we are incredibly lucky to have such a knowledgeable, nuanced, and endearing voice to bring it to us. She is a marvel. You don't get better than this."

—LESLEY CREWE, national bestselling author of *Recipe for a Good Life*

"In *Threshold*, Carol Bruneau makes visible those almost imperceptible moments when what one believes, or what is expected, begins to unravel. Nothing, it turns out, is stable. The logic of time, of how things unfold, collides with the truth—that everything will fall apart. In these keenly observant stories, beauty and fear comingle, but Bruneau's protagonists roll with life's little tsunamis because, well, life simply goes on, no matter what."

—SHANI MOOTOO, Giller Prize–shortlisted author of *Polar Vortex*

"These are stories of great power and insight. Bruneau illuminates her fictional world with a light so clear and bright that in it we can see into the shadows of our own world, into the usually unuttered spaces between human action and intent, between what we mean to each other and our usually inadequate attempts to articulate that meaning. And the source of that light is Bruneau's powerfully controlled language, never flashy or extravagant, every sentence perfect unto its purpose. *Threshold* is an admirable and inspiring work."

—LEO MCKAY JR., Giller Prize–shortlisted author of *Like This* and *What Comes Echoing Back*

"Masterful. With deep heart and deft prose, and a true understanding of the short story form, Bruneau presents characters jostled out of their complacencies and colliding with forces they can neither fully understand nor control. The characters in *Threshold*, who might easily be your neighbours, are by turns hilarious, petty, loving, and self-absorbed as they blunder, stumble, hop, and fall towards recognition of failure, empathy, love, and, perhaps, grace. As do we. Shall we cross the threshold?"

—MICHELLE BUTLER HALLETT, Thomas Head Raddall Atlantic Fiction Award–winning author of *Constant Nobody*

BRIGHTEN THE CORNER WHERE YOU ARE

Longlisted, 2022 DUBLIN Literary Award

"Dazzling! A poignant imagining of Maud Lewis's life; as colourful and joyous as Lewis's art, as bleak as an abandoned garden in February. Bruneau's vivid imagery and deceptively simple prose create a portrait of a woman so full of pluck, talent, humour and compassion that it will never leave me."

—LAUREN B. DAVIS, author of *Our Daily Bread* and *The Empty Room*

"An unforgettable character portrayal, Maud's companionable voice will stay with readers long after the last page."

–EMILY URQUHART, author of *Ordinary Wonder Tales*

"This book is beautiful, as rich and uplifting as it is a literary masterpiece."

–KERRY CLARE, author of *Asking for a Friend*

A CIRCLE ON THE SURFACE

Winner, 2019 Jim Connors Dartmouth Book Award for Fiction

"Told with a meticulous eye for detail, Bruneau's voice is simple, elegant, arresting. A portrait of a partnership in peril, *A Circle on the Surface* lingers for days after its final page is turned."

–TORONTO STAR

"A quietly brilliant novel."

–QUILL & QUIRE, starred review

A BIRD ON EVERY TREE

Finalist, 2018 Thomas Head Raddall Atlantic Fiction Award

"This is no mere exercise in voice: this is a reflection of a writer utterly in touch with her stories... Bruneau is a master. We should know this by now, but *A Bird on Every Tree* is a powerful reminder."

–QUILL & QUIRE, starred review

"12 beautifully crafted short stories. Her exceptional prose reveals how much there is to discover in the everyday.... Bruneau does not settle for cliché. Her prose is accessible and lean as she flits into her characters' lives."

–PUBLISHER'S WEEKLY

"Each of Carol Bruneau's stories is not so much told as meticulously shaped with exacting and mesmerizing attention to every gorgeous detail. Bruneau submerges the reader entirely in the physical and emotional worlds she so vividly evokes."

–LYNN COADY, Giller Prize–winning author of *Hellgoing*

"In *A Bird on Every Tree* we run through a wide range of twelve beautiful and genuine stories, all connected through the considerable pull of Nova Scotia.... The tying knot pulsing through these stories seems to be that you can leave, but you will still be tethered to Nova Scotia. Perhaps by some long invisible salt chain, a guiding light reminding you of where you come from, the sea-bound coast; home."

–ATLANTIC BOOKS TODAY

For my dear ones, especially Elijah

Bless the procession
of night owls
that do not fear the spectre
of unknown roads.

–Edith Stein, "Lord Bless All People"

A threshold is not a simple boundary: it is
a frontier that divides two different territories,
rhythms, and atmospheres.

–John O'Donohue, *To Bless the Space Between Us*

Perfect love drives out fear.

–John 4:11–18

Turn Our Mourning into Dance

THE MOST RECENT SIGHTING WAS PURE BLINK-AND-you'll-miss-it, though it unfolded so vividly it left Charlotte weak-kneed. It was a February afternoon. Wet snowflakes swirled and jitterbugged. Her mom was huddled with some people waiting for a bus outside a boarded-up shop on Barrington Street. She was doing a little dance to keep warm before she turned her back. But it was her all right. Anna, her mother. No question. She had on black winter boots and her maroon coat with its black fur collar. She didn't see Charlotte waving, frantically, from the opposite sidewalk as the bus pulled up.

By the time Charlotte crossed over, dodging cars, the bus was inching into traffic. She glimpsed her mom taking a seat as the bus lurched away. She kept waving, but Anna didn't see her. In a matter of seconds she was gone—again.

The sighting before this, Charlotte had spotted her mother, the back of her, from a distance going into Sobeys. The same coat and boots, but this time Anna was wearing a hat Charlotte didn't recognize. A black loop-knitted thing that, well, would appeal to what she remembered of her mom's tastes. Yes, it was her all right, pulling out a tissue and running it over the cart's handle—a bit much. But, being a nurse, she was something of a germaphobe. She had managed to glide past a table of kids collecting money for hockey. Charlotte wasn't so lucky, stuck behind the hockey moms. Before she could call out, Anna had disappeared inside the store. Her mother always was quick on her feet. She had also been into eating healthy, so Charlotte hoped to head her off in produce, or possibly seafood.

But her mother was not to be seen in either section.

Charlotte continued pushing the cart she'd grabbed by the entrance. Force of habit. It was hard to enter the store without a cart; she was always here picking up something. With a husband and a teenager to feed, the place was her second home.

Too late, she glimpsed a flash of maroon at the far end of Pet Food & Detergents. Fine, she would catch Anna in Baking Needs, her mom's favourite section, though it had been years since Anna had baked anything. Thank goodness for when she *had* baked. Charlotte blinked, savouring thoughts of brownies tasty enough to counter other memories of Anna's cooking. Three hundred ways to serve lentils and save the planet.

"You can dress them up all you want, Mom, but you can't hide what they are." She still remembered complaining, her mother biting her tongue. What a relief when they'd gone back to pork chops. Anna never was the most attentive cook. But, having a family of her own, cooking endless meals, Charlotte could empathize, albeit thirty years too late.

In Baking Needs the only shopper was a guy on his phone discussing prunes. Since they were right there, Charlotte threw a couple of bags of chocolate chips into the cart. At the end of the aisle she caught a whiff of something familiar—the way her mother's top bureau drawer used to smell. The dust of spilled talcum powder on costume jewellery. Cedar and a sickly sweetness.

Her mom was from a time and place where nobody threw things out. *You never know when you might need it.* Like an older sister's worn-out coat, cut down to make a new one. For herself.

Who even thought about such extreme recycling these days? But Anna had grown up that way, a born whiz at letting out and taking in. Making old stuff new, making stuff last.

"You've been wearing that forever. You could buy a replacement," Charlotte had said, before her mother got sick.

"Replace *this* colour? But, it's so becoming."

Charlotte still remembered rolling her eyes. "Becoming *what?*"

The cedar-perfumey scent drifted from one aisle over, Pasta & Canned Vegetables. Charlotte ditched the cart, never mind the chocolate chips or her pretense of shopping, and bolted toward it. She narrowly avoided toppling a tower of boxed cereal.

The fragrance clung to the air exactly as it had to Charlotte's fingers when she was small and would pick through her mother's treasures while she napped. Anna's naps had enabled her to clomp around in her mom's high heels and pink ball gown, clip-on earrings and plastic pearls.

Her mother would open one eye, smile, and say nothing. Charlotte couldn't really remember Anna using talcum powder, though the tins were always half-empty and its smell followed her.

Despite the scent's vague, lingering sweetness, there wasn't a trace of Anna in the next aisle or the next, Cooking Oils & Condiments. Beside the ketchup Charlotte stopped, emboldened enough to call in a loud whisper, "Mom?"

She considered going to customer service, having an announcement made over the PA: "Would Mrs. Batherson come to the desk, please. Your adult daughter's looking for you." An ask no different from those of mothers with wandering little kids.

Anna would have killed her, though, for drawing such attention—except, after all this time she might find it amusing?

A sense of humour helps, Charlotte recalled her mother saying, though as Anna's illness had progressed this outlook had eroded.

Suddenly, the scent was gone. Not a trace lingered.

Charlotte swallowed a bitter taste in her mouth. Then, just to be sure, she checked the last aisle, Frozen Foods. Nada. Squeezing past the speedy checkout, she heard the cashier ask, "Find everything you were looking for today?"

Just outside, there was Anna—no, her lookalike—loading grocery bags into an SUV. The sort of vehicle her mother would've found too big and flashy. The woman turned; of course it wasn't her. Yet Charlotte distinctly heard a voice like hers: "Oh my, don't those Cape Bretoners love their cars—live in a shack as long as they can drive a Gran Torino."

The remark was chased by her memory of a phlegmy laugh and her mother's words when she had stopped laughing at things. "If I'd never left Cape Breton I'd never have gotten sick."

"And you wouldn't have had me," Charlotte repeated it now.

"Sorry?" said a man getting out of his car.

She shrugged, arranging her smile. Fought a stray tear, watching the SUV drive off.

At home she checked for messages. There was just one, a voice telling her the warranty was up on a car she didn't own. The way the caller skipped over the first O was how her mom had said Toyota.

She started fixing supper, a frozen lasagna Anna would've loved except for the price. Any minute Ted would be home from work and, she hoped, Bethy would emerge from the basement. Of course the two would expect a feast to have been whipped up at a text's ping. Forget that Bethany kept herself holed up, lounging all day while supposedly looking for work.

"Charlotte!" The voice came as if from the next room, caught her unaware. A chill slid from her ear to her clavicle, the space at the bottom of her throat. Bold, desperate, even a little angry, it had the same tone as Anna's words when she'd come home from hospital. "What am I supposed to do now? Wait for a cure, or hell to freeze?"

Charlotte dropped the lettuce she was rinsing, crept

into the family room. The 24/7 news channel played soundlessly over the flat screen. More footage of killing in various places around the world, a too familiar ad for a sugarless drink. A crooner wearing a tux mouthed lyrics to the song. Anna's voice filled in the sound, a melodious rendition of Nat King Cole: "In time the Rockies... crumble, Gibraltar...tumble /...only made of clay." On the coffee table lay her mother's tattered blue paperback copy of Betty Friedan's *The Feminine Mystique.* Somehow it had migrated here, and Charlotte left it on display not completely as a joke, hoping Bethy might read it.

She picked up her phone, tapped in the number. Scary how after so long it was still right there in her head. But then she heard Ted coming in and hung up before the call could go through.

"Who was on the phone?" He touched her arm lightly. "Bethy needs a ride from somewhere?" As if Bethy had left the basement.

"Nobody. It was nobody." Before she could muster a smile she watched his chin slacken. The jowly look he'd always had, perhaps, before she had really noticed it. Maybe even before they were married?

"Charlotte. For Christ's sake. When are you going to accept—?"

His look made her want to scream. "I do. I totally accept it. Not like there's a choice, is there?"

Ted looked away, clicked on the volume. The news had an item about dancing. Stooped seniors shuffled around an institutional-looking room. The couples made her think of winter-weary birds slow dancing. Birds that had been frozen then thawed, waking, and in a time-lapsed video, whirled stiffly around a ballroom with disco lighting.

Then an updated image flashed of the same pairs. Smiling, laughing dance partners twirled once-rigid mates by arms grown suddenly limber, guided their suddenly gliding feet.

Partners too cheery and well-rested to be their mates' life ones.

"Dance therapy provides big relief for sufferers of Parkinson's," the voice-over blared. "Simple as one-two-three."

Stunned, Charlotte listened with her hand over her mouth. Why had the therapy only now been discovered? How could it have taken so long?

It was as if Anna were trapped inside an eggshell, trying fruitlessly to peck her way out.

Bethy slouched in unannounced. She was wearing floral pyjama pants. "Holy crap. Those folks look like Grandma."

Charlotte fled in such haste she almost knocked Bethy over. A photo of Grandma, Bethy meant, that Charlotte couldn't bear to look at but could not bring herself to rip up or throw out. She still didn't know what had made her take it. Anna's mask-like face turned aside, head propped against a pillow, all but her narrowed eyes frozen, virtually lifeless.

She had snapped the picture without her mother knowing—at least, at the time she thought Anna didn't notice. She'd been very quick stealing the shot. Something inside her knowing exactly what she was doing and why, determined to keep it from her mom. A play at toughening herself up, promising herself not to forget the disease that had stolen Anna little by little. As if she could forget; that's how flighty she had been at nineteen. Bethy's age. But even as Charlotte clicked the shutter the person behind the lens was older, a stranger to her. Someone old enough to anticipate the worst. The inevitable. Viewing Anna's suffering with an instant's coldness had been a way to dull her own.

There was something profane about it. The picture was a secret that reflected badly on her, she knew even then. She had barely glanced at it after picking it up from the drugstore where she took the film to be developed. Instead, had buried it in a shoebox in a series of attics, its latest hiding place one that Bethy—with too much time on her hands—had recently been poking through.

Could you even buy film anymore?

How selfish, how callous, to have captured her mother in a way no one would choose to be captured. A double betrayal, really—punishment for Anna's betrayal of *her* by getting sick in the first place, and a betrayal of Charlotte's own youthful arrogance. How the photograph and her snapping it sharpened then sealed Anna's silence. Shouted Charlotte's insolence: *Here I am, alive and healthy, unlike you. Because you are not me, Mother, and I will never be you. We have always been separate, even when I was being knit inside you.*

So the sightings might be Bethy's fault, Charlotte mused. In a way they were. After unearthing the picture, Bethy had left it on the kitchen counter, a surprise Charlotte stumbled upon one day and absorbed before she could whisk it into a drawer. Having the photograph dredged up after so long refreshed Charlotte's grief, fanned her guilt and the creeping, crawling sense that she and her mother had unfinished business. Left her feeling as bitter and raw as she had felt when Anna passed.

"I'm just waiting, love. Waiting to die," her mom had said, before the disease robbed her of speech. Anna's endearment had been as commonplace as the one store clerks in Cape Breton had for customers, only a little less impersonal.

Dying wasn't to be taken personally, after all.

In the kitchen Charlotte went about making salad. But everything she tossed in the bowl smelled bad—not rotten but acidic and medicinal, like urine saturated with chemicals. The way her parents' house had smelled through the worst years of her mother's illness, despite the best efforts of her dad and the caregivers.

As she set the table Bethy reappeared, still looking like she'd just woken up. What was wrong with her? She was nothing like Charlotte had been at her age, nowhere near as responsible. At Charlotte's prompting she rinsed a cucumber. Then dug her phone from her hoodie to forward a link to something she was actually jazzed about.

Charlotte set down her paring knife, found her phone, and clicked on it. It was for something called a sugar glider. A what? A drink recipe? Some saccharine cocktail like a Singapore sling? She opened the picture. The small grey and white animal had a face like a bat's, a marking on its forehead like a widow's peak. Some type of marsupial, an exotic pet that called to mind Anna's ratty fur collar.

Bethy leaned against the counter, eyeing Charlotte. Texted, *I want 1.*

Charlotte texted back, *U need 2 figure out yr life 1st.*

Bethy sighed, fingered a piece of lettuce, and glowered.

Ted was as sympathetic as anyone could be. "You ought to talk to someone. You really should. Someone to help you get over it." As if she were a baby and "getting over it" was as simple as slipping out of a onesie. A onesie she wore on the inside of her body, invisible to everyone but as warm and fluid and as much a part of her as capillaries and corpuscles.

Interstitial. Anna's presence was interstitial. Though the sightings left Charlotte shaken, she didn't really want them to stop. Having them stop would mean relegating her mother to the fully dead, the place and the state prefigured by the photo.

By Charlotte's own hand, really.

The therapist, a hipster sporting a soul patch, was young enough to be her son if Bethy had a sibling. Post-bereavement hallucinations, he labelled her "experiences." "Doesn't mean they're not real. But you *do* know your mom's not there." His inflection suggested she didn't, quite. "Actually, you should count yourself lucky. The imagination is a powerful tool. The sightings confirm your bond."

The whole time he spoke, her mother floated near, invisible to him. Instead of her maroon coat, Anna was wearing the swimsuit she had bought when Charlotte was thirteen, just before she'd fallen ill. Anna had loved the beach. Charlotte could picture her popping up between waves, shrieking with glee at the cold.

She and the therapist could have been meeting on the sea bottom while her mom breaststroked overhead. In his company Anna remained resolutely mute.

Charlotte thanked him, thinking what a goddamn waste of money and how she wouldn't come back. Before she could escape, he assigned homework: list your top five memories. Happy ones, he stressed, not from her mother's illness, and certainly not the memory Charlotte had divulged, clenching her fists to keep from getting emotional: Anna in her casket, the fine line where the edge of her face had been sewn to her scalp at the hairline, post-autopsy, as if it were a mask. Not this memory or that of a friend placing a single red rose atop her casket, or of the photograph and the feeling that she had let her mother down. Dark memories schooled, so many fish in so much murky water. The only solace she could find was in a childish hangover, the memory that *she* was the one who had felt abandoned.

Bethy, meanwhile, mounted a campaign pleading for what she called the pet of her dreams. "I'll feed it, I'll clean up after it, I'll carry it everywhere in my pocket. Who cares if it's nocturnal and might swing from the curtains all night? I *will*, I promise." Of course she had no money to buy it herself. Fending off suggestions that she front the cash—"just until I'm working, then I'll pay you back"—Charlotte pulled a barstool up to the island and opened her notebook.

Ted and even Bethy had the grace to leave her alone to make her list. But the memories that surfaced only reflected the therapist's earnest queries.

"Did your mother dance? Did she not undergo any alternative therapies?"

Trapped inside an image of her dad spoon-feeding her mother, Charlotte had bristled. How to say that skepticism and despair would have squelched whatever mind-over-matter miracles the ablest healer could've summoned? If her mother had danced, she didn't know about it. Not even pretend dancing with a broom like a sitcom housewife before there was Betty Friedan or brown rice.

Happy memories for Charlotte, or memories Anna would find happy? A tear slid from her chin into her turtleneck. Could such memories be one and the same? She drew blanks.

Except, there was one memory, just one, from when Charlotte was a toddler. It was captured in a black-and-white snapshot, and though too young at the time to recall much about the actual moment, she could fill in the colours. Her mother had strawberry blond hair and her sundress was pale green. She was perched on a whale's back, the sea's hard blue sparkle visible behind its glistening granite.

She was smiling at Charlotte's dad behind the camera; her smile was for him alone. Anna was twenty-two or twenty-three. But where was *she*? Charlotte was out of frame, but now she remembered: standing on the sand below, reaching to be lifted up. In her mind's eye she could see the sand on her toes. Its grains were bits of finely crushed shells, mauve, pink, and white; she could feel their sharpness.

Anna's dress would've been good for dancing, with a skirt made for swirling. Charlotte imagined her twirling around, singing along to "Moon River" and "Spanish Eyes" on the radio, songs her mother sang to the room when she, Charlotte, was tiny.

She made up the rest. Anna scooping her up, holding her tight, spinning, laughing. True or false, the fantasy was so real she felt Anna's breath on her cheek as she jotted this down. She dabbed a splotch of wetness from the blue-lined paper.

Ted tiptoed in and poured her a glass of sturdy red wine.

That night she dreamed about her mother: her mother was a kangaroo, and she was riding around in her pouch, not born yet.

But there was an earlier photograph, Charlotte remembered, upon waking. Who knows where it had got to? A black-and-white eight-by-ten of Anna at her graduation ball before she got married. The valedictorian of her nursing class, she was sitting at a banquet table, wide-eyed and lovely and looking tipsy, flanked by partiers. A man in a grey suit, not Charlotte's dad, was laughing and lighting her cigarette. Despite the occasion's happiness, something lurked in Anna's eyes—a wariness? Resignation? Maybe her date, nameless and unmentioned, had been a mansplaining bore?

What Anna *had* spoken of—roused from her nap one afternoon when Charlotte's childish snooping produced *this* picture—was her gown: an over-the-top, ruffled, off-the-shoulders confection with sleeves puffed at the top and straight at the wrist, unlike anything Charlotte could imagine her wearing. It was tightly fitted to show off her mother's narrow waist, and the ballooning fabric in her lap suggested its billowing skirt. Just looking at the photo you could imagine the dress's rustle. My "Madame Pompidou" dress, her mom had called it. She had only worn it the once. Shiny, dusty-rose taffeta, enough material for four dresses.

Had Anna danced in it that night? Charlotte's dad, who had entered the scene a few months later, wasn't a big dancer. In the picture, Anna's date looked a bit too tanked to be much good on the dance floor.

Eventually Anna had, with uncharacteristic haste, cut it down into a child-size one for Charlotte for Halloween. Haste that belied her usual skill, because Charlotte had decided at the last minute not to be a ghost or a witch but a princess. Resized, the dress was still too big and long for her to safely twirl around in, even wearing her mother's pumps.

What had her mom thought, pretending to doze and watching Charlotte thump and scud across the bedroom floor, playing dress-up? Who knows what had become of the dress and its remnants before they disappeared altogether?

Bethy was actually up and making coffee when Charlotte came downstairs. A concerted pitch for the cash to get herself a slinky, exotic pet? As she sipped from the cup Bethy handed her, Charlotte could feel the slither of pink taffeta against her shins.

If only she had known at nineteen what she knows now about the strange, secret, ongoing body bond between a daughter and her mother. If she had known, she might not have been so afraid. She might have lifted Anna out of her wheelchair, taken her mother into her arms and held her upright, barely breathing, until the magical, medicinal notes of a dance tune had unlocked her brain's frozen pathways. She would have held onto her until, just like that, bingo, Anna whirled away under her own separate, ethereal steam. Released.

As it happened, the final sighting took place outside the mall a couple of months later. Charlotte was driving Bethy to pick up the sugar glider the girl had ordered. She had gotten a part-time job and managed to save up for it, undeterred by the apparent fact that hers wasn't the wisest choice of pet, sugar gliders being prone to sickness, several sources said online. A veterinarian's nightmare or cash cow, depending. Worst of all, females couldn't be spayed, the procedure considered too risky.

For one of the few times in her life, Charlotte could've kicked herself for living in Nova Scotia. In many places, most of the United States for starters, owning one of these creatures was illegal. But not here.

Naturally, Bethy had ordered a female, was angling to adopt a male too. "It'll be so cute if she has babies! They carry them around in a pouch just like a kangaroo!" Apparently gliders are highly social, too, and make "more successful" pets when adopted in pairs. Bethy was getting on well at the grocery store now, trying to get more hours, and it was her money, and maybe having something other than herself to look after would be a good thing?

A light drizzle ate away at ridges of ice along the curb, the stubborn remnants of winter. Music blasted from a car window along with gusting vapes. As the engine idled, the driver cranked the sound. Michael Bublé crooned, "Save the last dance for me."

A bus pulled up, disgorged a full load of passengers.

Bethy, meanwhile, had hurried ahead, more excited and enthusiastic than Charlotte had seen her in months, *months*.

Then, suddenly, there she was—Anna, a few paces behind Bethy. Bethy skinny as a stick in black yoga pants. Her mother was slipping through a knot of pedestrians. "Oh darlin'," the singer's voice rose above the hiss of wet tires. He sounded like he'd inhaled honey by the spoonful.

Anna began to run. She was hurrying, gaining on Bethy heading toward the entrance. She lifted the hem of her rustling, shimmering dress to keep its pinkness dry. It was astonishing how gracefully she moved, hardly wobbling in her high-heeled pumps, the bone-coloured ones Charlotte had always thought were elegant. The heels more than a little worn down. She must've been freezing, half-bared shoulders an opalescent blue. Drizzle beaded her freshly waved hair, netted it with jewels.

For a fleeting second, her mother turned and saw her, grinned. As she waved, Charlotte felt those slender pink arms encircle her, felt the chill of gathered taffeta brush her cheek.

Then her mother slipped right through Bethy, with a sound exactly like the swish of fresh leaves. A scent wafted, clear and blue as the sea's, mixed with the smell of exhaust.

Bethy turned, held the door impatiently as Charlotte caught up. "Hey, they close in like twenty minutes, Mo-ther."

Behind them a fresh bus pulled up, *Out of Service* rolling over its digital display. Bethy grabbed her arm and held onto it, pulled Charlotte close enough to give her a quick peck on the cheek.

"You are the best, Ma. I mean it. I know I never say it. But you are." Who knew if Bethy's words were wholly sincere? But they were enough in the moment floating between the two of them, the vapour that was Anna now dissipated into thin air. Because there is no telling how or when a mother and daughter would betray each other, just by being themselves. *We betray each other from birth, even before our bodies betray us.* Not that it mattered, Charlotte realized, not so much.

Animal Kingdom (or What Women Want)

SISTERS, "DREAM BIG OR GO HOME": EVER GET SICK OF that line? Can I just say, gal pals, my ambitions were never so either/or. But they were complicated by a dream, one of those dreams that clings to your brain like a soapy film to skin. In it a couple of customers who found a turtle in a parking lot, a snapping turtle, chose me to carry the creature safely to water.

God knows what sparked the dream. All I know is that, except for the fact it only had one eye, the turtle looked a lot like my boyfriend, Ritchie—he's a bit short on hair and keeps his head shaved. The way the turtle thrust its neck out was pure Ritchie, him in a shirt and tie trying to get comfortable.

Maybe it's time I invested in a dream catcher, or even started stocking them? Although I'm not sure that would be appropriate and the last thing I want to do is step on toes or hurt anyone. Now, I've read on the internet how turtles have special meaning for the Mi'kmaq and other First Peoples across Turtle Island, as it's called. The turtle, a sacred figure, represents Mother Earth and played a huge role in Creation. Seems Indigenous folks would know, they've been here the longest. Turtles mean good health, long life, and wisdom, among other things I discovered, googling. Apparently, the markings on a turtle's back represent the cycle of the moon and the workings of a woman's body, meaning fertility. And as one of the oldest animals on the planet, the turtle supposedly signifies truth.

Personally, I think sometimes truth tellers can be bores. *Hey, Cher. It takes one to know one,* Ritchie might say. One more thing I learned is that snapping turtles make good soup, which the Onondaga fed to newborns and people with sore throats. Reminds me of Ritchie's issue with button-down collars, though that is beside the point.

The point is, the turtle in my dream only wanted to bite.

"You're braver than us, Cheryl," said the gauzy, faceless ladies who appeared and urged me to rescue it.

"Think nothing of it, gals." Never mind the creature had me quaking in my flip-flops, where, seconds before its appearance, I had been happily stocking shelves, merch for stagettes. Items to make the wildest girls' night out shimmer like gold lamé.

Never mind that in real life my business is bed & bath and silk flowers, much tamer stuff. The stuff of ordinary women's dreams. When I told Ritchie about *mine*, his response was not surprising.

"What were *you* smoking, Cher?"

We were sitting in the truck, sipping our first double-doubles of the day, contemplating our walk around the lake, this routine we had, to hit the park before work. He is never in the best mood until he's downed that all-important Timmie's.

"But what do you suppose it means, Ritchie? Reptiles totally creep me out."

"Frigged if I know, Cher."

I got out and started walking.

Ritchie soon caught up. "What's the matter?" He sucked in a gulp of fresh air. He's a plumbing contractor, likes to remind me about the "sore" gas he deals with—"sewer" gas to the rest of us. "Come on now, don't go all *sour* on me." For once he did not need correcting. "You know your dreams make me twitchy."

I kept quiet; the morning's warmth was already dampened. I don't even like walking; in fact I hate it. But these daily strolls were a chance to see dogs, any number of breeds out for their constitutionals before the owners went to work, probably left them crated all day.

If not for the dogs, I would have gladly chilled in the shop until opening time. Ritchie, however, was not a dog person, could take them or leave them. Evidently he was not a turtle person either.

"Hey. Did you know the Mi'kmaq ate snapping turtles during lean times, Ritch? Survival food. It says so online."

This information garnered a blank stare, which annoyed me. I was simply trying to make conversation. And no one ever said I had to support my partner's efforts at getting fit. I could have easily spent the hour arranging purses instead. The ones I bring in are the closest you will find to Gucci in Fairfield, can I just say? The smell of their pleather is every bit as delicious as that of a new doll at Christmas. Why, two bags had practically sold themselves the day before: a python tote to a gal who works cash at the Canadian Tire, an alligator clutch to her friend from the Pharmasave. It was their first time in the shop.

"How've you been here so long and only now we pop in?" one of them wondered.

"You tell me, hon."

I'd tucked a complimentary sachet into each of their bags. Jasmine, a fragrance that shouts *airport, duty-free, Jamaica.* Leaning over the counter, I beamed a fresh, wide smile. "We're not called 'What Women Want' for nothing, you know."

The name, actually, had been Ritchie's idea.

Recalling their purchases made me think of the turtle's legs and neck, and I could not withhold a shudder. Replaying their visit in my head, as Ritchie and I ambled toward the lake, a chill rippled through me. The purse gals were the ones in my dream.

I thought, *Is an actual turtle about to slither from the bushes, stare us down?*

Ritchie held my hand. He was already breathing rather heavily. I worry about him. Until a month before, his idea of a walk was from the truck to the Tim's counter, his favourite exercise devouring crullers. He was the one who decided we should turn over a new leaf. Together.

Well, all around us the trees shimmered with lots of new leaves. The air was filled with birdsong. But none of this wiped away my dream. Well, less my dream, perhaps, than an image from my reading filtered through my white, one-eyed way of seeing, as the Indigenous folks might call it. The image of something viscous and green being fed into an infant's mouth.

Just as I needed a dose of reality, a jogger slipped

by with a Shih Tzu in tow. Both were moving too fast to allow me the faintest hope of petting the little furball. As I peeled back the tab on my coffee to take a deeper sip, Ritchie nudged me. "What kind of dude walks a mutt like that?"

Scalding my lip, hot black coffee sluiced down my wrist. My dress was brand-new, ecru, with these fantastic bell sleeves, see-through lace. "Shit, Ritchie!" As I dug around for a tissue, a girl with a pug bounced past, wearing neon green shoes. Narrowly avoiding us, neither she nor her dog so much as glanced my way.

Ritchie held my coffee, dabbed at my arm with the napkin from his cup. "Jeez, pumpkin."

"Seriously? Can you not call me that?" It was almost as if reptilian claws were scrabbling at my skin.

"Come again?"

"Oh, right. I forgot. We're not those people who call each other by their real names, names like 'Cheryl' and 'Richard.'" Nor do we have the kind of relationship I imagine many of my customers aspire to, I was careful not to add. Gals who appreciate marketing events like Queen for a Day. (Buy two or more décor items, draw for a prize. A tiara, a card with instructions for hubby, boyfriend, partner, whatever, on how to pamper you.) I was not that kind of woman, nor did I plan to become one.

The dream twigged again, this time even more sharply. I folded back my sleeve, could almost feel turtle jaws clamping down on my flesh. At least the staining was minimal. But the scald reached halfway to my elbow, a stinging pinkness under soggy lace.

It forced me to focus my thoughts elsewhere—away from the dream, away from Ritchie's shortcomings. (Who doesn't have shortcomings?) Why *not* get into stagettes, I asked myself, make pre-nuptials fun even for those on the sidelines? "In this animal kingdom not all are the favoured ones," an older customer once griped.

"But many don't want to be." After all, I had wanted to add, who even gets married these days?

"I don't see the need for it myself." That would be my man.

Ritchie steered me down the first path to the lake. "Give 'er a dunk, that'll help. So much for dressing for success, Cher." It was a little joke between us. His coveralls had *Why Sleep with a Drip?* machine-embroidered on the pocket. I fantasized about designing similar coveralls for women, only personalized with things like *Life Coach* and *My favourite food is wine*. Success means knowing exactly which nut to turn on which bolt, just as Ritchie says, understanding people's desires and letting them know these aren't just worthy but doable. Affirming not just likes but dislikes too.

"Seriously," I'd told someone just the other day, "light this pine-and-balsam candle and he will never make you go camping again. Repeat after me: 'Hey hon, why camp when we can create the perfect outdoor ambience right here in our bedroom?'"

The customer bought three, one for herself and two for friends. "For such a young thing, Cheryl, I guess you've been around the track a few times?" She even winked. I chose to take her presumption as a compliment. Forget brand loyalty; forget having thick or thin skin. Sticking by what you see as true necessities is what counts.

I downed the dregs of my coffee. Ritchie chugged his, then crushed our cups, one in each hand. Before us the lake loomed perfectly still, such a soothing reflection of the sky. If I'd been wearing my swimsuit I would have jumped in. Then the dream crawled back, as though moving on all fours. It raised the fear of something cold-blooded and leathery lurking under the surface.

Ritchie gripped both flattened cups in his teeth, dug for his keys. "Go for a *skinny* dip, Cher?" Muttered, not quite to himself, "Dream on, eh." He's a nice guy, a lovely guy, but sometimes that didn't stop him from projecting his weight issues on me.

By now, apparently, he was the one who had had enough of walking.

"What, tired already?" I was more than ready to leave. Yet, gingerly, I crouched on a rock, slipped off my flip-flops (gold glitter, new that season). Held back my sleeve and dipped my arm, managed not to fall in. The scald was as pink as some scarves I'd draped in the window for curb appeal.

Ritchie squatted beside me. Nudged me closer to the edge.

"Smarten up!" The dream's squirm factor gripped me. "I bet you liked pushing girls in, didn't you. When you were a teen. Just when they trusted you."

"That's me." But beneath his laugh he sounded hurt, the way he had after our discussion once, a debate about men getting what they wanted ninety-nine percent of the time. As though stung by a hornet, he'd said, "Really? You really believe they do?"

Out in the lake a tiny solitary island appeared to float on the surface. Ritchie pointed to a tent pitched there, no sign of people or a boat. It looked like a prop abandoned from *Survivor* or *Amazing Race*.

"We could both skinny-dip out there, Cher, no one would see."

I refrained from commenting on his belly, then could not resist. "Fair enough, *pumpkin*." *Arse*, I kept to myself. I imagined being at work, happily arranging crystal angels on mirrored shelves. Setting up the sidewalk sign: *BOGO Celebrate U!*

The morning's constitutional was shaping up to be a bust, certainly on the dog front. Though as I slithered from the rock, a border collie appeared, towing a girl. The girl removed its leash and flipped a ball into the lake. Instead of fetching, the dog sat there barking.

"Poor pup." I smiled. "Hates the water, does he?"

The girl didn't take her eyes off the dog. "She sure does."

Ritchie huffed and puffed. Made a joke about what dogs wanted and what people heard.

"Hon, it's 'what *people* say, and what *dogs*...' Hey there," I piped up, "mind if I pat your pup?"

"What? Oh. Sure, whatever." But as the girl leashed her pet and I reached out, the dog spotted a squirrel and was off, dragging her behind.

I wished my dream had been that elusive, watching as a pair of loons flew closer. Their shivery cries made my throat tighten. For a second, being there was like being in the boonies—the true wilderness, I mean—until the hum of traffic brought me back to reality and thoughts of business. How pine-scented bath salts would pair nicely with those balsam candles. Throw in some *Nature's Call* CDs and, *voilà*, boxed sets.

Ritchie's thoughts must've been ranging elsewhere too. His first work order of the day was a bathroom reno.

But he could not have been pokier strolling back to the truck, as if we had all morning *and* afternoon.

"Those birds up there, see them?" He gazed upward. "Better hope they don't crap on us. A pair of hawks, bet you five bucks."

"You've never seen a loonie? Really, hon."

"You like critters so much, Cher, how come you didn't go into pets? Now there's a way to make loot."

Leading the way up the trail, I stopped and waited for him to catch up. Hopped on one foot, flicking grit from my flip-flop. By now I suspected he was being slow for a reason. He had something up his sleeve? Every once in a while Ritchie shocked me by demonstrating in some playful but tangible way that he knew me better than I thought he did. His boyishness was, or could be, lovable—the reason I devoted a display unit to stuffies that only in a perfect world would appeal to adults as much as to children. The cutest among them was a velour tortoise with a sequinned shell. This hit me like a gut-punch, tamed a second later by the more mundane realization that these walks made zero difference on the bathroom scale.

A weariness, you could call it a longing, suddenly set in. "Ritchie, do you realize how lame it feels, being a dog lover walking day in and day out without a fur companion? Being here rubs my nose in it, actually. Never mind being man's best friend, dogs are women's besties too."

"Hey, aren't I your bestie?" He had this nervous energy as he spoke.

He fired our cups at a trash can, missed. Forgetting that his latest tat was just beginning to heal, I slapped his arm. "You know there's a fine for littering." I bent down to retrieve the cups, dunked them. If there's one thing I can't stand it's Tim's cups lying everywhere. Worst of all is when people leave them on my shelves, to share space with treasures for kitchen & bath.

Ritchie grabbed my hand, squeezed till it almost hurt, then kissed the back of it. Gazing at me, his small, greyish eyes were shiny, suddenly dead earnest. Forget my fear: I felt an urge to run back to the lake and jump in, swim fully dressed to the island though I'm not the best swimmer. Crawl inside the tent which could not possibly fit more than one person, and stay there, though I am no camper. If not for my fear of snapping turtles—or should I say the one in my dream—I might have done it. No, I would have, had I guessed what Ritchie was about to say.

"Okay, Cheryl. Here's the deal." Coming at me, his voice was pinched, almost shrill. "I'll give you a dog if you give *me* a baby."

I felt myself go white—well, whiter. I had the same slo-mo, klutzy feeling you get the instant you drop something hopelessly fragile, a piece of glass swag so delicate, just look at it the wrong way and it breaks.

Until that moment I had never so much as thought of babies. Let me correct that. A baby.

We both went silent as the boulders along the trail. *Stone* silent. You could have heard bird poop landing on a rock, salamanders wriggling in the dirt underneath its weight. Ritchie was joking, of course he was joking. Though he knew I had wanted a puppy since forever, long before he even entered the picture, I had given up trying to talk him into adopting one, had finally quit showing him dog videos on Instagram. I was afraid of being accused of never being satisfied. Of always wanting something, as if having him and a business weren't enough, as if nothing was enough.

"You're kidding me, right? Quit messing with me, Ritchie. I mean it. Do. Not. Mess. With. Me. Who even thinks up something so stunned, let alone says it? A 'deal.' Right. More like blackmail."

The most experience I had with kids was driving past the daycare by the mall. I had a rule, no babies in the store. *Break it and it's yours at full purchase price* is posted everywhere. Moms knew it was targeted at them, a subtle nudge to leave children home, where they belonged.

Babies. Wipes, bottles, cases of diapers, formula, accessories, the dreadful pastel accessories. The crying, oh shag it, the crying. Never leaving the house without a puffy quilted bag crammed with all this crap and, hell's bells, a stroller. *A stroller*. And not far behind, a car seat! A crib!

Visions of pink extruded plastic swarmed my brain. No way, José. Not in this lifetime. Not for *this* mama. Never.

Ritchie stroked my tingling arm. At least the scald had faded. The colour in my head switched to powder blue, a whole Walmart's worth of it.

Not to suggest for a moment that stuff, goods in and of themselves, is bad. Wanting stuff makes the world go 'round, we all know. And babies, I gathered, create the biggest consumers of all.

"So. What do you say, Cher?"

Insanely, I tried to focus myself on the reward he held out—the potential reward. A puppy. I thought of all the various breeds there were to choose from. French bulldogs, sheepdogs, Jack Russells, cockapoos, doodles. Pit bulls, shepherds, Rotties, boxers, huskies, beagles. But my thoughts slid to turtles, not just any old turtles but the snapping one in my dream. The way it had pulled its head into its shell defensively right before thrusting it out again, thrashing in attack mode.

Ritchie led me toward the truck. I stopped thinking how the turtle resembled him and decided instead that it resembled me. That perhaps I resembled it.

"If you need to think things over for a bit, I get that."

His voice was gentle enough. But I felt myself recoil and shrink into myself, not unlike a turtle. Other ripple effects of his proposal started to sink in.

"Having a baby...I'd have to take classes for that, wouldn't I?" Where was I supposed to find the time, for starters?

"Classes?" He seemed embarrassed. Mortified, actually. Like the time he had unclogged someone's septic and called me to report that there were condoms spewed all over the front lawn.

"Well, *yeah*. I would need to learn to *breathe*."

Maybe it was my tone. He looked as if a boulder had rolled out of nowhere and was pursuing him, aiming to flatten him. Pure disbelief. "You have to take classes for that?"

A long, breezy pause ensued. A passing beagle ambled up, sniffed Ritchie's shoe, and lifted its leg. Ritchie did not seem to notice, not even when the owner lunged. "Winston, get over here! Now!"

But his voice was resolute when he spoke. "Couldn't you just watch it on YouTube, Cher? They've got videos for everything."

By the time we got into the truck he was in a mood. "You know, babe, you're not exactly a teenager."

No shit. We had just celebrated our thirty-fifth birthdays, one week apart. I gazed straight ahead. "No need to be in a snit, Sherlock. I never said I wouldn't. Consider it, I mean."

"Whoa. Chill, okay? It's not like I asked you to tie the knot or anything. It's just—"

"You want a kid."

"And you don't."

I took a deep, deep breath. Pushed the thought of turtle slime from my mind. "I *never* said—"

"See? You don't know *what* you want! Cher. Like, fuck, what is your problem?"

We drove in silence. When he swerved into my tiny parking lot, I almost fell getting out. I slammed the door shut. A sleeve of flyers lay on the doorstep and a half-eaten Big Mac. What no one wants is someone else's trash to clean up. "Don't let the gas get to you," I hollered as he peeled off.

Inside the shop the scent of pumpkin spice—an early order for fall—calmed me, until its hominess whispered, shouted, trouble. *Lots of women have babies. You won't be the first, Cheryl Ann Lahey. And you certainly will not be the last.* This left me as chilled, as discombobulated, as the dream had.

More than a little desperate, I grabbed my phone, googled. "A snapping turtle can amputate two fingers with one swift bite," said the Wiki entry, which was not helpful. I delved deeper, frantic to decipher what the dream *meant*. Scrolling and scrolling. I finally landed on a tweet by a Mi'kmaw artist, enjoining, "When the turtle spirit guide appears to you it's time to slow down, stay true to your path." The tweet recommended calling "on this spirit when it is time to reconnect with the Creator."

What? *Meet my maker.* Was that what all of this meant?

Pushing away the dream, I spent the rest of the morning scrolling puppy videos. Suppose I did take Ritchie up on his offer? If his offer still stood. I mulled over breeds, what an ideal dog would look like. A bulldog mix with some lab thrown in, because we needed a dog with decent walking legs (for Ritchie's sake), not one that hunkered at the end of a leash like a lump of melted lard. Add a bit of pit to fend off pervs and possibly the break-and-enterers that plagued the spa next door. (So much for my notions of expanding into nails and eyelashes.)

A man sauntered in and took forever choosing a paperweight, a locally sourced beach stone painted with butterflies. After he paid, I phoned Ritchie.

"Did you actually mean it? A dog for a baby. You weren't just arsing around?"

"Can I call you back?" His voice sounded distant, as if he was speaking from inside a vanity.

"No, wait. You really want to be saddled, tied down like that—?"

A trickling noise coming through the phone triggered a terrible urge to pee.

"Babe, have I ever jerked you around?"

Then the line went dead.

My dreams ramped up when the test showed positive. Granted, I'd picked it up at the Dollar Store and figured the result wasn't one hundred percent reliable. But, the doctor confirmed it. I was gobsmacked. Ritchie was over the moon *and* scared shitless.

Like striking out on a whole new business venture, thrown for a loop I grew weirdly excited. I decided, I did, to embrace it.

The dreams were of the recurring type. In them

a cradle rocked by itself in a bedroom while a bonfire-scented candle burned on a dresser top, all to the sound of whale songs playing on a loop. In the dream I was a whale? I thought of the picture a customer had pulled from her purse once to show me, something her daughter had drawn: her favourite mammal, a human.

It was all like something out of Stephen King.

For seven whole months I dreamed the same thing night after night, regularly waking in a sweat at 3:13 A.M. It isn't the best scenario, lying awake while the rest of the world snores on. It left me exhausted. I ended up opening later and later each morning. Not that business suffered. Customers came in to coo over and feel my stomach and rarely left without buying something. At first I felt like every dog's lamppost, public property. But once I got over this, for the first time ever, being rotund proved to be, dare I say it, desirable.

Under the circumstances, our fitness regimen was the first thing to go. Perhaps it was the lack of exercise, for Ritchie started dreaming too. Would wake up whimpering about substances dredged from drains—nightmare scenes, he said. Solidified fat mixed with hair had faces. Reptilian faces, eyes with flat-line pupils, no noses to speak of, and dangerous, chomping jaws—toothless, at least. But once, he woke up shaking because the turtle—it was definitely a turtle, he insisted—had latched onto his wrench-turning hand and would not let go.

"Get a grip on yourself, hon. It's okay. You can quit freaking out."

By then my stomach was like one of those exercise balls you sit on. It was appalling, really. Except, I was dazzled, thrilled, and not just because I had to be. Maybe it was hormones, the body's betrayal of the rational mind. At this point I had no choice but to welcome what was happening.

Oddest of all was that I completely lost interest in Ritchie's end of the bargain. I unfriended people who posted dog videos. I overcame my distaste, my loathing, for baby products and accessories. But because of the toll insomnia took on my waking hours, I caved to his advice and went to YouTube for Lamaze instructions.

In my dreams, at first the rocking cradle held a turtle. Then the turtle developed puppy breath. Grew long silky ears, a feathery tail, had a soft, lolling tongue like a slice of ham.

The only fly in the ointment was that my passion for business began to flag slightly. A lot of those beautiful purses gathered dust. Plastic fatigue became a problem, along with the sun bleaching items in the window.

Dust and fading, a shop owner's worst-case-ontario, Ritchie clucked. "Maybe Junior's trying to tell us something?" Lounging beside me on the chesterfield, he pressed his ear to my baby bump.

"Oh she is, is she? What could it be, I wonder?"

Meanwhile, Ritchie developed a sympathetic addiction to maple-glazed donuts, sinking, as far as I could tell, to a new level of weakness regarding diet, a weakness in him I had more easily ignored before.

"Keep eating garbage and watch, you'll have a heart attack when I go into labour."

"Doesn't sound to me like a catastrophic blockage," I heard him tell someone on the phone one night after hours. But he quickly downed his rye and Coke, said he was going out.

"This late? If it's not an emergency—?"

"I need a walk" was all he said.

He came home at 3:00 A.M. stinking of weed. The way my space had smelled when I first assumed the lease from the head shop guy who rented it before me. (Location location, I believed back then, was everything.)

"Babe? I'm not sure how to tell you this." Stricken with the munchies, he tore open a large bag of Doritos with his teeth. Then, gazing straight at me, he said, "Look, I'm not ready to be a dad or a dog person."

"Give. Me. A. Break. Are you for fucking real?" The acid reflux that plagued me at night literally singed my throat.

"Okay, okay. Please don't go ballistic. I'm sure I'll come around."

"Goddammit, Ritchie. Buck up! You're going to have to."

The morning my water broke Ritchie googled the pound. "There's so many homeless dogs—I just can't see going to a breeder, can you?" His voice might have been steady, but he was a wreck. "Not when there's all these little guys with nobody—"

I can barely think about much of that day. Put it this way: I wish the word *delivery* applied solely to UPS shipments, like those of the purses I was starting to think would have to go on Kijiji. *Things don't always go as planned, aren't I right, ladies?*

Through a haze of pain, all I saw was the doctor in his white coat. He had a nasal voice and a sharp-nosed face like a bird's. His questions seemed to issue from a beak.

"Cheryl? Cheryl? Can you hear me?"

I did not know where exactly Ritchie was at that juncture. I guess he was there.

Eventually, after what was surely days, weeks, from a corner of the room came a sound not quite human—like a lamb bleating, or a sheep. "What is that?" I kept crying.

"Congratulations!" People, nurses, were cheering.

And then Ritchie was gazing into my eyes and weeping. They were happy tears. He was leaning down over me, so I felt their wetness. *Don't sleep with a drip,* said a tiny voice inside me. *How's that for too little advice too late?* I barely heard it, as I was crying and laughing. Ritchie was holding a little bundle. The baby's tiny, red, scrunched-up face had Ritchie's eyes and nose, and, bonus, was crowned with a shock of hair. Except for the hair, our child looked just like him, a miniature Ritchie. This mini version had been swimming around inside me for nine months.

I have never seen Ritchie happier, before or since.

"About the promise I made you." He stumbled on his words. "Are you sure you want to forget about it?" For I had been having severe second thoughts about how I would juggle a baby *and* a dog.

As the baby latched on to my nipple, he could have been a pup, suckling with all the fierceness of a baby pit. Eyes like the lake reflecting gentle rainclouds, and, as the redness started to fade, skin the colour of a Timmie's that was mostly cream. The wrinkles around his tiny neck and elbows, knees, and wrists were adorable. Honestly, in the state I was in, I could have mistaken the cord for a docked tail.

The one thing I had gotten wrong was guessing the baby's sex. Oh, and much later on, the part about worrying what would happen when he grew big enough to walk and talk and—.

"Holy good shit," Ritchie said over and over, kissing that beautiful, wrinkly little face.

We named our boy Rio. In my half-drugged state, ambushed by love, I imagined someone putting a clicker in his tiny hand to start Ritchie's clicker-training in being a good, solid dad. Ritchie just kept wiping his eyes and thanking me, thanking me for giving him a son to grow up to be just like him someday and maybe even take over the plumbing business.

As the baby nursed, his cheeks moved like a little pair of bellows fanning a flame.

"You can't have it all, Cher," Ritchie had once said, well before his fitness jag. Before our walks in the park. Before any of our crazy dreams.

In my mind I was already clearing inventory to make room for the cradle. Oh, yes, and by now I had a line on an artist in Sipekne'katik who crafted dream catchers, the most beautiful ones imaginable. Fingers crossed she would agree to be my supplier.

Postscript, ladies. Turns out Rio is an added draw. What woman doesn't love walking into a shop and discovering the unexpected?

"Can I hold it?" even the crankiest customers say, and I will never turn them down.

"Be careful what you wish for, hon." Hey, it's not easy being a 24/7 milk-and-cuddle machine. Especially with a business to run that could use a little resuscitation at times. Despite its name. Which might be its best asset.

"Hang in, Cher. Soon enough it'll be flip-flops and margaritas-at-the-cottage season. That'll bring them in in droves."

Easy for Ritchie to say, bouncing Rio in the air. He counts on things the rest of us do not want or would ever ask for. Burst pipes, broken toilets.

"I'm rethinking your end of the deal." I raise it now and then only to keep him on his toes. Up to my eye teeth in motherhood, what would I have done with a dog, anyway?

It's a damn good thing, a lucky thing, men don't always come through with what we ask for.

Ritchie sucks in his gut and looks at me. "You're kidding, right?" But when he sees that I am, he starts in. "Now you've got it all, Cher, how 'bout what the guy wants? This guy, I mean. The guy you're looking at. A little bit of attention would be great."

Sit, stay, heel, I think. *Down. Off. Free.*

Rio reaches out. I take him and hold him close, gaze into his steady, bottomless eyes. Then I kiss Ritchie's cheek. "No problem, hon."

What people say is one thing, but what people hear is no less than what they want.

Believe me, I know.

Alpha Frontier

A BITE MARKED THEIR FALLING OUT—A BITE! POSSIBLY from a spider? Julie figured this might have been the moment things truly unravelled. But she waited till she was safely home unpacking before she teased it out, a moment rivalled by many.

Emptying her suitcase on the bed, she wondered if Tobias could similarly identify such a moment. If he thought that deeply. Not that she gave a crap what he thought. She extracted her passport from the heap of balled-up T-shirts, underwear, and dresses, stowed it in a drawer. Plowed the clothes into a pile on the floor, and shoved him from her mind. Again.

What was it Magda said about people living rent-free in your head?

She went into the bathroom, unpacked her baggy of toiletries. The spider plant in the window had sprouted a baby in her absence. She set her toothbrush in the mug with Magda's. Stuffed loose tampons into the shaky metal cabinet over the toilet. She had started to bleed on the plane, not the greatest timing but a relief. A big relief.

Would Tobias even be thinking of her? Would he remember her by the fall term? At least she'd graduated, wouldn't be running into him in hallways, at exhibitions, openings. Wouldn't be facing that stare he must figure was super hot or super cool, like the man gaze in films noir he'd made them watch in class.

Embarrassment tightened inside her, and anger—she felt it swell and push at her ribs. She needed to talk, wanted nothing more than to drink tea and laugh. Where was Magda, how come she wasn't here? She should've been home from school by now. Being roommates had made their schedules more or less predictable.

But, about Tobias's stare, that fucking stare. Now that she thought about it, it resembled a hawk's. If a hawk had a weak chin. She wondered when his stare had stopped making her feel special, chosen, and started making her cringe instead. That was harder to pinpoint. It might've happened near the start of the trip, on the flight from Rome to Palermo.

She splashed her face, listened for Magda's footsteps on the landing. Remembered Tobias staring at the flight attendant, a woman wearing ridiculously high heels, a little green hat tilted at a flirty angle. Handing him his bottled water, she had stared back the way you'd stare at a sticky restroom doorknob. A look made for assholes.

And yet, flying over the Tyrrhenian Sea, its green glimmer directly below, Julie had hooked her arm through his, happily, and snuggled closer.

Flying home alone, the recollection had made her

squirm. By then, of course, she was already deciding how she'd describe the trip, make it funny. Except Magda would freak at the part about the spider. Magda had this phobia about arachnids—kind of pathetic for someone doing their PhD in science. Geology. Of all things.

She could not imagine doing a PhD in anything, spending how many years in school? To become a prof and teach art history like Tobias? No way. She'd made up her mind ages ago, she would be an artist.

The trip to the island of Sicily had been his idea. The perfect way to celebrate finishing her undergrad, he'd promised. "The food, the wine, the cultural mix, the cross-currents of political, economic, and historical struggle. An island raped and pillaged by every imperialist colonizer going, also the Mob. Plus the food is great. It'll be the start of your real education, Jules. You haven't lived till you've sucked the juice of a blood orange right from the tree. Trust me."

He was working on an article he needed to publish in order to get more courses. No better place than Palermo to do the research, he said. His topic was the power of art to fight crime.

"Oh, like murals cutting down on vandalism? Or, like, looking at something beautiful makes someone forget about dealing drugs?" She was careful not to say, *You need to leave Halifax to find this out?*

"Organized crime, Julie. Like in *The Godfather*."

A movie he raved about, from, like, the last century, as she recalled.

"Everything boils down to economics, controlling the means and mode of production," he'd told them all on the first day of class. He had fixed her with his disarming stare. Snow had pelted the windows, the first blizzard of January. It was a one-semester course on Marxism and outsider Italian art. "Before you think about creating anything, friends, never forget, struggle is struggle." People were pissed the school didn't call a snow day, but she was glad. Mesmerized.

They had barely landed in Palermo before he started to "share" his research, never mind she was bleary-eyed from flying. Riding the airport bus to the city, she laid her head on his shoulder, silently absorbed the rugged, treeless landscape flying by, until he shouted in her ear.

"Check it out!"

A monument of some sort flashed by—an obelisk, maybe? She looked up in time to see a bunker on a hillside, a squat building with NO MAFIA painted on it in huge dripping letters.

"You see? Graffiti's a *major* instrument of social and political change." He was gleeful, his enthusiasm endearing. Youthful. It summoned a kid version of him: sandy blond curls with no grey, child-size button-down shirt, black jeans, hiking boots.

The bus hurtled past piled trash, past crumbling high rises and villas crammed along the seashore. The colours were a complementary marvel of terracotta and electric blue. Tobias railed against the Mob contractors behind such derelict housing. She felt terrible for people living in squalor but said she and Magda would have made do for the view.

He laughed, nuzzled her ear. "What you need to do is

check your privilege." Maybe this was a little rich? Three and a half weeks earlier, they were sitting on the couch listening to Magda making KD when it came up: "You're kidding me—you haven't been to Europe? Not even Italy?"

Her roommate had set their bowls on the cable spool they used for a table. He left his fork where it was, massaged Julie's nape. "Sorry, ladies. By no stretch is this pausta."

Magda had rolled her eyes, fleeing to the tiny kitchen.

Then he had popped the question. Would Julie come with him? His treat.

The very next day, a safe distance from campus, he'd slipped her the tickets.

"Wait. This isn't. For real?"

"Don't thank me, thank my alpha frontier."

"What the—what is that?"

He paused, amused by her bluntness maybe, more than her ignorance. "Financial jive, it's nothing. Listen. How else you figure I get to do shit I care about? I'm lucky admin even offers the course. They could shut me down faster than a—. It's family money, that's all. No biggie. I'll explain at dinner, okay?"

By then they had been dating for almost four months.

The B&B was located in a mystifying web of tiny, winding streets. Ramshackle buildings stood amid bombed-out ruins Tobias said were from the war his grandparents remembered. In the distance, the city's sprawl was hemmed by bare, mist-wreathed mountains, each shaped exactly like Marge Simpson's hair. The landscape conjured

Greek myths she had learned about in high school. The round white sun was like Cyclops's eye.

After checking in, they set out on foot to visit sites he'd bookmarked. The first was a church, a Baroque confection of lemon-yellow stucco that reminded Julie of a wedding cake, statues perched on tiers, like Moonie brides and grooms. The sun made stubby shadows of palms as lofty as the church's spires. She had never seen a more dazzling sky, could not stop looking up. It was only the first of June but summer seemed full-blown.

A banner draped over the doorway proclaimed the *Year of Mercy*, whatever that was, and an anniversary: *eight hundred years of faith*.

"Okay, back home, no fucking way you'd catch me in a church." Tobias spoke the way he talked in class. "But here? Wait'll you see.

"The magistrate? That monument we saw coming in? Commemorates Falcone's assassination. A car bombing. Though it's bizarre, Giovanni Falcone winding up *here*. The guy was a communist. I mean, sure, being a magistrate was how he carried out his day-to-day struggle. But his goal was freeing the people from the oppressor. The tyranny of the Mob. And he ends up in a *church*?" He wiped away a smile.

A priest waved them in, greeted them in an Italian unlike its airport version. The inside was a spectacle of carved, curlicued, and inlaid marble flooded with light. Old people dotted the pews. The total silence had a chill.

What Julie really wanted was sleep.

Tobias barely lowered his voice. "It was Giovanni's buddy Borsellino who was the Catholic. Ultra-right. Pretty crazy since they grew up together."

"I heard the Pope's a Marxist." It was all she could think of to say. She whispered, "Is that true?"

"Only what they want you to think." His footsteps echoed ahead of her. Up near the front he called out, "Here! Here he is!" She could feel people's eyes burning through her as she caught up.

He stood before a slab of pale grey marble, thumbed wetness from his cheeks. The slab was showered with hundreds of slips of paper, so many the tomb's inscription was hidden. *Grazie, Giovanni. Mille grazie*, said the notes she could read. She reached for Tobias's hand. Remembered the Post-it notes plastered over his office corkboard, thought of him writing one word on each in green Sharpie: *Guns, Farmers, Trade, Coffee, Oil, Bombs*. Though a few had statements (*Eat the rich*) or phrases like that puzzling one, *Alpha Frontier*.

He had tried to explain the meaning over supper in his loft apartment. She had heard of alpha animals (as in packs of dogs) and frontiers (as in outer space, brain science, and installation art), areas with boundaries to push. A brochure on his engineered wood table had the phrase in boilerplate letters, something to do with investment.

"Let's get out of here." His eyes glistened. "Find us some drinks."

In a nearby street—the oldest of the city's marketplaces, he said—they stopped at a little shop, drawn by its outdoor furniture. Tables made of orange crates, kindergarten-style chairs. Magda would have loved it. A sign in the window advertised *arancini* with Gorgonzola. Her first taste of Gorgonzola had been at Tobias's.

"Here?"

He scanned the window for more: the sign declaring the owner's refusal to pay *pizzo*, he explained. "Protection money" to keep the Mafia from blowing up the store.

A thin, smiling man waved at them to take a seat, plunked down two free *arancini*. Tobias ordered Prosecco for two. Sitting on her tiny chair, she felt like a parent at a parent-teacher meeting. Tobias grinned, watching people, scooters, and tiny delivery trucks winging by. One was piled with stovepipes and tin buckets. For the first time since she'd finished, she missed school. The metal shop especially, where she had crafted the bird that sat on her and Magda's front windowsill. She'd found the scraps to fashion the piece in a dumpster a few doors down from the flat.

Her first glimpse of Tobias was at a fourth-year crit in October. Her studio instructor had invited him along with a few of his students. The following month, he'd turned up at Julie's pre-grad show. She knew he taught something political but that was all. She had done a series of paintings of vulvas riffing on Georgia O'Keeffe, only adding sparkles. Some boy had made a gross remark and Tobias had flinched. Standing near enough that she could hear him breathe, he had admired her use of Dollar Store glitter, but questioned the ethics of materials from China. "Sometimes, though, maybe the end justifies the means," he'd said, and winked.

She was studying gender politics and, at the time, was into questioning her cis identity. The possibilities of identifying as queer were a subject she and Magda talked about late at night after beers. The asexuality of minerals was what drew her to geology, Magda said. Which made sense but didn't sound like a lot of fun.

The cure for jet-lag, Tobias insisted, was to keep moving until you dropped. After a couple of glasses of Prosecco, Julie let its buzz and the city's diesel-laced squalor claim her. A splendour of wandering dogs, feral cats, decayed churches and palaces, the urban streets were filled with people of every colour and ethnicity. Leaning into him, she dodged shit in the *vicoli* and *calli*, his words for alleys and lanes. She had trouble seeing straight as they wound their way to another marketplace. The vendors had packed up for the day. Parched yellow dirt was slick with the run-off from emptied stalls and rotted fruit.

She was starving but everything seemed closed until evening, so they agreed to go back to the B&B for a nap.

His kisses were deep and long, a bit too long. "Don't want to waste time sleeping, Jules." He had a ton of energy for a guy almost forty and knew what she liked. Or what he seemed to think she liked. "Hey. I get it. You young things need your rest."

Noise poured in through the darkened window when they awoke. They threw on fresh clothes, stumbled outside. Earlier, the square had been filled with stalls displaying faded postcards and tablecloths. Now it was jammed like a flash-mob scene. Men cooked mystery meat on makeshift grills, sold shots from pop-up bars. People her age milled about elbow to elbow, dancing, drinking, and glued to a soccer match playing over TV screens that had sprung up out of nowhere. Lurid flashes of green, blue, red, and the white of a spinning ball. Thunderous applause. Clouds of smoke and the smell of sizzling meat permeated the air.

Tobias nudged her. "You might want to wear your pack frontwards, babe." He peeled a hundred-euro note from the roll in his moneybelt, bought beers. Stuffed the change into his pocket with his phone, apparently unconcerned with his own earlier warning about pickpockets. He leaned against the bar, arm looped around her. "What do you feel like eating? A spleen sandwich?" She felt her tongue curl, horrified. He laughed. "Don't worry, something more upscale—how about that place around the corner?"

The restaurant near the yellow church was totally touristy. But she was ravenous, and he was paying.

The pasta didn't taste so different from what she and Magda made when they bothered to cook from scratch.

Tobias was up and dressed, keen to head out when she awoke late the next morning. She was a little surprised, almost disappointed, having kind of expected more sex then a leisurely breakfast. He'd exchanged hiking boots for sandals, jeans for cargo shorts. His legs looked spindly and white, like a fifty-year-old's. He tossed a dress at her. The green linen one she had borrowed from Magda and somehow remembered to hang up.

"Do I at least have time for a shower?" She was a teen again, negotiating with her parents.

"Why not?" Staring at his phone, he continued scrolling.

Downstairs in the breakfast room, a girl with a tattoo of the *trinacria*, a three-spread-legged figure with a face where you'd imagine a vagina, poured their glasses of juice. It was orangey red and citrusy, delicious. Tobias cut slices of cake for them both, carried their plates to the table.

"For *breakfast?*"

"It's Sicily, Jules. You have to love a place where anything goes."

"Hey. I *think* that's a boy's name? Like, how 'bout I call you Toby? Or Tobes?"

He winced. "No."

The news in rapid-fire Italian spilled from a flat screen TV. A woman in heavy makeup read out headlines, the camera panning to newspaper pages marked in yellow highlighter, like Magda did with particularly pertinent sections of her study notes. A story about migrants landing at La Cala, the city's port, refugees camping out on the waterfront. Palermo was a haven, the city groaning under their weight, Tobias translated.

"They defy death to escape African hell-holes we can't even imagine." He drained his juice, picked up his espresso, sipped. "You watch. The Eurozone's consumerist elite are gonna pay for their privilege. Not fucking soon enough."

Thinking of her own good fortune, she imagined Magda boiling chai tea in their Canadian Tire saucepan. Pictured her room packed with art supplies and Magda's with rock specimens. Their upstairs flat could have been on a whole other planet.

The heat belted them in the face when she and Tobias stepped outdoors. Heat and a hail of grit: the sandpapery wind blasted like a hair dryer set on high. The piazza was deserted, a desolation of smashed bottles, dog crap, and swirling litter. Through the debris, hazy sunlight streaked the buildings' facades and a fountain's heart-shaped centrepiece. A naked man bathed in its trough. Braced against the gusts, a worker in a fluorescent vest swept up glass, flung it at an overflowing bin. The sound was like ice being crushed in a blender (a cheap one, not the kind Tobias had for mixing drinks).

The air stung Julie's eyes. It singed her throat and lungs. "The wind is in from Africa," said Tobias in a not quite tuneless voice. "We've got ourselves a *scirocco*, feel it? From the Sahara? You know about these winds, right? A good day to hang by the sea." A big part of his research meant checking out a city on Sicily's western coast—the city where he said Judge Falcone had picked through the Mob's money-laundering paper trail.

Shielding themselves from flying candy wrappers and grocery bags, they found the bus station. The departure wasn't until late afternoon. She studied a travel poster while he bought return tickets, good for a couple of weeks. "*Mille, mille grazie,*" she heard him tell the clerk as he stuffed them into his moneybelt.

In the meantime, he had another monument on his list. She wiped sweat from her neck.

The towering black twin columns occupied their own huge traffic island in the middle of a freeway near the waterfront. Gripping her hand, he darted out in front of whizzing traffic to get a closer look. A pair of policemen in what looked like riot gear patrolled the opposite sidewalk, appeared to pay them no mind—even when the wind whipped Julie's dress up over her head. She pressed her palms to her thighs to pin it down.

The columns commemorated all the innocent victims of organized crime, Tobias explained, reading out the plaque. *Monumento Ai Caduti Nella Lotta Contro La Mafia.*

An unobstructed view of the mountains captured her eye. Grey-green slopes were dotted with orange and not just wreathed but shrouded with something—thick grey smoke? She had to yell to be heard. "Are they on fire?"

Tobias squinted into the distance. "No big deal. Grassfires. They happen in June. The mountains are all rock anyway."

He pulled out his phone to snap a photo of the massive monument; coins flew from his pocket into the roadway. His face went suddenly pale, a panicked look crossed it. He unzipped his moneybelt, pawed through it.

"Fucking *fucking* shit. Can you believe it? I think I've been robbed!"

She could see the police watching from across four or five lanes of passing cars. Her gut flip-flopped. Melting, dripping sweat, she felt for her daypack, rummaged inside, relaxed. Her little stash of euros was there with her passport. Safe.

Perspiration streaked Tobias's cheeks. Underneath it they looked waxy.

"Seriously? You lost *coin*? I mean, serious coin? I watched you check at breakfast, your cash and everything. We haven't been anywhere super busy. Crowded. Today, I mean. Yet. And you—"

"My cards. My *passport*, man. Fuck!"

She should have been upset; she *was* upset. But this shit could be replaced, he had said so himself: money was no big deal. Part of her, the part that enjoyed sharing secrets with Magda, felt nervous laughter bubble up. Childish, selfish giggles—the worst. They gripped her then spilled over in all their meanness. "How…can…it be?"

He glowered. He looked old. Super old. "Glad someone finds it funny."

The scorching wind didn't help. Her eyes felt burnt, her throat baked. "I'm not—I don't. You can get new ones, right? You can…still…do…research."

"Yeah, but—a large fucking *but*." He waved his phone. "A clusterfuck of a but."

The policemen were staring now. One of them raised his hand, casually directing traffic.

"You don't need your passport to travel to—" The wind spun the long, fine hair from the unshaven side of her head into a hive, then flung it into her eyes.

"Trapani." His voice was brittle and small: he had shown his passport for ID to charge the tickets. He sounded even more pissed than when students plagiarized. ("You know the word *plagiarist*? Guys, in case you're interested, it means kidnapper.") Parched, she tried swallowing, swallowed again, gathered what saliva she could in her mouth. She'd have killed for a glass of cold water. How many hours before they caught the bus, air-conditioned with any luck, to this other place by the sea? A fishing port, she'd read, like towns in Nova Scotia but famous for sea salt; it might be cooler. Fine that it also happened to be where Tobias's hero—justifiably—had done the "forensic accounting" to "nail the Cosa Nostra's kingpin."

"What was dude's name again? The guy you said was a monster?" Distraction, she knew, could help calm someone down.

"Who? Oh, fuck—Totò Riina, you mean."

"So he got busted. Then what happened?"

Tobias eyed her as if she was completely stunned. "He spent years in jail."

"And then what?" She actually wanted to know.

"He died. Last year."

"That's it?"

The cops, meanwhile, had stopped traffic. Five lanes parted to let them across. Still distant, they strode closer, approaching the monument, and lit cigarettes.

"My lucky day." Tobias waved his phone impatiently, summoning them.

"Perfect timing." The sweltering heat made it hard to sound fully on side, sincere. Julie forced a cheerful cool she didn't quite feel. "Even if it takes a couple days to get a passport, it won't keep us from seeing art." In spite of herself her voice did an uptick at the end. But it was true; every surface around here was decorated with murals by street artists almost as famous as Banksy, as well as random tags. *And not just graffiti*, she thought. Obviously, churches were stuffed with statues. *If you're into that kind of thing*.

"Betcha they're checking for vandalism." Tobias spoke under his breath.

"Directiones, per favore," he yelled above the traffic noise. The island was marooned by speeding cars. "I need the polizia stazione."

Their backs to the monument, the cops stepped closer.

An artist she'd read about had filled entire churches here with stucco figures and friezes, she heard herself say. "*Plaster of Paris! That's freaking tonnes of gypsum!*" she imagined Magda gushing. "Worth a look." She nudged Tobias. "The stuff sounds, like, sooo beautiful."

Both cops were heavily armed. They scowled, obviously *non comprendo*.

"There's more to art than beautiful *things*, Jules." Tobias's voice was a hiss half swallowed by the roar of wind and traffic.

The larger cop waved his rifle; it had a scary-looking blade, a bayonet, at the end. "No photos, no photos," he seemed to be shouting at Tobias, but Julie couldn't be sure of the words, not with the accent.

"But I wasn't—I was just trying to—"

The other cop made a grab for Tobias's phone, never mind Tobias was clutching it like a lifeline. Knocked from his hand, it landed on parched grass. Oddly, neither of the cops moved to pick it up.

"Shouldn't we just go back to the B&B," the noise swallowed her whisper, "make some calls?"

The cops gripped their guns, motioned the couple toward the curb. In a flash Julie pictured the Post-its. Pink, blue, lime green. *Fugitives of the creative economy. Imperialism. Revolution. Police violence.*

"Scusa, scusa." Tobias held up both hands in a stagey surrender and backed up to rescue his phone.

The cop who had tried half-heartedly to confiscate it smirked and shook his head. Was he amused? He raised his hand. Traffic screeched to a halt, pavement bared like a sea floor in the lee of a tsunami, and she and Tobias stumbled across it to safety. His back to the cops, once out of their view, he poked at the phone with his finger. "Bastards thought I was trying to shoot them!" His laughter sounded unnerved.

"What?" Now she was confused.

"You're not allowed to photograph the cops. I should've known."

"Really? You're kidding me. But you weren't. Were you?"

His sigh sounded the same as when students forgot to do assignments. Like the assignments didn't count, like little he said in class counted—which it often didn't, she had come to realize, since she'd gotten the credit and graduated. But suddenly it seemed as if he was grading her. Keeping score, tracking things she didn't get. Which was unfair, even condescending—enough that it gave her reason to wonder. Because she should know. In case it came up, and for future reference. Like how much she owed for her half of the trip. Not just the trip but other stuff. And if she owed him, did the debt have terms, like her student loan? Was there a time limit, would there be interest?

Now wasn't the best time to come out and straight-up ask. But she could poke around the subject of finances. Get him thinking along these lines, lead up to it—not that she was quite ready, yet, to hear, accept the numbers.

"That thing, like, you know, the alpha whatever? You never actually defined it."

His tug on her hand was too sharp to be playful. "When performance outdoes benchmark."

She swallowed, picked dirt from her eye. "What does that even mean?"

"Let me rephrase." His voice oozed a chill impatience. "When outcomes exceed expectations. Obviously, it doesn't happen all the time."

Okay, fine. So they were both dancing around things.

She channelled her dad. "Like, getting the biggest bang for your buck, you mean?"

Tobias eyed her. "We all want what we want."

She bristled at this. "So isn't it kind of about greed? Like, end-times capitalism. Stuff you talked about in class."

His gaze dimmed to boredom. Unmitigated,

unblinking boredom. Maybe even disgust. "It's human nature, for fuck's sake. It's the way things work."

He set his gaze on something ahead. A building, its grand, pillared entrance draped with rainbow flags. The wide, sweeping steps were carpeted in deep crimson. "Teatro Massimo. That's where they filmed *Godfather III*'s famous last scene—where Michael Corleone's daughter gets killed?" He shook his head, sighed again. "They've got this major pile here, and tons of government offices. But for us the nearest consulate's in Rome—can you goddamn believe it?"

"They email you a form, you email it back. Presto, passport." She made her voice sing-songy, never mind her heart was clogging her throat. "You phone the bank, they send new cards. No biggie."

Even dimmed, his look just then could have melted plastic. "Sweetheart. This is Italy."

They went back to the B&B, where he spent all afternoon on the phone. He hadn't bothered going to the police station, what would be the point? They would go to Trapani another day, he said without much conviction. After dealing with banks and the embassy, he needed food. Until the bank sent his e-transfer and new cards—her Visa was at its limit—all they could spend was what coin they had on them. He needed something to cheer him up, he said, to remind him the day wasn't a total waste.

"We'll grab something at del Capo—the market on the way to the Palazzo di Giustizia." This was the court where Falcone and Borsellino had tried and put away Totò Riina, the boss of bosses, he mansplained. The efforts that got both men assassinated.

Once again they arrived too late, only to find stalls stocked with nothing more than picked-over veggies and fruit. Still, Tobias managed to suss out fresh mozzarella, sesame bread, dried salami. They ate standing up, washing everything down with one-euro wine. This cut the need to talk but cleaned out a third of the euros in her stash. If she could have, she'd have gladly forked over another third for more cheese. But before she could suggest it, Tobias started to shoulder his way through the crowd. The teeming market street was obviously a shortcut to somewhere else.

She sidestepped dogs, squeezed past a gauntlet of men hawking cellphone cases. Getting farther and farther ahead, Tobias could've been cutting a trail for himself through snow. Except it was still stinking hot, the sun blazing through a smoky haze that held in the smell of rotting food. At least the wind had died, but it left the air thick with the smell of things burning—from the fires they'd spotted earlier lighting up the mountainsides? She had changed into Magda's other offering, a sundress. Its Indian cotton flagged against her body, already damp with sweat. She ducked around a man carrying a swordfish over one shoulder.

Tobias must have thought she was close behind. He did not glance back.

Beside a crate of discarded tomatoes, kittens fought over a fish head. They were so cute—didn't Magda keep saying they should get a cat? A woman selling light fixtures from a stall called out and fixed her with a hopeful gaze. Above the vendor's head chandeliers glistened palely, a dusty rococo opulence. Engine noises rose in a deafening blast, and Julie turned in time to see a fleet of scooters shoehorned into the piazza outside a church. Another volley of revs erupted, a salute to a bride and groom joyfully descending the steps. The riders were decked out in flashy, beautiful clothes. She stopped to watch the bride toss her bouquet. A girl perched on the back of a scooter caught it.

When Julie looked for him, Tobias had disappeared from sight. She felt an instant panic merge with something like relief. Then she spotted his curls, saw him turn and wave.

She was glad he had missed the wedding salute. He'd have had something to say about it: what a waste of fossil fuel? A throwback to anti-feminism? She wished Magda had seen it. They would have laughed, cynically of course, amused but quietly envious. Not of the bride or groom but of the scooter people in their party clothes, well, not so much them as their thoughtless, carefree exuberance. All those young "things" in skimpy gowns, arms around handsome macho drivers in all their incorrectness.

Caught in a human gridlock, she watched a puppy perched atop a crate lick himself. Next to an empty banana crate, a scrawny black cat gnawed something bloody. She stepped aside to let people pass. Aimed *puss-puss* sounds at the cat. The feline did not look up.

Then, all at once, she felt it: a piercing jab. Like a fine, fine needle stabbing her calf. The sting was sharper than a pinch, sudden and fierce. Even as she lifted her skirt to look, it began to throb with a fiery pulse.

A cluster of three tiny puncture marks. The wound looked like an adaptor had been plugged into her leg, the kind of adaptor Tobias had for plugging in his electric razor.

Had she been attacked by fleas? The puppy and cat

hadn't moved. Rotted bananas half-filled the crate, a nest for insects? Oh God, could the culprit have been a tick?

Once again Tobias was all but out of sight, elbowing his way forward. She dug at the wound with her nails. If not for the crowds, the lack of a place to stop, she'd have plunked herself down, gathered enough saliva to spit on her fingers, and rubbed it—anything to ease the shrieking itch.

Hawkers wheeled past, hauling collapsed stalls on broken baby strollers.

Fear watered with anger flooded her. Was it too much to ask for him to wait up?

Struggling along, head down, skirt hiked as she kept scratching—scratching till the wound wept—she finally caught up. He barely acknowledged her. Muttered about globalization, free markets.

Couldn't they just enjoy the city? But first, take a short break until the sting and the itch subsided?

But there was his plan. The palace of justice lay somewhere nearby on a major street. It closed in fifteen minutes, he said, couldn't she walk a little faster?

To distract herself she tried imagining what a Mob monster looked like. How a Totò Riina would eat and sleep, say, while being responsible for the murders of hundreds of people for the sake of money, power?

She scratched until the wound bled through Magda's dress, left a dark red spot on its flowered print. Balancing on one foot, still scratching, in spite of herself she gripped Tobias's arm to keep steady. Doubled over to take another look, she hooked that heel into the other knee, held a wobbly tree pose. What if it was a tick bite? The thought of a tick latching on, gorging on her blood, spreading Lyme disease, made her hyperventilate. If it was a tick, by now would she see it, the rash people watched for?

Tobias shifted, restless. Obviously unhappy. Finding a patch of bare sidewalk, she squatted gracelessly to take a closer look. He eyed her with something that felt like disgust.

The more she scratched, the more the bite itched. Who cared if her dress rode up, that a man dismantling a dishtowel display nearby was enjoying the view?

"Can't you pick it up a bit? The place is only open till five-thirty." Tobias sounded totally pissed off.

"*Official* hours. *You* would know."

Outside the fascist-era edifice—stark, ugly lines and rectangles of concrete, marble, and glass—a squad of armed guards lounged, automatic weapons slung at their sides. "The Carabinieri," Tobias murmured, just letting her know. The braid on their blue uniforms looked tarnished against their brilliant white bandoliers. Before he could pocket his phone, two of them pointed at it: "No photos, no photos." Nodding, Tobias mansplained to her some more about Falcone and Borsellino working here thirty years ago.

A guard lit a cigarette, waved it. Spoke in heavily accented *inglese*. "The Palazzo of Justice is not open to the public."

Tobias dug out his phone, consulted it. His mouth tightened. "It doesn't close for another seven minutes." He stuck out his small, stubbled chin as he spoke. "The sign says."

Julie pictured the Post-its. *Doritos, palm oil, petroleum by-products.*

Always resist authority, he had drilled into the class, when authority thwarts fairness, the common good.

The guard raised his gun. Tobias backed off then, muttering about police states, tyranny, individuals' rights.

The guard smirked, blowing smoke rings. "*Turistos.*"

"If you hadn't been so slow." Tobias's voice was jokey, but the look in his eyes was distant. Cold. Yet, as they slouched away he laid a lank arm around her shoulder. A gesture of apology or defeat?

"Maybe I should have it looked at?" The bite, she meant. By now it had swelled into a bump with the circumference of a loonie.

He didn't seem to hear.

They wandered back toward the B&B, taking a different route through yet another closed-up street market. He talked about Nigerians taking over the heroin trade from Sicilian Mafia traffickers the law had sidelined. She'd seen it in the *Globe and Mail*, right? No? Wandering down an alley filled with funeral supply shops, they passed a pizzeria whose TV livestreamed a pilgrimage to Mecca. Its call to prayer poured through the open doorway, where the cook squatted, cradling a cat in his apron.

Fugitives of the creative economy. Fundamentalism. Religion. Revolution.

She bent and lifted her hem. There was no sign of a target rash, white encircled with red. But the punctures had closed over, the flesh around them shiny and tight. It took everything she had not to tear it open, rip out whatever might have wormed its way deeper.

The smells of cinnamon and nutmeg from the pizza place scented the smoky air. A group of men in ragged clothes huddled nearby. Their voices made her uneasy.

Big oil. Cartels. The Philippines. Colombia. Commodity pricing.

"My guess, it was a spider, maybe a tarantula." Tobias could not have sounded less concerned. "Definitely not a viper—they have these too, here."

That night she wondered if sex might take her mind off the bite. But the room was stifling and Tobias wasn't in the mood. He kept his nose in a book—research—read with the light blazing as she tried to doze.

"Everything's dog eat dog," he said, finally turning it out. "In a market economy the rich will kill to thrive. It's not about survival, it's thrival, thrival of the fattest." He rolled over, immediately started to snore.

The itch burned with a rabid intensity. She willed everything inside her to resist it. Holding still, hands tightly clasped, she wondered if remaining cisgender was the best choice.

A woman would not have turned her back. A woman would have helped her find a doctor.

And she wondered how in the name of everything that was right and good she would survive eight more days. Eight more days until they flew home.

"You okay?" Tobias did ask at breakfast. The news on TV was scary. The wildfires—the fires they'd seen starting on the mountains—were the top story, and now he was more interested. Keeping his eyes on the screen, he translated. The Cosa Nostra set the fires deliberately to force the owners off their land, apparently. It happened every year. Excitement gave his voice a lilt. "Holy good shit, there's got to be graffito about this."

It was the first time in ages he'd mentioned art, the crux of his paper's thesis. Not that she was keeping score. But as far as she could tell, his research was about dodging its point.

Land grabs. Agritourism.

"But...with that wind, the heat...Don't people die? And animals, what about the animals?"

Financialization. Partners. Costs.

"Look. We're not talking the Apple Dumpling Gang. Scorched earth diplomacy. 'Give me what's yours or I'll kill you.'"

She set down her glass. Took out her phone. Eight more days, and this one had only begun. Polishing off his espresso, scrolling through his messages, he complained about the bank. "What could possibly be taking so long to send the e-transfer?"

As he spoke she tapped in her dad's email address. Eight days. How many hours was that? *Do the math, eight times twenty-four.* She hesitated, then tapped in the message. If there was any way he could maybe possibly send an advance against Christmas and her birthday...her twenty-second was in just a couple of months. Rent was due and she was short of...

She looked up when Tobias's phone pinged, and his face brightened.

Love, Julie, she typed. She was about to press send when Tobias punched the air—Yes! The transfer had come through, and if she wanted he would give her the cash to change her ticket.

Change her ticket and fly home early, he repeated. As soon as she liked. The earlier the better?

Magda was wearing a weird orange backpack when she finally came home. The backpack had a clear plastic bubble at the top, like a window, and as she turned to shut the door it looked like she was wearing half a space suit, something out of Kubrick's 2001: A *Space Odyssey*. She had a plastic dishpan in one hand with some cans in it and in her other hand a sack of kitty litter.

Magda nearly fell out of her skin when Julie slipped from the bathroom. "WTF? Aren't you supposed to be in—?" Their hug was warm and sweet and lasted quite a while. Peeling off the backpack, Magda started laughing like a loon. "Like, I'm not going to say 'Told you so.' I promise. Except, he sucks, right? Tobias sucks. I had a feeling he would. Mr. Hot Shit Pausssta mon. There was just something about his—"

"Words?" She couldn't help it. Her lip wobbled before she let out a wounded giggle. A giggle that fizzed in her ears, then unleashed more giggles that came straight from her belly, somehow bypassed her heart.

"You okay? Really, I mean."

"No. Well. Yeah. Sure. No worries, okay. I'm fine. Like, totally. But what the…?"

The sweetest furry face Julie had ever seen peeked through the bubble window. Orange stripes and cobalt-blue eyes. "Don't tell me, is it ours?" *Vet bills, cat food, litter,* she was already thinking.

Unzipping the carrier, Magda knelt to release the

kitten, laughed as it sniffed their toes.

"Hey Julie. Meet Georgia. Georgia, meet Julie. Welcome home, girlfriends."

Julie squatted low to scoop up the kitten. Closed her eyes, held it to her cheek. Felt the softness of its fur and the scrabbling of tiny, teeth-like claws. Instinctively, the fingers of her other hand slid to the swelling on her calf. But she clenched them, resisted.

Magda grimaced. "Crap—*what* did you do to your leg?"

Fleas. She smiled, shook her head. "Hey, you know, this thing happened, but I'm okay."

Outcomes exceeding expectations, or falling short of them. Gains versus losses. The line that divided them was gel-tipped-pen fine, she thought. Some things were harder to figure out.

Flea or spider, for starters; she would never know.

What a Friend We Have

THE FRENCHYS BIN OVERFLOWED WITH PLUSHY SANTAS and reindeer, glittery balls and bows, and—as Grey dug deeper—gold! A green plastic pickle covered with sparklies, so ugly-ass it was fire. It had Ty all over it; she would have slipped it into her pocket if cash lady hadn't been looking. She moved to a bin of socks with candy canes on them. The radio blasted "Simm-ply haaa-ving a wonderful Christmastime" with sleigh bells like a bag of quarters going *shake shake shake*.

She returned to the pickle, held it up. "How much?"

"Fifty cents."

Forget it. Ty probably wouldn't even laugh. Anyways, she already had his present, from dude in the next apartment. A real nice guy. Sometimes she thought it wouldn't be such a bad idea to move in with *him*. She felt in her pocket. Dude was always giving her stuff while Ty was busy sleeping or playing N64. And he called her April, which nobody had since grade five. Dude said they'd go out driving sometime, though so far his car had not left its spot.

So she walked. Walking was no big deal if you had nowhere special to go. She felt in her pocket again, closed her fingers around the tiny gift—it would suck to drop it, especially here. She felt for her money.

"You can pay me later," Dude had said. Maybe *he*'d like the pickle? He could hang it on the plant in his window.

She dug through the sweaters bin, found a purple shirt, girls' size something. Found a hoodie, just right, size zero, a skull on the front in gold glitter. Grazing men's T-shirts, she yanked up a black one with *You Got My Back* on it. Too perfect—why wouldn't she have Ty's back? He could be so sweet, going with her to buy food, for instance—except when he'd scammed the checkout with a fake coupon for chocolate milk. Dialling the manager, checkout bitch had given them both the finger.

Now the Frenchys lady was watching, so Grey went up and paid, left with her bag of stuff. Outside, it was raining, slushy rain. As she passed the Canadian Tire, cars went spitting by. Passing St. Jude's—its sign asking *Guess Who's Coming for Christmas?*—she heard singing. "What a friend we have..." She felt for the pill. It had begun to burn a freaking hole in her pocket. She pictured Ty waking up. Maybe he'd make her hot chocolate. Just the thought...for a second she was April trucking along in pink snow boots with a Hannah Montana backpack—back when Mom and them had given a shit and her biggest worry was what snack was for recess.

She closed her fist around the friend, let it dig into her palm. Maybe she would wrap it in some toilet paper with a sticker from the junk mail. Maybe she could find a tree and put it and Ty's T-shirt underneath. He might even put something there for her. A tree—there were woods behind St. Jude's, in behind the new townhouses where she'd seen baby Christmas trees, going back there a few times to party.

The townhouses were all lit up, though it wasn't yet dark. Airless Frosties lay like muddy sheets on people's lawns. She found the path. By now the rain was mushy snow, making everything so quiet she couldn't hear traffic anymore. She reached the clearing full of dead cars—cars that might have driven up and down the road when Mom was a kid. The snow sat like cake frosting on their rusted-out dashes and windshield frames, the woods so silent she imagined Mom sitting in one of them with some guy, maybe making out.

Now the pill burned a hole in her hand—what she *really* wanted was to stop and put it on her tongue, catch some snowflakes, tip her head back, and feel it go down. She knew what it could do. "But it's for Ty, I'm keeping it for Ty," she said out loud. The friend was his present.

A tree would take her mind off herself?

She kept going because of Ty, because a tree would make things perfect. She had a nail file on her to cut one down with, or she could snap one off at the roots. Pulling her hand from her pocket, she bent to check one out, touched the trunk: stickiness on her fingers.

The tree wasn't skinny enough. The trouble was, none were.

The snow was falling thick now, the woods turning from green to grey. Her sneakers left brown tracks, a mash of dirt and dead leaves in the shape of footsteps.

The swing caught her by surprise, hanging there,

hanging from its big, tall tree, perfectly still. Its plastic seat was white and purple—lilac, like some Zuppies at Frenchys. She had seen it before with Ty, looking for the lake, the day he'd ducked under so long she thought he had drowned. It marked a fork in the path, either way leading to the shore. A sign they'd almost made it.

Something told Grey this was where to stop.

The seat was crooked and way too high to climb up on—some asshole had wrapped the ropes around and around the branch it hung from, wrecking anybody's hope of swinging. Not like when Ty had boosted her up, given her a push. Just hanging there now, it didn't even move when a coating of snow fell from it.

Forget Ty forget Ty forget Ty, the woods and the snow were saying—the ropes too, creaking when she pulled on them and rested her chin there. The cool of the seat and melt trickling down her neck and down inside her jacket said, *Forget him forget him forget him.*

The wind picked up.

Stick your tongue out, said the friend, *why not?*

Ty would never know.

Snowflakes swirled. *What a friend we have, what a friend.*

But her fingers were stiff with cold, and the pill slipped. Before she could save it, the gift fed itself to the snow. Its greyness bleeding, dissolving into white.

Ship Time

"IT'S THE PERFECT WAY TO EXTEND THE HONEYMOON." Krista squeezed his hand as the grinning captain and crew welcomed them aboard, along with a tide of other folks in flashy cruise wear.

"You're right," Sam agreed, "a floating paradise—it'll be great, sweetie." Though he wasn't exactly jazzed about the holiday she had booked. An extended Mediterranean cruise was his idea of a trip, especially since their honeymoon, eight weeks past—Bordeaux, Lisbon, Barcelona, Nice—was now a hazy memory.

Crystal Seas Cruises was not one of the biggest lines and the *Bounty* wasn't its most luxurious ship. But it was the itinerary Sam found wanting, a guarantee he and Krista would simply spend the week on board, overeating and drinking, doomed to use that *state-of-the-art gym*, or buy bigger clothes once they got back to Hoboken. Of course, shopping would ease the letdown Krista always complained of after trips she wished went on forever.

"It'll be a chance to fall in love all over again," she'd promised. "And, hey! It'll be fun to see where your folks came from." Krista was one of those people who could lose herself forever on ancestry.com.

There was a reason his great-greats had left Canada for the States more than a hundred and fifty years ago. The allure of sailing up a barren, northern coast—stopping at places that barely rated being on a map—was beyond him. He wasn't even sure where his forebears had emigrated from, only knew the Maritime provinces were small, poor, sleepy places, according to his grandfather. For all his buried, watered-down-to-the-point-of-not-existing Maritime roots, genes, or whatever Krista wanted to call them, Sam was not an oceans person. Growing up in New Jersey, with only the odd foray to Long Island, where his parents were, he preferred cities, suburbs, *land*.

He'd tried to sway her. "Why not the West Coast, or the Caribbean? We could always do the Dominican." Exactly, she'd said; they had the rest of their lives to see these places. Wasn't that the greatest thing about being married?

"Well, it's not *quite* what the photo showed," Krista admitted, settling into their room near the front of the ship. Still, she cooed over the décor. They had only been a couple for ten months—two of these wedded—but he already knew how quickly she spotted flaws.

No family, friends, or work to get in our hair, she texted him from their tiny private balcony, the two of them perching there, watching Staten Island become a dot. He texted back an upside-down smile. Her grin reminded him of the first time he had noticed her, at the start-up where they worked—he as junior counsel, she as a programmer. Love at first sight for both.

She was anxious to check out the pool on the top deck. Up there, Sam was surprised to see so many folks already lounging around it. Late afternoon, the sun behind clouds. The pool water looked surprisingly still, given the engines' rumbling, how many decks below? Most of the sunbathers were leathern and elderly, many of them undoubtedly Trumpites, he thought cruelly. Others were the slightly older, slimmer, wealthier, more successful versions of himself and Krista. Exemplars of why people like his ancestors had chosen the States over backwaters like the one she wanted to see.

"Let's wait for a warmer time—this'll be great in the mornings, though. You're such a good swimmer, Sam. Like your great-grandpa." She'd heard his father's boast about the old man's crawl. With the sigh Sam found winsome, she added, "Your great-grandpa must have been so ancient." She pressed toward the elevator, curious about the wet bar. "It's so cool you can remember him. That you have this...connection. To your past, I mean. A lot of people hardly even know where their parents come from, let alone their parents' parents."

He slid his arm around her. In the elevator, with no one looking, he slipped his hand under her shirt, stopped respectfully short of brushing her breast. "Oh yeah? I prefer living in the present. In case you haven't noticed." They forgot about the wet bar and instead hurried back to their room. In bed, he kissed her ear, then the hollow at the base of her throat, toyed with the gold chain he had given her on their engagement. It seemed ages ago.

"See? I knew this was the perfect way to spend our

vacay." In a way she was right. Much as he loved his job, its challenges, it was too bad life didn't include a little more downtime, he realized. Damn, could that mean that somewhere in his blood he was a lazy Maritimer, the way his mom described his dad's forebears? A scary thought. Divorced, leaving behind Hoboken, his parents lived separate lives in Larchmont.

He and Krista had no sooner shed their clothes than a bell sounded, a digital alarm of some sort, and a voice blared from the speaker beside the cabin door. "On behalf of myself, Captain Burleton, and everyone at Crystal Seas, thanks for joining us. Just one thing. What happens at sea stays at sea." A suggestive laugh. "Forget your cares, folks. We are officially on ship time." The crackle of feedback, then a reminder that even crossing into international waters the time on board would match Manhattan time, "the same as if you were strolling Fifth Avenue."

The announcement continued, providing an explanation of bells, of all things—a throwback to the old days of sail? The bells signalled changes of watch. "Unlike the ones you hear on land, the ship's don't match the number of the hour. Eight bells in total, one for each half-hour of a four-hour watch." A chuckle burst from the speaker. Sam imagined the captain's grin, teeth like the grille of a pricey new SUV. As if this wasn't sufficient, an explanation of the crew's activities during each watch ensued, one mysteriously dubbed the first dog watch, another the last dog watch, all of this followed by the assurance that passenger safety was the number one concern. "Please take a moment, if you will, and read the terms posted in your room, the ship's rules and regulations."

Sam's imagination flew instantly to news images of

the Italian cruise ship *Costa Concordia*, which had sunk off Tuscany five years before. Protracted litigations. A messy case.

"TMI." Krista reached too late for the speaker's volume button.

"Not if something happens, actually. Remember all the old folks on board." Sam couldn't help thinking about the on-board emergencies he had read about online, and not just medical ones—fire being the worst, people falling overboard a close second, not to mention odd things happening at sea. The fact that people simply went missing. Suicides, most likely. Add to this the issue, evidenced by a case his dad had prosecuted, of passengers being wrongfully accused of crimes and held in the ship's detention facility, "the brig," until the ship reached port. It was reassuring that the *Bounty* was well equipped with cameras, if troubling to know they were all being watched, except in their rooms. A necessary evil, he decided. A ship like this could be the scene of countless wrongdoings and accidents. Falls. Pool mishaps. Drownings.

"You know there's a morgue, right?" Krista teased, seeming to read his mind.

Elbowing her playfully, he reset the volume. The captain was *still* speaking, in that chummy tone Sam had already grown to dislike. "Just so you know, *Oscar* is code for person overboard. Shipboard safety is everyone's responsibility, folks."

By now Sam had retrieved their tickets to read the fine print. Details about additional charges. The warning that itineraries could change, as docking was at the captain's discretion. The one condition not subject to change was that departure times were firm. Passengers travelling on their own on land excursions would be out of luck if they missed it. The ship waited for no one.

"We did opt for the 'free' Wi-Fi, yes?" Krista held up her phone. It kept going to data, the signal buffering.

"I forget how much extra it was, but, yeah. And a genie. Worth the extra fees."

She looked a little miffed. They couldn't be that far out to sea so soon, although when he stepped out onto the balcony, Long Island—he guessed—was a faint blue line on the horizon. When Krista tried to call her dad in Syracuse, just to say they were on their way, the signal was out of range. "What the—? Oh, don't forget to put your phone on airplane mode, Sam. We don't want to get dinged for roaming charges. Even with the all-inclusive—"

"Hey, isn't this what we wanted?" He did his best to sound upbeat. "Time to ourselves." *How incredibly fortunate neither of them had promised to work remotely.* "We can spend the whole week in bed, sweetie. But right now I'm starving. Let's go eat."

They had completely missed happy hour. All through dinner—six courses, champagne, all the seafood they could eat—he resolved to follow Krista's advice to him, given back at the Manhattan Cruise Terminal, to "chill." Yet, notions of risk niggled at him. But didn't everything come down to some kind of risk, even marriage?

After dinner, sipping from each other's glasses, they necked on the dance floor. The music was cabaret style. He drank more than he was accustomed to. The flush in Krista's cheeks reminded him of last November. He had known by Christmas that he wanted to marry her. By New Year's Eve they had begun planning the wedding.

"I guess you know what you're doing, Sam." His

mother hadn't sounded so sure. "You can be impulsive like your father. It runs in his family. The tendency not to look before they leap. Make this kind of mistake and you'll pay for a long time, dear."

Undressing for bed, he glimpsed himself in the bathroom's tiny mirror. Thought for a second how, even at thirty-seven he resembled not his dad but Krista's. A well-meaning, martini-swilling guy who had promised in no uncertain terms to put Sam's balls in a vise if he hurt his daughter. "*Dared* to hurt her," Mr. Osterhausen had emphasized, munching hors d'oeuvres at their engagement party. At that moment, Sam had experienced his one and only fleeting bout of cold feet. Since the wedding, only once or twice had he wondered how it was you could be smitten with someone yet at times "not know her from Adam," his great-grandfather's expression. Whoever Adam was.

He had begun to think there might be something to Krista's urge to learn about her ancestry. A few weeks before the ceremony at Hoboken City Hall, before a justice of the peace and both sets of parents, she had dropped everything to order a DNA kit, again to spit into the tube the website provided, and send it off.

"I just want to know. Before we tie the knot. That I don't have some bad apple lurking in my background. Something that might embarrass our kids or our kids' kids."

Sam hadn't even contemplated kids. She was joking, although he'd replied as if she meant it. "I'm sure you don't." But she had planted the seed. Albeit vaguely, he wondered the same about himself and his gene pool.

Tipsy, perched on their balcony wearing only the

fluffy white robes that were an add-on, together they peered up at the night sky, no stars to be seen. There was only the distant throbbing of engines, a sloshing far, far below. The waves had heightened into swells, creating a heavy, rocking motion. Never a big drinker, he regretted his fourth margarita.

To make himself feel better, he thought of his grandfather and his great-grandfather, how amazing it was his great-grandfather had been around when Sam was small. He thought about the things he might have asked the man, had he known what to ask. Things about *his* father, and his mother for that matter, not to go down too deep a rabbit hole. The mysterious past his grandpa rambled on about from his care-home bed—TMI, as Krista would say—stuff that had to be from two or three generations removed, at least, any sense attached to it lost to time, no loss at all, probably. About their "people" going to sea, in sailing ships when the world still had them. A bunch of romantic bull, Sam's dad said. Crazy old tales of how Sam's great-grandfather and *his* father before him went to sea as boys, sailing between Canada and Boston, New York and the Caribbean, even across the Atlantic and around Cape Horn. His grandpa's dementia talking, blurring the generations.

"Went to sea? A ship's boy? His old man? News to me." Sam's father had said this, snapping shut his briefcase, jammed with files he brought home in case of a fire or break-in at his firm.

"Wow. That is so paranoid," Krista had remarked when Sam mentioned this. "Honey, promise me? You'll always leave work at the office?"

They woke to fog at the porthole, greyness like a never-ending dust bunny. A drizzling mist enclosed the balcony, nothing about it enticing. From somewhere overhead came the screeching of gulls. When they tried their phones, hallelujah, the Wi-Fi worked. Sam texted the genie—a sort of personal shipboard butler—and asked to have two black coffees delivered to their room. The genie texted back so promptly Sam wondered if he/she/it, provided at cost, was AI. Ten minutes later, a knock on the door. A small, swarthy man in a white uniform handed them their beverages. "Can I get a breakfast sandwich to go? Do you guys do that?" The man shrugged and told Sam to send another text.

"Oh, babe." Krista looked disappointed. "But I really want to do the breakfast buffet. I guess a swim is out. Unless we did the indoor pool? No, forget that."

So they dressed and rode the elevator up to the restaurant on the deck below the vast one where they had eaten dinner. From its wraparound windows the view was a solid grey. The captain's voice came over the PA, announcing that they had passed Boston an hour earlier, run into some confusion over berthing times. Krista gazed into space, sighing. Her silence made Sam uncomfortable. The thought of having been so close to Beantown, now distant, made him uncomfortable. He could barely face the buffet, despite the fact that it was an astonishing smorgasbord.

Krista picked at her food. "We could check out the gym."

But the thought of getting on a treadmill made his head hurt. "Maybe later, okay?"

On the way back to their room they passed a steward wielding a spray bottle, wiping down the railing with a cloth. The man smiled and nodded, moved to wipe off a door knob near a section marked *Staff Only*.

Sam guessed Krista mistook his hungover silence for "a mood."

"It's okay, Sam. I'm sure we'll hit Boston on the way back."

A bell sounded just as they entered their room—the arch, lingering ding-dong he hated to admit he had gotten used to—followed by that familiar, jocular blather. Krista reached to mute the speaker but stopped, alerted by a change in Burleton's tone. "—Come to our attention...we may have a possible case of Norwalk on-board. No need for concern, the passenger is in good hands. Ladies and—"

Germs, Sam imagined his great-grandfather's voice, the joke that no one had laughed at, and he himself had been too young to get. The man had lived to be one hundred and four; Sam was seven when he passed. "Rest assured, I repeat, there is no cause for concern."

"It was all the fish my father ate as kid," his grandpa had said once from his bed, explaining the eldest man's longevity. Sam's own father had a ticking time bomb for a heart. He found himself hoping his great-grandfather's special gene hadn't skipped his generation too.

"Yuck!" Krista grimaced, racing to wash her hands. He couldn't help but think of the ship's wastewater, a plume of it trailing the *Bounty*'s crystal wake—the waste from twelve hundred functioning bodies. Where was it dumped? Twelve miles offshore, he had read somewhere. Was that nautical or real miles? Not that the difference of a few feet would matter much in the ocean.

"It's probably just me—but I don't feel so hot," she said, lying down.

If she's a hypochondriac, I would know by now, wouldn't I? "The power of suggestion is a thing, Kris." He stroked her arm. It didn't help that the rocking motion, the noise of the engines, seemed to have deepened. He thought of the bunker sea fuel propelling them, the foulness belching from twin stacks—all to drive a floating city.

"We should have booked a room lower down and in the middle—the centre of gravity," Krista moaned, draping an arm over her eyes.

When he picked up his phone to quietly google *cruise ship emissions*, the Wi-Fi was on the fritz again. He turned on the TV, but none of the streaming services they had signed into were working. He peered out at the fog, so thick he couldn't even see water. *Is this what could legitimately be called a liminal zone?* A very fine line separated them; it must, he thought. The coastline and now the ocean itself were absolutely invisible: one or both could be near or very far away. They could, possibly, not exist at all.

Just don't think of rocks, he told himself, as Krista squirmed beside him. Complaining of a stomach ache, trying to get comfortable.

Don't say anything, he thought. *Keep still, keep quiet.* After all, who knew, any kind of dispute, a foul word, a noise complaint real or perceived?—could land a person in the brig. *Oh, wait. Now I'm getting like my dad?*

He pictured Krista in her shimmery dress at last night's cabaret, thought of her pressed against his chest, her bare arms encircling his neck. The disco balls' spinning, speckled light: there'd been almost too many of them to count.

Was it possible to get seasick on a ship so large?

"Hon," her voice wasn't more than a whisper, asking him to buy her some Gravol.

At this point he was glad to escape the room with its see-sawing motion, the fog pressing at the porthole and balcony door.

It was an adventure grabbing an elevator that wasn't full. When one finally came, the older couple on it—speaking in southern accents, thankfully not wearing MAGA hats—asked how he was doing and if he'd been to Canada before. "Folks up there are different. Friendly but slow. Kid you not, nothing stays open past six o'clock—they eat so damn early! Five o'clock, some places. Though I guess given ship time we're the early birds, aren't we, hon."

"Makes you appreciate home, I guess."

In the gift shop folks were lined up for Gravol; Sam was lucky enough to score the last package. While he was paying, a dog-eared paperback wedged behind some candy bars caught his eye. He reached to pick it up; it had a campy cover with the title *The Flying Dutchman and Other Ghost Ships* in spooky, gothic script. The clerk held her hand out to retrieve it. "Ha, don't know what that's doing here. Folks 'gift' us stuff like this—see? Watch this, straight into the trash—" But before she could take it, Sam tucked it under his arm. The rest of the books on offer were a mix of no less shlocky romance and detective novels.

"Okay, well I'm rescuing it," he said, pocketing his debit card.

When he returned to the room, he realized he'd forgotten to pick up something to wash the pills down. Krista sighed. She had her hand clapped over her mouth and her face was pale. He texted the genie, who appeared minutes later with two bottles of water. Krista chugged back a pill then disappeared into the bathroom. Mercifully, he heard no sounds of retching. But stumbling out, staggering onto the bed, she looked awful.

Curling up, she pushed his hand away when he tried to rub her back. "Just leave me be. It'll pass. I've been seasick before..." A few sullen minutes elapsed, then she was asleep.

It was not how he had envisioned this or any trip. The sound of wet—rain? waves?—slashing at the porthole made him shudder. So much for stepping out on the balcony for a little fresh air. One false move and he might find himself in the drink, as his great-grandfather had apparently called it.

"Mind if I read?" He touched Krista's shoulder ever so lightly and snapped on the light. She did not stir.

The pages flipped open to a chapter about the *Mary Celeste*. The name sent a frisson of recognition through him. The story was a tale Sam had listened to sitting on his great-grandfather's knee—about a sailing ship in the 1800s that was found abandoned and adrift somewhere, maybe off Portugal? "The ghost ship was found by her salvagers in a dishevelled but seaworthy state, sails set but her lifeboat missing," the chapter began, "not a single sign of her captain and his family and crew to be seen." Sam read on. "Her cargo of alcohol was untouched, the belongings of Capt. Benjamin Spooner Briggs, his wife, their daughter and crew of seven were undisturbed." The author explained that the ship, "cursed from the start," was eventually scuttled and her "relics" could be seen in a museum "very nearby" the site in Nova Scotia where she was built and launched.

The writer also tossed around ideas about what might have happened—foul play, mutiny, piracy—including a theory that the people aboard had been overcome by the cargo's fumes. Sam's attention flagged when it was suggested that they had been pulled overboard by a giant squid.

Meanwhile, the room's rocking and rolling gave him a headache that soon became blinding, making it increasingly difficult to focus. When the story veered into the paranormal, Sam closed the book, reached for Krista's Gravol and took two. As he lay waiting for sleep to salvage the afternoon, he thought of the captain's words—Burleton's, not Briggs's from the *Mary Celeste*'s log quoted sporadically in the book. *Norwalk, receiving care.* Weren't cruise ships famous for harbouring viruses, due to the sheer numbers of folks on board, dining, dancing, and drinking in such reckless proximity?

By mid-evening the seas had calmed and Krista was feeling somewhat better. "Thank God it isn't hurricane season!" She rolled over to accept his hug.

"No kidding." He still had a headache but, thankfully, his guts weren't in an uproar. Agreeing it would be better to dine in, he texted the genie and ordered more water and two plates of everything the supper buffet offered.

They awoke the next morning to a deeper calm; the ship felt like it was barely moving. Back to her cheerful self, Krista kissed him and rose to peek outside. "Sea life. I want to see sea life." *Think of your cruise as a luxury whale-watching expedition*, the website had promised. *The Gulf of Maine teems*

with dolphins and porpoises, humpbacks and right whales, and even a few great white sharks! A sight for every nature lover's bucket list. But they were beyond the Gulf of Maine and must be in the open Atlantic—though when Sam google-mapped their location the signal just kept spinning. And when he joined her at the railing the fog was still so thick he could barely see his wedding ring when he held out his hand. Krista stumbled back inside. Joining her, he encircled her in his arms, nuzzled her neck.

"Guess we're bound to get fog at sea." He didn't mention how it must be treacherous cruising along a coastline that was exclusively rock—it must be, judging by the online photos of Peggys Cove, the place Krista was hell-bent on seeing.

It felt good to leave the cramped cabin, and reaching the breakfast room early, they avoided the crush. The fare was croissants, Danishes, muffins, and fruit that could have been fresher; scrambled eggs, home fries, sausages, and pancakes with "real Canadian" maple syrup.

"Fill your boots, hon. We've got a busy day ahead of us." Krista's high spirits buoyed him. Once again, as if on cue, the captain's voice blared over the PA, as buttery-toned as ever, saying they would soon be docking in their scheduled port of call: Halifax, Nova Scotia. "A great little city" from which tour buses would take them to their "iconic" destination, "the place everybody comes up here to see. And, more good news," it went on, "looks like we're in for clearing conditions later tonight." They would disembark soon and the departure time wasn't until 4:00 P.M. "Copy that, folks, that's local"—*crackle crackle*—allowing "ample opportunity"—*crackle*—to enjoy "the largest city on Canada's eastern seaboard."

"Finally," said Krista, as they went off to shower. Cheering, "Yay! We even have reliable Wi-Fi," while waiting for the elevator. She clicked on the cruise's daily bulletin, showed Sam details about buses and locations.

"There will be lots of folks to direct you," interrupted a smiling hostess he recognized from the cabaret. "No worries, you can't get lost. How is it possible to get lost in a city with less than half a million people?"

"You tell me," Sam said.

While Krista showered, dressed, and primped, he returned to the *Ghost Ship* book. Reread how the sailing ship's captain and his wife, Sarah, had brought along their two-year-old, Sophia, but left their son, Arthur, in the care of Briggs's mother in Massachusetts. How the captain and crew of the *Dei Gratia*, also from Nova Scotia, had set sail for Genoa too, following the same route from New York, only eight days later. How they reached the *Mary Celeste*'s position, "midway between the Azores and Portugal's coast, on Wednesday, Dec. 4, 1872 land time, or Thursday, Dec. 5, sea time." In Briggs's last log entry, dated nine days earlier, his ship's position was recorded as four hundred nautical miles from where *Dei Gratia* came upon her. Elsewhere, the log mentioned vague rumblings from the hold.

"Listen to this." He started reading out loud, about allegations against the salvagers, lawsuits that had arisen.

"And? This matters?" Krista rolled her eyes, loading her daypack with bottled water, extra socks, a sweater. "Peggys, here we come."

Something about her determination fuelled him. He googled Spencers Island, the birthplace of the ghost ship, then google-mapped it, and while Krista fidgeted impatiently, he googled museums. The first one that came up was just a few kilometres, not many miles surely, from the ship's launching site. Krista tapped her foot. She was wearing the yellow rubber Chelsea boots from L.L. Bean that she'd chosen especially for this excursion.

As he gazed back at her, for the first time since they'd met he longed for a day to himself. Just one day. If absence made the heart grow fonder (another of his grandpa's sayings—or maybe his great-grandfather's, passed down), being cooped up together in a twelve-by-ten-foot cell for two days and three nights might have the opposite effect?

He texted the genie, the genie texted back. *Yes, we can arrange a cab, no problem. The driver will be waiting for you outside the pavilion, where the buses are.*

Sam chose his words carefully, springing his plans on her.

Krista's response threw him for an unexpected loop. "Are you kidding me?" Incensed, she threw what his mother would call a rather major hissy fit. "You *aren't* suggesting we separate!?"

"Sweetie. The litigations alone—the *Mary Celeste* was one of the biggest insurance scams of the nineteenth century."

"And I should care about that?" Her expression could have been a knife flashing. "Fine. Suit yourself."

He didn't bother reminding her they would meet back on board for dinner, that the evening's scheduled entertainment promised to be something they would both enjoy—jazz and even a little reggae, for the fun of it. *Hold the samba dancers and flame throwers.*

"This way you have time to shop without me tagging along, babe. It's just this once, okay?" He kissed her and held her hand all the way down the gangway, stepping for the first time in what felt like months onto steady, solid if rain-slicked asphalt. He watched her slip into the lineup for the bus, then went to find the cab.

The cabbie waved, called out, "Mr. Sam?"

"Dewis. The last name's Dewis," Sam said, a little impatiently.

The cabbie shook his head, seemingly amused. "You sure you know *where* this place is, bud?"

"You sure you know how to drive?"

The cabbie made a face and set the meter. The cab was a late-model Camry, the time on the dash—9:23 P.M.—absurdly inaccurate. But Sam had his phone. According to it, the city nearest the destination was a place called Parrsboro, just an hour and a half away. No problem at all, he would be back well before Krista, especially knowing what she was like. Get her into a store and you could kiss the day goodbye.

It was going on noon by the time they reached the outskirts of what was not a city at all but a small town, with no more than a tiny main street and a park with a statue that looked to be made of papier mâché—the figure of a man with very red skin wearing a loincloth.

"What the heck is that?"

The cabbie shrugged. "Just another thirty kilometres, dude."

"Can you say that in miles?" Sam was already thinking Krista's bus would have arrived in Peggys Cove an hour before, probably longer. What would she do there, besides buy souvenirs and snap some selfies? He hoped the fog had cleared enough that she'd be able to see the lighthouse. There was likely more to do there than in the remote, forested part of the world he soon found himself speeding through, uphill and down. The terrain grew steeper, the road narrower and more winding the farther they went, a little like the roller coaster at Coney Island. Were they going where he'd asked?

A sliver of fear passed through him. Maybe the cabbie had his own agenda, was taking him somewhere to rob him, leave him for dead? So much for people disappearing at sea. Plenty more disappeared on land, he would be willing to bet. He tried texting Krista but his message came back, undeliverable. As soon as they got back to Hoboken, that's it, he would insist, no more trips out of range. His head started to ache again and just when he thought he'd lose his mind, a sign appeared: *The Age of Sail Museum*. At the foot of a hill, on a hairpin curve. Two cars in the parking lot. A building with the lights on, thank God, or somebody.

"I'll just be a couple of minutes," he told the cabbie.

"Your time is my money. No rush."

As Sam got out, he half expected the guy to peel away. *Being abandoned in the middle of nowhere would be better than winding up dead at the bottom of a cliff.* The wide, red-mudded bay he had glimpsed intermittently beyond the endless woods was half shrouded in mauve mist—beautiful, even though it was on the ocean. *Just call me a sucker for punishment.*

Inside the museum, an elderly woman and two youthful guides swarmed him. Was there something they could help him with, something he was there specifically to find? He felt like a schoolboy nerd murmuring, "the *Mary Celeste*." But there it was, his fixation, an urge, a need to get to the bottom of the mystery. There had to be a logical explanation, some solid science about what had happened. The world had had almost a century and a half to figure it out.

A pimply teen led him straight to a dusty display case, a few small, crumbling pieces of wood inside. A typed-up card identified the rubble as the only known remains of the brigantine's wreck, discovered by divers off the south coast of Haiti. *Brig.* Sam could think only of a tiny, dark, enclosed room in the bowels of the cruise ship—a cell, no luxury cabin with ensuite. Not only was the ghost ship a two-masted brig, but so was the ship that had kept her from wandering the eastern Atlantic possibly forever, ensuring that her story became legend.

There was also a plaque that named her builder. A man called Joshua Dewis, Esq., who lived in the same hamlet where she had been built and launched in her first incarnation, *Amazon.* All Sam could think of was a Prime deliveryman ringing the bell on his front porch: *Dewis, parcel for you.* He could not have made this stuff up! It dawned, slowly, how his grandfather got spooked whenever anyone mentioned Amazon. But all this was beside the point. *A Dewis from Nova Scotia.* It wasn't that big a place. Could they be related?

Sam hurried to the foyer, poked his head outside. The cabbie was still there. He returned to his browsing. Another display case had an antique photo of a woman named Emily Jane Spicer Dewis—the family name again—who had married a Captain Robert Dewis in the 1860s. The pair had raised their children aboard his ship, *Calcutta.* Three daughters and one son. There was a little typed-up story, about how the family was shipwrecked off Manila, spent two weeks in lifeboats, all living to tell the tale, except two daughters who died when they finally made it ashore. Emily, the mother, had paid everyone's passage home to Nova Scotia with gold coins she had sewn into the hem of her dress.

He snapped a photo, in a dazed kind of awe. Clicked on the arrow to send it to Krista, along with a quick text.

A minute later, miraculously, Krista's reply popped up: *Where r u? C u soon?*

By now, the cabbie had come inside, was chatting with the lady at the desk. He had left the engine running. Middle Eastern hip hop blared from the sound system.

"You coming, man, or what? Said you wanted to be back by 3:00, right?"

"Not 3:00, a bit before 4:00 should do it." Yes, for sure, he'd entered it—*Departure isn't until 4:00 P.M.*—in the notes on his phone. Accuracy was everything; in his line of work if you weren't accurate you were toast. Naturally, he had lost track of time a little, his mind whirring with conspiracy theories, the layers of possibility swirling around the mystery ship. The photos in the *Ghost Ship* book showing Briggs, his wife, and child had wormed their way into his brain and would not let go their hold. A two-year-old lost at sea, that would be the worst. Then he thought what a good thing, a lucky thing, his great-great grandparents, wherever they had come from, however they might or might not be related or connected to this crazy, gripping saga, had survived whatever they had survived and started a family not on the ocean but on land. The land of the free, the home of the brave.

But the mystery itself, of just what had happened aboard the *Mary Celeste* to cause the disappearance of those people, continued to goad him. There was one more site he had to see. It felt like a shadowy hand on his shoulder, directing him.

The cabbie was recalcitrant. "Spencers Island? Listen, man—I *know* it's not much farther. But, blink and you miss it, okay. It's gonna be that kind of place."

"Drive," he said.

Just up the road, past a few more deep bends, lay a field with a little white painted sign. Its black lettering and picture of a ship were faded but unmistakable: *Home of the Mary Celeste*. At the end of a bumpy turnoff was a wide pebbled beach, a boarded-up café beside a dirt parking lot big enough for three or four cars. To the left, an RV park extended just above a battered dune, and to the right, the remains of what might once have been a wharf jutted from rock-strewn sand, while in the distance loomed the small hump of an island. Straight ahead stood a cairn, a squat, tidy pyramid of reddish stones cemented into place.

Aside from providing a couple of dates—the ship's launching in 1861, her being driven ashore in a storm in 1868—the plaque simply stated the story's barest facts. All that was known, and ever could or would be known. *Welcome to the world where things defy explanation, don't have to make sense.* He felt a foolish, echoing dejection. *Even when you search high and low for the reason.*

The cabbie, meanwhile, had pulled an impatient U-ey, tires spitting grit. Music blasted from his open window. Climbing in, Sam checked the time on his phone. It was a little after two o'clock. Plenty of time to make it back to the dock, if they hustled. He texted Krista: On my way. Added a cruise ship emoji and a thumbs up.

Maybe it was the hilly ride or the fact that he'd had nothing to eat since breakfast, regardless, he felt increasingly light-headed, then queasy. He wished he had brought along a couple of Gravol—but why would he have, sticking to terra firma? The nausea grew all too real when he had to ask the cabbie to pull over, at a ninety-degree turn in the road. There went breakfast's watery remains into the ditch. The cabbie barely blinked, as if Sam had merely needed to take a leak.

"You'll feel better when we hit the 102."

For a while, the cabbie was right about the four-lane highway. But then, passing a wide, muddy river, just beside an overpass, he begged the man to pull over again. This time was worse; there was nothing left to come up. The ride was at least another forty minutes, he guesstimated—time for a snooze, which might make him feel better. It had to be all that rich food, the strange bed, the cramped quarters—literally being at sea—that had thrown off his system. But when he woke he felt no better, and now he needed the bathroom. Luckily the cabbie spotted a gas station off the exit ramp ahead.

When he got back into the cab, he didn't even want to look at the time, let alone the meter. The drive was a costly add-on he could have completely avoided. The clock on the dash now said 3:43 A.M. No worries, he told himself. According to ship time, it's only 2:43. But when he checked his phone, why would it lie, it said 3:56.

The cabbie looked in the rear-view and grinned. "Electronics, eh—nice when they work."

In a panic he texted Krista. *B there soon.* He was in a lather now, a cold, shivering sweat. His armpits felt spongy, perspiration stung his eyes. He needed to stop again. With cars whizzing past as if on a turnpike, he doubled over, spat bile.

On his phone it was after 4:00. *The ship waits for nobody. We can't be expected to hold up twelve hundred people for the sake of one.* As they pulled into the lot beside the pavilion, a fleet of tour buses was leaving. He paid the cabbie in US dollars, added a two hundred dollar tip. Hoped against hope that—

For one fleeting moment he felt his hopes rise and hover, answered. A cruise ship's upper decks towered like a gigantic, monstrous light fixture above the squat brick building before it. But the logo on the stack wasn't right: *Carnivale Cruise Line.* Somewhere out in the fog was the shuddering thunder of engines, the deafening blast of a horn.

He watched the cab, dwarfed by a transport truck, disappear.

He loved Krista, he wanted only Krista, could not imagine being anywhere but with her. He pictured her feeling abandoned, angry enough to dump him. Calling her dad in tears, sure she had been stood up.

A failure the Briggs and Dewises somehow might have taken in stride? He thought of Captain Briggs's mother seeing her son and his family off. Of Sarah Briggs's father (had he been there to see *his* daughter off?), waving from the New York City dock. Not knowing, never knowing. Perhaps people back then—giving themselves up to the whims of wind and water—were better equipped to weather the unknown.

C u @ *the next port, sweetie.* He pressed send, heard his message zip away.

Her reply, a purple heart, told him she'd received it.

A Procession of Night Owls

"WE NEED IT HERE BY 4:00—4:00 A.M., SI, NOT 4:00 P.M.," I enunciate. Carefully. Flip through the phrase book, jot down the words to make myself extra clear. My husband shoots a smile at our host: *Don't mind Rosa, she's always been like this, a Type A worrier.*

Domenico's nod, full of understanding, could not be more gracious. Our lack of Italian and his spotty, faltering *inglese* have never been an issue. "Si, si, no problemo, signora." Always wise to book the cab well in advance, he agrees. It'll be arranged straight away, he promises, in so many words.

"Perfect," I say. We've found no finer home away from home than his B&B in the *centro storico*'s heart. Have stayed numerous times over the years, which, I don't know, might say the same about our spirit of adventure as it does our budget?

"The flight leaves Capodichino at 6:00—tomorrow morning, *not* this afternoon," I can't resist repeating.

God knows why she booked the earliest one, says Tom's, my husband's, shrug. To avoid twenty-four hours of horribly tight connections *and* crazy layovers, I don't need to explain. Wasn't travelling easier the first few times we came here? Delayed and cancelled flights now *de rigueur.*

Domenico smiles. His eyes are the bluest of blue. Just leave the keys on the desk in the morning, he gestures. He kisses both my cheeks, shakes Tom's hand.

Arrivederci.

Then we step out for the day. Our last in our favourite metropolis. Until next time, of course. Goodbye would be painful without the assurance that, God willing, we'll return. How could we not? Even so, tomorrow's departure weighs on our delight as we hurry down the stairs and out into the fray. The bliss of being footloose and carefree running out.

Like most love affairs, ours with this place is a little complicated.

Of course we will make the most of everything as the hours tick down.

The very first time Tom and I set foot here, stepping from the *stazione centrale* into Piazza Garibaldi we were drop-kicked into a parallel universe. A circle of hell, we'd wondered. A circuit-jamming sensory overload of glaring sun, stench, noise. Wild, careening traffic, migrant hawkers waggling trinkets. Faces gleamed with sweat; eyes full of desperation had mimicked how I felt. Bogged down with luggage, we dodged them and barrages of scooters, pedestrians, and kids kicking soccer balls along curbs piled with trash.

We had an address, but how to reconcile a dot on a map with chaos? I had let Tom take the lead, though he's the more directionally challenged. Braver too—possessing an ability to tune out what's not useful—he had moved by instinct. He pressed ahead, turned to make sure I hadn't got swept in a different direction. Even with the sun blazing down, his face was winter pale.

Camera bag, messenger bag, and daypack for body armour, I towed my suitcase like a pet. My tailored shirt, cardigan, crisp jeans, and sneakers were all wrong: mid-April could have been mid-August. I'm sure my cheeks must have been the bright pink of my blouse. (At home in Halifax, dead grass would just be peeking through snow.) Grit and car exhaust stung my eyes. I nearly tripped over a small boy dandling a soccer ball. He glared through me. Stick legs below shiny yellow shorts, stick arms poking from a ragged muscle shirt.

Boarding the train in Rome a couple of hundred kilometres north, I was not prepared. Nothing could have prepared me. "People either love Napoli or hate it," was all the travel agent had said.

Tom gripped my hand when I caught up. We'd soon celebrate our twenty-third wedding anniversary, together long enough words weren't necessary.

What were we thinking, coming here? What had we done? Our son, Marcus, who'd backpacked Europe, had warned us off: we were too soft, too set in our ways, he had hinted, to survive let alone enjoy this city. Stick to Tuscany, he'd said.

"I didn't know Italy was developing-world," I yelled into Tom's ear that first time. A passing siren swallowed his reply.

Bookended by crowds of people, we got up the nerve to cross the street. Stepped out into traffic, stumble-ran across four or five lanes. Vehicles flew past honking. My heart bobbed in my throat. Bobbed like the floaty thing in a toilet tank. Any faked *savoir faire* had been instantaneously flushed.

Better than I was at spotting signs back then, Tom pointed, yelled. "Via dei Tribunali—that way." All I saw were dead mattresses folded like bread around fillings of dirty Pampers. We skirted trashed furniture and baby car seats, rotting food and dog shit. I rummaged for the printed email with our booking, our itinerary so carefully plotted. Breathed the way I'd been taught to breathe giving birth—pant-pant-blow—to keep from pushing too soon. Twenty-one years later my body remembered perfectly; odd how the body tries to soothe itself. So mine did as Vespas bore down, whole families aboard them. The drivers the only ones wearing helmets.

More scraggly children scraped past, then vanished behind what resembled a prison: barred windows, bell tower, peeling white stucco. A fountain behind twisted iron fencing leaked rusty water from sculpted lions' heads. Past a sidewalk barbershop-and-café jammed with old men, the street became a canyon. Decrepit buildings walled it, so deep in shadow it could have been night. Shops were, literally, holes in walls. A thin seam of sunlight lit paving stones slimed with melt from a fishmonger's. Eels and tiny silver fish teemed in buckets.

The street was a solid, pulsing crush of humanity. The

boy who'd almost tripped me—I think it was him, I recognized his yellow shorts—slipped past. Hard to tell his age: six or seven? Far too young to be free-ranging through this mayhem.

"It's only for three nights, thank God," I yelped into Tom's ear. Chanted barely under my breath, "We can do this, we'll get through it, it'll be okay. We'll survive. Somehow."

More scooters and tiny delivery trucks streamed past, vehicles dodging pedestrians at breakneck speed. I soon lost sight of the boy. He had easily melded with another swarm of kids the same size, darting in and out of traffic, past graffiti-slathered storefronts and through the crowds. People of all descriptions. Young and old, men, women, mothers, grandmothers, teenage girls and boys, virility bursting at the seams. Scuffed black leather, shredded denim. Tight-tight jeans, skimpy T-shirts, spike-heeled boots. Schoolchildren and toddlers tripping past with parents quarrelling, pestering, babies wailing. And overhead, laundry hanging every which way from crumbling balconies. Women in housedresses perched there gossiping, peering down. Keeping an eye on everything.

I must've stood out like Pollyanna in my blouse and white linen sweater. Or I flatter myself thinking I was noticed. That awful floaty feeling inside made me pant-pant-pant-blow until I got light-headed. As surely as his birth had been tricky, Marcus's warning was to blame for landing us here. No one told us where we should or should not go. Italy wasn't new to us. We had been before, to Florence, Siena, Rome.

The street suddenly widened, gave way to a piazza with the pedestalled statue of a saint perched high above it. Pigeons roosted on his light bulb–studded halo. Tom spotted the street number we were looking for on a crudely tagged green door facing the square. The B&B was listed in faded handwriting below a buzzer that didn't work. A troupe of bigger soccer kids scuffed past, shouting.

A man in the tiny café opposite called out, "You are here for Domenico?"

A small, fortyish, dark-haired fellow with the bluest eyes I had ever seen soon appeared. He grabbed our suitcases, led us up nine or ten flights of stairs. Pulled out chairs for us at a little Formica table, served us tepid bottled water in disposable cups.

Our room was bare-bones serviceable but spotless. Its heavily shuttered window and the cool of cracked tiles offered respite. A black velvet painting of the Bay of Naples hung above the bed, Mount Vesuvius's silhouette overlooking everything. It was sanctuary enough to bolster us against the craziness below.

Changed into lighter clothing, bracing ourselves, we ventured downstairs and back outside into sun-splashed crowds, shouting, and the incessant whine of scooters. Behind the saint's statue stood a massive church, its portico of ancient Greek columns looming over the square. I made a beeline for it. Tom followed. Inside the church's vast, echoing emptiness, gazing up at its ruined frescoes, I coached myself. *You can do this, you can get through two days and three nights: embrace it. What option is there?*

The smell of damp plaster, the chill of marble calmed me.

Tom held onto my hand as we descended the church's many steps into the hot, sunny piazza. *Let the wild rumpus begin*, I thought, an image from one of Marcus's childhood storybooks drifting into my head. I pictured our son back home studying for his history degree.

Re-entering the crush, we let it pull us into its flow. A blur of sunlit faces, noises, smells. By the time we had ventured a block or two further, the chaos began to rub away our agitation, our bougie whatever, as our son would say. Our stiffness melted away, the street's anonymity bathing us in its rampant *carpe diem.*

In short order, it turned my cautious nature inside out, my fears into a drug. Tom and I fell for Via dei Tribunali at pretty much the same moment, with the same speed. How to list the ways the street and its hordes captured our hearts? Like listing from memory every wrinkle and mole on another person's skin. Impossible.

For the next two days and nights, we wandered streets filled with garbage, orange and lemon blossoms, and wisteria, vines' scent like incense. We climbed endless stairs set into a cliff overlooking the whole city and huge bay below, a blue heaven as far as the eye could see.

We breakfasted on blood oranges from a hole-in-the-wall fruit seller's, cappuccino from the barista who'd called out that first afternoon. We lingered at his one street-side table to watch the flower vendor arrive at the start of each day to display his blooms. The care he took made me teary.

Surrounded by these and other delights, we imbibed beauty, pure beauty, amid filth.

Seeking a shortcut from the Duomo di Napoli to the Museo Archeologico Nazionale—the place stuffed with Pompeiian treasures—and back again to Domenico's, we got lost circling the sixteenth-century hospital for syphilitics: sufferers of the French disease, the Italian disease, the Spanish disease, variously named for its incurable carriers. On every corner, in every nook and cranny of the streets' sprawling labyrinth was a shrine to somebody. Saints, soccer stars, the newly dead, souls in purgatory. Tiny plastic people standing waist-deep in red plastic flames, arms raised in supplication to the One who could save them from sinking deeper.

After two days and three nights, Domenico's had become home. Napoli already a strange, dark craving I'd suspected even then would never be satisfied.

The theatre of its streets reminded me of Grimm's fairy tales. Having these read to me as a kid, savouring their horrors while sitting safe and secure on my dad's knee.

Packing, Tom and I polish off the end of a bottle of wine divided evenly into glasses purchased nearby. Souvenirs to take back with us, or leave for Domenico? The alarm is set for 3:00. Bedtime's rituals. Then I crawl under the covers to grab what sleep I can. But the quiet is punctuated by street noises. Sleep is a mirror dropped from a window, shattered on paving stones below; monkey-mind swings from dream-ledge to dream-ledge. Tom doesn't bother trying to sleep (no point), stays up with the overhead light glaring. Each time I lift my head from the pillow, he's surfing the net, slumped on the sagging loveseat surrounded by our luggage.

We need to be at the airport no later than 5:00—that's pushing it for an international flight, plus online check-in is on the fritz. What *was* I thinking, booking so early? At the time it seemed smart: nothing rattles me more than navigating massive airports with minutes to clear customs, locate gates, clear security. Luckily Capodichino is nearby, a quick drive even in heavy traffic—as easy to navigate as Stanfield, aside from the language. (This eases my recent memory of tearing down the concourse at Fiumicino, a luggage-laden bat out of hell flying ahead of Tom sauntering toward our flight to Toronto. Or Zurich. Or Paris, or Berlin, or wherever we'd been bound.)

As soon as Marcus moved out, Tom and I made it our mission to see Europe. Being creatures of habit, mostly this means Italy. Our privilege is not lost on me. I favour places where English isn't the language, a dare to myself. But I'm not looking forward to the next twenty-four hours in transit—four major airports between here and home—home, where by this time tomorrow night we should be back in our comfy suburban bed. No harsh yellow light bouncing off broken tiles, charming as Domenico's is in its modest way. No street racket bouncing up to the window and in through the shutters, the shouts of night owls processing, staggering, past. I'm ready for our quiet, safe reality, as Marcus calls it. Not that he's one to talk these days.

After that first flirtation of a visit, we resolved to feed our addiction. None of our return trips was ever long enough. In Napoli's gritty paradise the sacred and profane rivalled each other in exuberance. The Catholic and the pagan made a feverish chiaroscuro of faith and superstition. A world where the veil between the living and the dead wasn't just thin but holey.

The place changed, though, after our initial stumble into its chaos. With each visit it got slicker, its streets cleaner, choked with a little less garbage. Its draw for tourists brightened, but this made us dig deeper. If this city has a colour, it's the yellow of lemons steeped in the azure where sea meets sky. A luminous mossy green shadowed by a sinewy black whose depths are bottomless.

Emboldened, I wanted to experience its knowable depths. Tom remained content to enjoy its sunniest surfaces. Sunny rivers of traffic and people, so many people. Women with big hair, thick ankles, kerchiefs, rundown heels, stilettos. Waifs and men with stocky, thickset bodies. Glamour girls and boys, bodies in expensive suits and bodies in rags, the well-fed and the hungry, all barrelling and boring through the city's oldest thoroughfares, a human drill—Via dei Tribunali and the decumani, Spaccanapoli a block to the south or the west (directions only grew more meaningless), which since antiquity split the place in two. A long, perfectly straight crack just wide enough to allow daylight in.

The B&B was in a six-storey yellow building glommed onto a thirteenth-century church. Both sat atop the ruins of the city's original ancient Greek marketplace. Wandering underground passages carved out of tufa offered respite from the throngs, but their silence made me relish Tom's preferences. We wanted only to be caught in the streets' dizzying swirl where, it's true, I never felt more alive. We ate pizza every night, washed down with blood-red Aglianico. We drank two-euro Prosecco in the street amidst throngs of partying youths, and lemonade made by an old woman under a lit-up picture of Christ and the Madonna. With gnarled hands she squeezed lemon juice into a beer cup, spooned in baking soda till it fizzed and frothed over like Vesuvius.

I took a sip, passed it to Tom. I glimpsed the boy again, that little soccer player, or one identical to him, hovering in an alcove. One of a thousand boys who looked alike, we had quickly discovered.

Each trip, we would see them everywhere. Playing on the concrete outside the bank where we withdrew cash to pay Domenico, and outside the sprawling basilica in Piazza del Plebiscito while a wedding took place. How many kids called the streets home? How many since the city's beginnings?

Tom wiped foam from his lip. I nudged him. Something about the boy reminded me of Marcus at that age, eight or nine? The gaze of hollow eyes caught mine before the child darted away with his ball into a *tarralli* shop—to steal supper? An almond *tarrallo* rather than macaroni slopped on a plate wherever home was. Or was I imagining too much?

The local word for street kids is *scugnizzi*.

That night in bed, sifting through the day's happiness, I heard gunshots. Three loud, unmistakable blasts in the street below.

I soon realized, gratefully, that I was mostly invisible. A fly on a wall of crumbling, piss-stained stucco adorned here by a Banksy saint, there by tagging. Blue plastic buckets delivering household supplies at all hours being lowered and raised over their grimy surfaces from balconies. Carousing voices. Laughter, curses. Milk, bread, dish soap, wine.

As Tom and I got to know the city, we teetered between pride that we knew it as well as we did and realizing how delusional we were. No one but locals whose people had lived here for millennia could know its layers, as unknowable as the boy with his soccer ball.

The boy who wove in and out of my dreams just as he wove in and out of our walks through the streets.

One evening before dusk, I glimpsed him through a doorway, the upper half of the door swung inwards to expose the room within. A gang of kids squeezed together on a couch, the boy perched at one end. A widescreen TV blared. Under the gleam of a naked bulb a woman stirred something in a pot. An old man and another woman shared a table wedged beside the stove. Against a wall was a bed. The picture above it showed Jesus exposing his sacred, glowing heart.

Eating something with his fingers, the boy swatted the others' hands from the bowl. The mother yelled. I could not help staring long enough to take all this in. A voyeur. Their poverty shocked me.

Looking back, it was like the time we took our granddaughter—Marcus's little girl—to see a touch tank. The creatures inside were fascinating to look at but the feel of their squishy bodies in the cold water made me recoil.

The instant before Tom pulled me away, the old man's eyes met mine.

We hurried off. A door slammed. Something slapped stone. A child's shouts echoed.

By 3:45 I'm showered and dressed. By 3:50 we've gathered up our bags—overstuffed knapsacks that cleverly convert into messenger bags, daypacks, a carry-on suitcase, and my camera bag. Already exhausted, we lock our room's strong door behind us, step out into Domenico's darkened office/lobby, and deposit our room key on the table. Even in the gloom, I see how the little chrome chairs fit under it like sections of an orange. From Domenico's shrine to Maradona—a wall plastered with photos of soccer plays, banners, and tributes—the legendary player peers from his portrait. In case we've forgotten anything we don't lock the outer door with its series of deadbolts. One of us will run back up and return these keys when the cab arrives.

Then the stairs. The long, knee-buckling descent down all those flights, sloped, cracked, and slanted marble steps, shaky iron railings, the stairwell all hard white light and our echoing footsteps, to the very bottom. Of course there's no elevator, never was; why would there be? Even after six or seven stays, we haven't a clue how many apartments or suites like our B&B the building houses, how many tenants. Tom and I are noticeably older, old enough that we've minded the stairs this trip more than we thought to mind them before. We were ten years younger that first time, more fit, more adaptable maybe, quicker on our feet. Back then, the stairs barely drew a blink. Raised heartbeats caused some breathlessness but nothing Domenico's hospitality could not revive.

What I learned early on? Tom had an adventurer's ability to weave past the misery we witnessed unperturbed. Or, at least, outwardly unperturbed.

"There's nothing you or I can do to fix it." The poverty, he meant. The inequity, the unfathomable swings of fate that lead some people to call a *palazzo* home, others a *basso* apartment open to the street. Like the boy we kept seeing, who barely seemed to grow older, taller, or less hungry-looking. And the mothers who crouched on the cathedral's steps, dirt-lined palms outstretched. *Per favore, signor.*

"The poor will always be with us, Rosa."

"And the rich?"

We took to walking through Forcella, one of the city's poorest neighbourhoods and home to the Camorra. Once, our destination was a *pasticceria* in the warren of streets near the train station, in the vicinity of the dreaded Piazza Garibaldi. Tom had read about its famous *sfogliatelle.* Along the way was a church I wanted to see. Santissima Annunziata had a museum. Its infamous Ruota Degli Esposti was still there, the guidebook said. A telltale square in the exterior's stonework was sealed with a small marble slab, the year 1875 engraved on it. It hid the trapdoor through which the unluckiest of parents for centuries deposited babies they could not care for. Like a slot for making large bank deposits when cash ruled, with a rotating drawer inside. Love having little or, perhaps, everything to do with it.

Along the wide, curving, litter-strewn street, the church's Baroque façade thrusts upward, refurbished stucco painted lemon yellow with a deep charcoal trim. *Ave Gratia Plena* was graven above its portal. "Hail full of grace," words the angel spoke telling Virgin Mary she would bear a son. "Seriously?" she surely said. The church of the Annunziata is one of the city's hundreds and hundreds of churches; at least one was crammed into every tiny, dense, surging block of the *centro storico*.

We stepped inside its grand entrance, turned left for the orphanage's museum. The place was deserted. We spoke in whispers. There it was, the wooden bin with its door to the outside, just large enough to hold an infant. No slot for paperwork, notes of introduction, reasons or excuses or pleas for mercy—no such thing as birth certificates. I ran my hand over its scuffed varnish. Tom fidgeted, keen to be on our way.

How many babies over the years? And how long had it taken the nuns to hear them crying, lift them from the drawer, and carry them to the nearby sink? Was the water from its single spigot warm?

In that closet of a room, a nun would strip the baby if it was clothed, bathe the grime from its body. Record in a notebook any identifying marks—eye colour, a birthmark on left cheek, say?—date and time of discovery. A scrap of ribbon around a tiny wrist? A ragged diaper or shirt, a saint's medal pinned to it? Anything to distinguish the child, known now as one of the Madonna's, or, in the worldly way, another Esposito in the ever-burgeoning family of Espositos, the name for kids without parents abandoned to the Church.

Children's drawings adorned a wall. They depicted Jesus in red, Mary in blue; nuns cradling babies before a row of kids sleeping in cots. Tom shook his head. I knew what he was thinking. Like everyone he's appalled by the depravity of deviant nuns and the horrors they and criminal priests inflicted on Indigenous children on our side of the ocean.

I thought of Chagall, his words artfully displayed in an exhibition we had just seen. "In life as in the artist's palette, there is a single colour that gives meaning to life and to art: the colour of love."

I couldn't help thinking of Marcus. Not just Marcus but our little granddaughter, Thea. Couldn't bring myself to imagine her or any little one left to this sprawling, gritty wilderness.

It took us the rest of the morning to find the *pasticceria*. We walked in circles, up and down, block after block, were about to give up when finally it appeared. Inside, a ceramic model of the baker and his assistant adorned the counter. Tom ordered his coveted treat, layers of phyllo filled with orange-zested ricotta and dusted with icing sugar. The street, more upscale than the others, was unnervingly quiet. No parentless children ran loose on its sidewalks. An elegant old woman wearing a beautifully tailored suit asked in near-perfect *inglese* if we needed directions.

Another trip, a year or two later, another occasion. Outside the Duomo, in the midst of a thunder shower I saw the boy again—or one who instantly brought to mind the boy of our earlier visits. Small, wiry-thin, brown-skinned, a street urchin noticeably older but not much taller or tidier. He crouched in a doorway taking shelter. A nervous jittery hunger filled his eyes. He held out a palm mapped with dirt. I reached into my daypack for a couple of euros.

Tom was already hurrying up the cathedral steps. The boy slipped the coins into his pocket, folded himself into a ball, cheek to knees. A greyness making itself invisible in the needling rain.

Beckoning me, Tom held open the humongous door. My cue to hurry up and take cover inside.

"Didn't you see him?"

Tom eyed me blankly. I didn't ask if he thought the boy had a home somewhere, or a school, a classroom, a teacher. Stupid questions, a stupider answer would have reflected the obvious: *Now what do you think, Rosa?*

Sometimes it is just better to keep silent.

Thunder roiled above the ceiling's vaults, rattled its dome. I imagined lightning hooking itself around spires and campaniles as rain spattered stained glass lit by an eerie yellow light. In silence we stepped down into the small, ancient basilica of Santa Restituta attached to the cathedral, and waited. The weather quickly passed.

When we stepped out into Via Duomo again, the boy was gone, of course. The sun was shining; patches of blue broke through charcoal clouds. It wasn't far to the Botanical Gardens on Via Foria, which I was dying to see. To clear my head of the city's noise, be wrapped temporarily in the quiet of plants.

At first the security guard in the little green ticket booth refused to admit us, mumbling about Mondays, the gardens off-limits to all but students. He relented, gave us special permission to enter. It had begun to rain again.

Inside the gardens, schoolchildren wended their way along twisting paths, a shuffling queue in rain boots and coats, carrying umbrellas every colour of the rainbow. Led by a pair of teachers, they threaded their way past the gargantuan cacti, barely paused to note the massive agave plant in flower—a phenomenon that happened only once every forty or fifty years, I've been told. A boy with a purple umbrella asked questions, his Italian sweet and a little shrill in the lashing wet. He had a brown leather school bag strapped to his back, looked to be eight or nine. Beneath the umbrella his dark hair was combed smooth, the lines of the comb visible. Another boy gave him a shove. A flock of girls erupted into cruel laughter. A teacher hissed a reprimand—well, I assumed it was.

I thought of Thea, now a toddler. Marcus's plans for her—engineering, law, med school?

The boy with the purple umbrella stooped to pet a scrawny striped cat. Part of a feral colony, it lurked beside an ornamental pool, poised to nab a goldfish.

Tom couldn't help himself: once a dad, always a dad. "Watch your fingers. Last thing you want is to get scratched."

The child paid no attention, ran to catch up with the others.

Anxious to be on our way, we reach the green steel door at the foot of the stairs that separates our haven from the street. Nothing like sleep deprivation to make you fixate on a singular goal: to be in your own bed. For now it overrides our fascination with this city, makes us keen to step back into our orderly lives an ocean away on the western edge of the North Atlantic, as far as it's possible to imagine from the Bay of Naples and the Mediterranean. Eager for rest if not the greys and dull greens of a Maritime spring.

Tom grips the latch, heaves at the prison-like door till it swings outwards—funny we have such fond memories of it from that first arrival. It's 3:57; the cab isn't here yet, of course. The street outside is empty, a novelty. A shock, really, to see it utterly deserted. Pre-dawn cabbies and fares in a city this size must be a matter of course. I anticipate the brightness of headlights swinging closer, illuminating the darkness.

Four o'clock. Not just yet.

The next time I saw the boy, the *scugnizzo*, he was outside the church behind the B&B. A funeral was in progress—a hearse and a few other vehicles were parked on the strip of pavement outside San Lorenzo's towering medieval doors. On a little rise separating the pavement from the tiny, teeming cross-street sloping from the piazza, tables and chairs tossed into place each day by another café across the way lent a festive air. Tom and I had stopped for an early *aperitivo*. The boy was with his friends—a clan of Espositos?—encircling the hearse. They were playing soccer (what else?), San Lorenzo's doors their goal net. Repeatedly, the ball slammed against impenetrable wood. I expected someone to come out and order them to take the game elsewhere. But no one appeared, and no one around us raised a voice or an eyebrow. Nobody paid any mind.

Nearby, a street crew painted blue bicycle shapes along one side of Via dei Tribunali. Cigarettes dangled from the men's mouths as they worked. Paint fumes singed the air. Under the shadow of San Gaetano's statue, the flower vendor was packing up his display as two stooped nuns in navy blue habits, last-minute customers, ambled up. They fussed over his wares, bought a huge bouquet of lilies, roses, and birds of paradise, then continued down the street. Scooters burbled.

The boys bellowed, racing after the ball. It bobbled along San Lorenzo's threshold, stone carved by the footsteps of countless generations coming and going. It rolled past the road crew, nearly bowled over their paint bucket. The boy, the one who was everywhere and nowhere, darted out and claimed it. The foreman looked right through him. Cursed at the other boys, hollered at them to watch out. We could tell from his tone what he was saying.

I pictured the boy running home. The *basso* with its half-door open to the street. Squabbling siblings, dinner boiling. The noise of early partiers and sightseeing tourists melding with the family's. The room a goldfish bowl lit by the dangling bulb, three generations fighting for a spot on the couch or in the bed. Maybe they don't sleep, I thought, just stay up all night. Or if they do sleep, it's in shifts.

A caged bird in a corner singing its heart out to rouse the sleepers at dawn?

Tom nursed his drink, observing passersby. I watched the boy dart across the piazza, climb atop a dumpster below San Gaetano's statue. Dig a half-eaten pastry from the overflowing trash, wolf it down. Even seated across the street, I could see his hands and arms streaked with filth. His face too, but beneath the dirt his cheeks glowed, rosy from the sun.

Still brilliant, the late afternoon sun covered everyone and everything, and the only things shielding us were the bright shapes of planes flying so low overhead we could read the airlines' names on them. Almost count the rows of porthole windows, blinds lowered, blinds half-raised. Their wings cast giant shadows over the orange, yellow, rust, and maroon buildings with their laundry-draped balconies and networks of wires dangling like broken trapezes and dripping, whirring heat pumps.

Their roar sucked the air from our ears, momentarily dampened the whine of scooters and the streets' thousand shouting, laughing, cursing voices. Inside this roaring bubble, their theatre churned on. The roar was just another form of prayer, really, in a place that was itself a raucous, rambling prayer, a prayer to the living, to the dead, and the almost dead—those whose memories are not allowed to wane or disappear. Like San Gennaro, patron saint, whose liquefying blood each September protects the city and its populace from the brooding volcano—Vesuvius's twin peaks ever-present in the distance—long overdue to erupt. A constant reminder of the destruction and darkness that thrives under sun-drenched surfaces. And San Gaetano, his statue's arms and face raised heavenwards, overlooking us all: the patron saint of gamblers.

By 4:05 the cab still isn't here, but no cause for concern. For all Italy's craziness, one thing that has always worked out for us, impeccably, is transportation.

Five minutes later, there's no sign of it. The dark, empty street is surreal, entirely other than the Via dei Tribunali we've known at practically every other hour. From the morning's stream of vendors opening shops and stalls; parents and children, teenagers, and university students heading to school; legions of old men gathering for espresso; elderly women shopping, shuffling between home and the streets; young women dressed to the nines for work; and young men in leather and jeans hurrying to day jobs; scooters, vans, cars, and delivery trucks squeezing by, to the steady afternoon parade of similar but different people hurrying to and from lunch, the day's siesta or sex or whatever, to the evening *passeggiata* crowd ambling along, wolfing street food, lining up for drinks at open bars and *enotecas*, then racing, shuffling, and shoving along for dinner and late-night partying.

Now, in the deep gloom, nothing moves—nothing so small as a mouse or rat skitters along the gutter, let alone a cat. The stillness is eerie and encompassing, as if a plague has blown in and carried everyone off. It's deader than the catacombs of San Gaudioso we visited once, skulls set into walls frescoed with details immortalizing the lives of their owners. In death we are awfully alike. Except, perhaps, for the nobles whose remains underwent special preservation, the Dominicans' fundraising practice of draining, flattening, drying, and displaying the corpses of the rich to give them burial befitting their lives' stations. Princesses, judges. And a lowly artist, an inconsequential Carracci, whose fresco work paid for his own auspicious burial.

At 4:15 the cab still hasn't arrived. I'm starting to get anxious. A lie. My stomach is a ball of knots. "Good thing," I say to Tom, "the airport's so close."

One Thursday, the twelfth day of the month—we deliberately avoided going on Friday the thirteenth—Tom and I took an excursion out of the city. Boarded the Circumvesuviana at the train station (crossing Piazza Garibaldi like we lived here), and rode it to Pompeii.

Instead of revisiting the town buried by Vesuvius's most infamous eruption, we caught a bus to visit the culprit. The death-defying route threaded its way up the mountainside, switchback after switchback, through charred olive groves and pine forests. Landed us and a mob of other tourists at a checkpoint at the end of the road.

From there, the trail to the summit was littered with chunks of lava charred and ruddy as iron ore. It was like climbing a vertical moonscape, the remote, sprawling city below washed in a yellowish haze. The Bay of Naples was a vast lagoon, the bluest of blues, the islands of Capri and Ischia rising in the mist. The sky overhead was a wispy blue, while underfoot and all around us were the colours of camo gear: dull grey, beige, khaki, a ruddy, dusty black.

Not a big hiker, Tom forged ahead, afraid if he slowed down he would lose momentum.

Just before the summit was a concession stand selling ice cream and little black plastic crucifixes, skulls, coffins, dolphins, and owls. A week or more had passed since I'd seen the soccer-playing boy, and near the stand was a child who resembled him, from behind anyway. The same clothes, hair that looked as if another child had cut it. Alone, he pressed forward, undaunted by the trail's increasing steepness. I wanted to catch up, pull him back to the counter, buy him ice cream. But I didn't, of course. I didn't want to lose sight of Tom. A hiker Nordic-poled her way between the boy and me. When I could see past her, he had disappeared.

The sun's glare was blinding. Tom grinned, winded but chuffed, waiting for me to hurry up. When we reached the final dip in the trail alongside the crater, the boy was still not to be seen. A shrine in the lava had a picture of the

Madonna and baby seated before the mountain's erupting peak. A rusty piece of scientific equipment—measuring barometric pressure?—was plastered with logos. Sports teams and businesses, *Amazon Prime*. Steam wafted from slits in the rock below. The only living things were lurid yellow lichens and stunted gorse bristling in the wind.

At the very top of the trail stood a wooden stairway that led to a railed observation deck.

The boy was nowhere. The thought shivered through me: had he gotten too close? Had he fallen in?

At 4:20 A.M., forget Piazza Garibaldi, Via dei Tribunali must surely be Dante's first circle of hell, or someone's idea of purgatory—an accident that a block or two beyond the piazza and San Gaetano's statue is the church of Santa Maria delle Anime del Purgatorio?

The street's a litter-strewn tunnel of blue-black ruin. The only glimmer of life is a watery thread of light thrown over the roadway by a single bulb suspended between two featureless buildings. Even Gaetano's halo is in darkness.

By 4:25 it's obvious the cab isn't coming. Tom leaves me watching from the doorway and races upstairs to try phoning. Domenico was adamant: if there's any problem, call me.

On our very last afternoon we visited the Cimitero delle Fontanelle. Who could resist the name? It made me think of Thea—more precisely, her skull before her newborn bones had knit together. Her mother, Marcus's partner, brushing wisps of baby hair over the pulsing soft spot; Marcus too afraid to touch it.

Finding the place took more patience than we had expected, traipsing up and down the narrow hilly streets of Materdei, another impoverished neighbourhood. A tiny chapel with a little bell tower; for a nanosecond a plane roaring overhead appeared skewered by its cross. The *cimitero* was a series of lofty caverns cut into the tufa, the burial place of thousands upon thousands, the poor and dispossessed, victims of earthquakes, volcanic eruptions and plagues over four or five centuries.

Inside, bones were stacked on bones. Bones, bones, and more bones piled like kindling, studded with skulls row upon row, festooned with rosaries and plastic roses. The numbers were breathtaking; it was ghoulish and captivating and banal—obscenely banal—the reminder (yet again) of how death erases the individual. The grim suggestion that human accomplishment and suffering led to the same dust heap. In life these folks were no different from Tom and me, save for our good fortune, I knew in my bones. They had felt love, grief, and joy; I hoped they'd felt joy.

A film crew was shooting a documentary. Well-dressed families with little kids browsed the caverns' echoing avenues, a labyrinth sanitized of the streets' chaos. Children swung from railings separating the living from the dead, played hide-and-seek, not a *scugnizzo* among them. Skulls could be adopted. Toss in a couple of euros, give one a name, pray for its owner to escape purgatory. As if grace could be bought or traded.

Tom was laconic but tired, I could tell, of humouring

my macabre fixation. Tired of living out of a suitcase, too. If he was anxious to leave, it wasn't because the sight was gruesome or scary. There was something mawkish and sentimental about how it glossed, or maybe defied, catastrophe and death. Still, gazing into empty eye sockets, I couldn't tear myself away, not until I was seized by the desperate urge to pee. There was no washroom, and because I couldn't think of anywhere closer, with Tom tailing me I raced through Sanità, down into Decumano Maggiore, and back to Domenico's, up all the stairs, and made it.

Running cleared bone dust from our nostrils. Then it was time for lunch. You only live once, we laughed, and stuffed ourselves with *mozzarella di bufala*, tomatoes, prosciutto, bread, and wine in our favourite salumeria. Elena Ferrante's novels shared a shelf with cheeses. Tom raised his glass, clinked it against mine. A weariness in his eyes I hadn't noticed until now.

My penchant for worry was, it struck me then, a luxury: a greedy attachment to good fortune.

After lunch, we trudged up to our room and made love, then decided how we would spend our last evening, free of plans.

It's 4:35. What the *hell* is keeping Tom? Panic climbs through me, waiting with our stuff at the foot of the stairs. Suitcase wedged in the door to keep it ajar, head poked out, praying even though I know it's futile that any second, against all odds, the cab might still show up. Superstition kicks in: give up; a watched pot never boils.

Stomach in an uproar, lungs in throat. That breathing

thing. Except it's shallow and fast because the panic leaves no room for air. Even as my breath forces it down, panic bobs up and fills my mouth.

How can it take this long to call someone, order another cab? Or to reach Domenico, who said to phone at any hour if there's an issue? We're not sure where he lives, only that it's in another neighbourhood. Forget our early assumption that he had the suite adjacent to the B&B, rooms filled with wildly fake Baroque bric-a-brac glimpsed briefly through an open door—not his style.

The stairwell's fluorescent light could be a cellblock's. Through the cracked door, a sliver of that light illuminates details outside that we'd missed. A hand stencilled on a cornerstone; its glowing white paint pops against the grime. Stop, it signals: watch out? Don't worry be happy? I want to take it as a sign that all will be well, a cab will come, we'll make it home. Instead I read it as a warning taken too late: You don't belong here, don't even pretend.

On our last *passeggiata*, the evening sun washed the façade of Pio Monte della Misercordia a peachy yellow. On our very first visit, we had marvelled at the rotting mattresses behind its iron fence, barricading the church that for centuries fed and sheltered the poor, and boasted Caravaggio's *Seven Works of Mercy* above its altar. Its doors were perpetually locked, mattresses a derelict testament to past mercies? Now, the place had its own tourist office.

Seconds before closing time, we ducked inside, saw the painting long enough to glimpse its entwined angels swooping down over scenes of human need and kindness.

Silently, I listed the Catholic acts of corporal mercy: feed the hungry, give drink to the thirsty, shelter the homeless, clothe the naked, visit the sick, visit the prisoner, and...?

We stopped at a street-side bar for a drink. Mercy sifted down like that soft light—or maybe luck was more like it, I thought, watching the helmetless roar by on scooters. We finished our beers and turned the corner to Piazzetta Divino Amore, a block below on Via San Biagio dei Librai: the entrance to Forcella.

Poverty spilled as extravagantly from windows, doorways, and balconies as the plastic dishpans and buckets that overflowed tiny, crowded shopfronts, and people went about the business of living. Shouts, rapid-fire chit-chat, screams, cries, and laughter poured out into the street. This was a world all its own fed by a ruthless energy—a world Tom and I could walk through but never inhabit, a world whose heart would be forever off limits to us. I felt at once glad and regretful, discerning a toughness in people that I found enviable.

Were they born impervious to disaster or made that way by deprivation? Was it from living in an earthquake zone under the eye of a roiling volcano? An admirable oblivion marked their faces. The rumble of sure chaos was the city's heartbeat. Doom perhaps the only certainty. Why worry about what you cannot control?

We wound our way slowly back to the end of Via dei Tribunali, to Castel Capuana, the old palace of justice whose crumbling white façade had greeted us the first day of our very first visit.

As we waded through the human tide, I felt chaos's charm drain abruptly into exhaustion.

"Dunno why," I nudged Tom, "but doesn't the name just kind of morph into Via dei Tribulation?"

"Oh, Rosa. You do like to catastrophize, don't you."

I laughed, indignant. In spite of myself, the fear I had kept carefully smothered inside, ever since letting it go our first afternoon stepping foot in the street, surfaced.

"Expect the worst and you'll never be disappointed," Tom teased, dredging up an old, outworn maxim of mine from when we first met. As if all these years later I was the same person.

Bobbing toward me down the stairs, Tom's face is ghostly pale. Domenico's not picking up, he announces. Voice mail says he's not available to take our call. Neither are any of the cab companies in the city, not a one.

It's 4:42. Tom takes off running down the empty street. There's a stop across from the cathedral where, by day, cabs congregate. From the doorway I watch him disappear, afraid of stepping outside in case the door swings shut and locks behind me, marooning me out there.

Daylight is hours away. Darkness is everywhere. Who knows how many dangers lurk?

I gaze out at the solitary street light suspended over the street, its bleak grey light illuminating the trash below. Unthinkable, Napoli sleeping. This hopelessly dense, restless city shutting its eyes, catching a few innocent winks.

There's not even a hint of starlight, only the surreal gleam of wings. A huge white low-flying bird—a bird of prey, wings outstretched, far too large to be a seagull: a falcon? an owl?—cruises toward me, navigating the street's canyon. Soars closer, swoops past at eye level. And then it's gone.

There are much worse things than missing a flight. But I have never felt so acutely alone, more trapped in consuming bleakness.

The squeak of hinges swinging either way feels, yes, catastrophic.

The seventh act of mercy? In my panic it comes to me. Bury the dead.

On our final *passeggiata* that last evening, we wound our way from Forcella back to a church across from Castel Capuana, a church we had visited once before. A gang of young men commandeered the entrance, possibly the older versions of youths we had seen on our previous stop here. The place supposedly housed a community art project, one that back then was conspicuously low-key, almost non-existent. As our last stroll's final destination, we decided to see if there had been progress.

The sun was sinking fast. The smell of weed wafted. Doused in shadow, the men stopped talking as we approached. They passed a bottle in silence. Their narrow faces were scowling, eyes sullen, hostile. Hard to guess their ages, but they seemed old to rely on such a spot for a hangout—a corner of the neighbourhood staked out as territory? Or home, a patch of sidewalk tucked away from the street and the traffic blasting by. I had the feeling the men had grown up here, the spot refuge and prison alike. I offered a nervous smile as Tom and I hurried past.

As we climbed the steps, one of them yelled. Ugly

laughter. My imagination, the flash of a blade?

It was the first and only time in all our visits I felt threatened—forget everything we'd heard over the years about Napoli being dangerous, crime-ridden. Forget Marcus's warnings about violent thieves and pickpockets.

The building offered shelter. The men's voices faded as we escaped inside, intruders starkly out of place. Its cavernous interior was submersed in gloom, the mossy light of centuries of grime and neglect. On autopilot I crossed to the nearest side chapel. On its narrow, crumbling altar was a little glass and gold-encrusted casket like Sleeping Beauty's. Inside reposed a pair of greenish bones, an anonymous saint's tibias crossed pirate-style.

Tom and I were the only living souls.

Never mind the massed bones at Cimitero delle Fontanelle, that marvel of commonality. These bones spooked me. The death they spoke of was singular and unilluminated by their surroundings—the artless ruin of their surroundings. Stackable plastic chairs replaced pews. The only light was dusk's seeping through the dome's sooty oculus.

I had never felt afraid in a church before. Wanted only to flee back to the land of the living. The land of those men on the steps just outside.

Cornered inside, we stood still, spoke in whispers.

Suddenly, a shrine to the Virgin flanking the towering main altar lit up. At the flick of an invisible switch, the electric candles around her head leapt ablaze—garish red and orange light. A door cracked open, admitted a sliver of yellow.

Through it a stooped old woman appeared wielding a feather duster. Without a word—not that we hoped or expected to be welcomed—she bustled over to the shrine. Gave it and its statue a few brusque swishes, the way you'd dust off an old TV. As silently as she had appeared she vanished behind the door again.

We were all ghosts, as off limits to the living as the mouldering relics.

The men were gone when Tom and I emerged. In their place a teenager leaned against a wall, gaped at us. His eyes were strangely familiar. It was as if he knew us, had always been nearby but just out of sight, watching us. As we descended to the sidewalk, he made a remark about Americanos and turned away. And I realized how privilege had enabled us to trespass on a world foreign to us, simply by letting us gloss over it. A world where *scugnizzi* became men.

I'm freaking out. Breathing through my mouth, loudly. Brain racing. Travel means moving, walking. Walking fearlessly. If I don't move I will hyperventilate, implode, die.

Tom finally appears, breathless. He hasn't spotted so much as an empty cab, let alone a driver.

We have no options.

"We can walk." My voice is an airless gasp. My feet take charge. Bags strapped over me, I lunge past him into the street.

He's behind me, yelling, "But we don't know how to get there."

It's true. Capodichino may be only five kilometres away but the route—I refuse to admit—is a vague, circuitous hodgepodge. The part we know is Via Foria, the long, mostly straight boulevard that wends from Via Duomo past the Orto Botanico and uphill before it becomes something else, narrowing and zigzagging past a jumble of shops selling terracotta flower pots, garden statues.

I'm running, every muscle fired with adrenalin—as fast as a well-past-middle-age person can run shackled with baggage. I'm tearing up Via Duomo. Tom is so far behind, he's but a punctuation mark in the gloom. Ahead, the only movement is a garbage truck pulling around a corner. I want to flag down the driver, beg for a ride. Too late, the truck is gone.

Light-headed, I turn to make sure Tom's still there. I fear for his heart. His bags are heavier than mine, he's older than me. Fast walking, sprinting, has never been his thing.

At the top of Via Duomo a sign shows an airplane, an arrow pointing right—reassuring. It's 4:50. Now I'm running up Via Foria—on the wrong side of the boulevard, I barely notice—should by some miracle any vehicle appear and happen to be heading the right way.

Dawn hasn't broken. The sidewalk is a crush of smashed glass from last night's partiers. In the street lights' gleam, I pause to see Tom turn onto Foria and creep along the opposite side. Could he move more slowly? He hollers to me, I don't know what he's saying, then realize, yes, it would be better if I was on that side of the street.

Crossing is a breeze with no traffic. It's as if Napoli is under some bizarre lockdown, each and every living, breathing Neapolitan confined to whatever place they call home.

My feet hit the dark, patchy grass in the middle of the boulevard before I spot it. The impossible: the roof light of a cab blocks away, speeding toward us.

Tom is flagging it down. I'm waving my arms like an unhinged airport worker guiding in an engineless jet.

Miracle of miracles, the driver stops. He's off work, he says in scattered English, not due to start for hours. I might as well be pleading for our lives: "Can you take us? It's an emergency."

He shakes his head at first. Tired, inconvenienced, annoyed but amused enough—kind enough—he waves us aboard.

Tom jumps into the front. "We need to be there in five minutes."

The man glances into the rear-view mirror as I squirm into the back. He doesn't say a word, screeching away from the curb.

An angel, what else can he be? An angel from Santissima Annunziata. An Esposito, I am convinced, despite glimpsing his licence clipped there, the name on it.

A race-car driver. For the ride uphill past the flowerpot stores and through a morass of winding streets is a blur. Squealing tires, no stops for lights, no lights—Formula One. Below us, the buildings' jumble is punctuated by domes, the city's crumbling sprawl bathed in an unearthly blue. I feel the strange, resolute certainty that we will never see this place again, never visit the unexplored buildings under their domes. Though washed with sadness, the certainty brings relief. We've done our time, have pushed our luck to the limit, let ourselves be tested, and survived. There are other cities to visit, other B&Bs with fewer stairs. We can let go, bid goodbye to our obsession with Napoli. Our addiction to it, to our fantasies.

Outside the terminal, I'm crying tears of gratitude, keep muttering my amazement at how the driver has saved us. Yes, saved us.

"God bless you," I say, as Tom pays. "God bless you."

The man shakes his head and laughs. The joke is on us: just a couple of crazy Americanos, I know he's thinking.

We stumble into the terminal in time to check in, a full half-hour before boarding.

My legs don't stop shaking until we are in the air circling Frankfurt.

Waiting for our flight to Toronto, Tom shoots Domenico an email, a curt one just to let him know the cab never showed.

Tutto bene, Domenico emails right back. All good. *Baci!* Kisses.

Settled into our seats, somewhere over the Atlantic all is more or less forgiven.

And on the last leg of the trip, before touching down in Halifax, we dream, however remotely, of returning.

More Fish in the Sea

GETTING THROWN IN WAS NOT HOW I EVER IMAGINED being dumped. A splash of red (a dying sprig of huckleberry?), eddying light, a crow's squawk: these were my last ties with you and your world. All were cut, washed away the instant I slipped under the November current, somersaulted over rocks and rapids rushing to suck the air from my lungs and between my ears. The burbling mimicked the engine of your souped-up Civic back in the clearing.

I imagined you fleeing the scene in it, sure I was done for, until my arms became fins. Hard to fathom that only seconds before, we were kissing on the slippery bank, at that bend in the river before suburbia tames it. You griped about cooking. My sneakers skidded. *Somebody's losing her head*, the crow cackled. Nothing to grab onto but a fistful of twigs. Not so much as a branch you might have tossed me, the nearest life-rings located downstream at

Canadian Tire, assuming these were stocked out of season. If you'd wanted to, you could've sped there, purchased one, watched for me racing under the bridge by the parking lot, stopped my acrobatic thrashing.

You could have saved us both the drama. I'd have understood. But, oh no. Rather, you'd tricked me: "Is that what I think it is, Meena? There, see? What kind of asshole dumps a bicycle? Shopping carts, maybe. But a bike?"

You had made me look closer. Ever the ecological geek, I fell for it. I peered down, felt your hands slip to my shoulder blades. "Cry me a river," I think you'd said when, earlier, I had accused you of weaseling out of chores. The whitewater churned like clouds as I reeled.

One long "Fuck you" curled from my cold-blooded tongue as I sluiced away.

Soon, knifing, spinning, tumbling along—the burble and froth laced with a wintry iciness, the cold of dead things—I grew a dorsal fin, then a tail. By the time the first of the beige houses appeared I was a trout, stronger and wiser than any smolt but far from mature. A rainbow trout, I imagined myself, in flashes of sunlight as the wind had its way with us, the flying river and its slippery passenger, me.

As the river surged near the mall, I understood you were well out of the picture. I knew I would make it to the ocean, no mere trout anymore but an Olympian one. And you, my friend, were prima landlubber saddled with your rust-bucket car, no doubt hangry, maybe even panicky, and stuck with an inertia that can't be cured by weather or changes of season.

You were marooned ashore, while I finned past a hook that dangled for one scary second from a line suspended from concrete—the concrete of a bridge—dangled there, then dragged on some eelgrass. Dodging it and you, whirlpooling around a shopping cart, for one short second I freaked, but then realized this trout, with all its slippery smarts, me-myself-and-I graced with them, was home free.

Ripple

WHAT I NEED YOU TO KNOW IS HOW THE AIR ITSELF was orange, an orange crush, the night of the Sturgeon Moon—a perfect August evening before you were a ripple in your mama's belly or a spark in your dad's mind. On the trail above the Arm a rufous deer lurked, vivid against the leaves' sun-splashed green. The dog missed it, impervious to everything but a different scent, following her nose down another path—the path that preschooler me and your great-grandma took many moons past to go swimming.

At the bottom of the path lay the narrow inlet, peach-coloured in the sunset. The sea flat as pavement—a dead calm. A heron fished from the breakwater's spilled rocks. Seaweed breathed in and out. Sailboats motored past, sails furled—without a lick of wind, the regatta was a stalemate. On the grassy hills that sloped to Fairy Cove, where the neighbourhood kids and I learned to do the dead man's float, new Canadians smoked hookahs. The same hills from which our white, freckling/burning/deep-tanning mothers trained lazy eyes on us: those mothers had trusted in lifeguards, teenagers like the one you will become if this world, our kaleidoscopic world, lasts.

If it lasts, you and your small aura will be every colour of the spectrum, and powerful—a prism, a rainbow. Back in that strange, old, white universe, only rain kept the mothers from sun-worshipping. They poured on baby oil; sunscreen wasn't yet invented. The highest neap tide could not breach the hand-built, stone-piled-on-stone wall guarding land from sea—the wall that's been replaced by granite blocks the size of Smart cars. (Will Smart cars still be a thing, once you're in the world?) Blocks as big as industrial-strength heat pumps, say, and the letters of the Latin words that encircle and codify the inner dome at St. Peter's. None of these structures will be any match for the rising oceans, the great flood bound to come.

But on the night of the Sturgeon Moon, little kids like the kid you will be played in the shallows of an ebbing tide. Grabbed floating plastic bottles, filled and threw them like bombs, yes. Parents shielded their eyes against strategically posted warning signs about bacterial counts, dangerous levels. Shielding their eyes against the sun's low blaze, along the seawall's fortifications fishers cast lines that wrinkled the same calm surface and hauled up mackerel like mackerel was going out of style. Life free for the taking, buckets overflowed with fish. (You are what you eat, I might tell you someday, if there's a lucky sea change.) Just out of reach, a safe distance away, a grey seal backflipped, bobbed upright. Could do nothing but keep watch, in case there were sharks.

And then the dark, seaward view opened up to me. I wish you could have seen it, I wish I could have held you high in my arms to look at it. The moon was a peach hanging over the Arm's mouth, its reflection was an orange shimmer tangled in a yacht's spars. Anchored there, the yacht was an ark full of partiers. People raising glasses, cheering on nightfall, their laughter bouncing from one shore to the next. Above this shore's trucked-in sand was a playground, where, call me wishful, call me blind, I hope to take you someday. A future promise—as I watched a man in a brilliant red turban push a tiny, cooing child on a swing.

Back in the ancient days, a canteen slumped nearby, a whitewashed shack with signs that said *Smoke Sweet Caporal Cigarettes* and *Drink Coke*, which you will never taste, at least not on my watch. The spot is a parking lot now, go figure, paved and filled with cars—hard candies, seen from the air? Past the sand, seagulls yank mussels from the rocks then levitate upward, drop them from a great height to bash the shells open on asphalt. A bedtime snack? Shards of mauve and dark, dark indigo are razor sharp—what damage they would do if you were to pick them up in your tender hands. What would I do to hold back the sting, the memory of red beading warm brown skin?

What I need you to hold in your heart is not the sharpness but the ease of light, the knowledge that from light comes colour. That our world had more shades, tones, and hues than you will imagine, than your parents will remember—reds redder than red, oranges more orange than orange—even as the storm waters rose. Even as the ocean waves rose cold and black, slipped their bounds, replaced air, crested over our heads, broke and washed it all away: each leaf, each bird, each fragment of shell—as you slipped by unseen and swam like a seal. Amphibious.

Scrubland

WE HAD IT PLANNED: MY PARTNER DROVE THE getaway car. We weren't wearing masks, tended not to bother, with just the two of us. Later on—looking back, a knee-jerk reaction—I would call this a mistake, just considering the toxic crud lining the ditch the afternoon of the heist. Though the May sun blazed down nakedly, the wind was razor wire: a mask would've provided warmth and protection.

The province, still under lockdown, had lifted a few minor restrictions—license that day for the gazillions of people sick of staying home to take a drive. So it appeared, judging by the traffic that poured out of town, traffic we got stuck in. Up until now, with hardly any cars on the road, no planes in the air, the skies had never been bluer or the birdsong louder. Driving was allowed, though you questioned the point of it with everything closed and nowhere special to drive to. It was different for Jeffrey and me, though. I had a project. A goal to give the day meaning, after two and a half months self-isolating at home; otherwise, I mightn't have got out of bed that Sunday.

Yes, it *was* a Sunday, never mind how one day bled into the next.

Unfortunately, the roadsides were hopeless for executing my plan—so many *potential* rubber-neckers on the loose. The location I had in mind should've been prime, a secluded area that, before the world had ground to a halt, was soon to be clear-cut to expand the nearby industrial park. Surprise, surprise, in the two and a half months since Jeffrey and I had last left our 'hood, not only had it been cleared, but also a highway interchange had been built, leaving nothing but scraped granite and fresh asphalt. A massive disappointment—if it hadn't been, I might not have ended up in hot water. Too late to fret about it now. I told Jeffrey to keep driving. He headed for a secondary route outside the city that eventually wound its way to Peggys Cove. The traffic heading out of town was, I kid you not, bumper to bumper.

I'd almost lost heart when, not two kilometres down the two-lane freeway, Jeffrey spotted the cul-de-sac cut into the woods. Actually, he spotted the sign first, *Evergreen Place*. "That's got to be meaningful," he said, signalling the turn. And, oh baby, it was. The pavement was lined on one side by warehouses catering to, well, bodily functions, all facing a wall of scrub forest. A reinforced steel fence formed a holding pen for dozens of Honey Huts, portable toilet rentals. Next door was a plumbing wholesaler, beside it a medical supplier.

Jeffrey pulled over onto the opposite shoulder. He stayed behind the wheel scrolling through his phone while I unloaded the gear from the trunk. I pulled on my gloves. Weeds and scrub spruce fought over what space in the ditch wasn't mulched with litter. Feisty little things, the trees forced their way up around rubber gloves, surgical masks, Tim's cups, and what have you, blown there from some nearby dumpsters.

"This is a rescue mission," I had reminded Jeffrey a few times—he needed reassurance, having been forced, asked, to help. Not that he needed coercion—he was as keen as I was to escape the house, our yard, our street. A person can only take so many walks around the same subdivision for two and a half months.

Aside from a coffee cup rolling across the pavement, Jeffrey peering at his phone, and me hefting my shovel, there wasn't a single sign of life, not even a bird. Evergreen Place was a veritable dead zone—it was gold.

I stacked my buckets and pots beside the car, left the rear passenger door open to ease the operation. In the front seat Jeffrey had the spray bottle of disinfectant at the ready. I started digging, had made a few minutes' headway when a car pulled in off the main road. It crept toward us, heading closer. Annoyed and, oh all right, self-conscious, I dropped the shovel and slouched behind the door, making myself invisible—not exactly easy when Jeffery and I were the only living souls in the area, as socially distanced as could be. Crouching there, I felt Jeffery staring more intently at his screen. The car crawled by, looped back, then finally sped up and left. I picked up the shovel and resumed digging.

The first specimen came away easily, tiny and perfectly shaped despite its necklace of trash. I heaved it into a green plastic bucket and slid it into the back seat.

Craning around, Jeffrey reached back and sprayed it down with Lysol, which I trusted wouldn't mar the upholstery under its plastic sheet. I was already eyeing the next specimen a few metres away, struggling to raise itself above a web of latex gloves.

"What is wrong with people? Such abuse of the environment would make you despair," I yelled.

Jeffrey wasn't listening. He was deeply engrossed in whatever he was streaming—CNN with the day's death toll?

This is *definitely* a rescue operation, I told myself. Being so close to the shoulder, these babies would fall victim as soon as the power company cleared its right-of-way, or the next porta-potty truck cut too close to the ditch. As I drove the shovel's blade through gravelly muck, another vehicle approached, parked a healthy distance behind us. The smell of cannabis wafted faintly. No worries.

Rescuing the stubby, yellowed specimen, I spotted another certain to be mowed down unless I acted. I dredged it up, homely as it was, and stuck it in a pail, then dredged up another and another, stuffing these into pots. The only sign any of them had been there was some scuffs in the gravel. The only one who could possibly mind was Mother Nature, a begrudging Mother Nature, I'd have to say, given what the sad little things had been up against. Besides, everyone knew they bred like rabbits. That's what I told myself, loading the four sad specimens into the back seat beside the choicer one.

Jeffrey unglued himself from his phone long enough to give each a good spraying. He took the virus *very* seriously—which is not to say I didn't. But did he really think it would attach itself to living things and stay active out in the elements?

Of course, we know how it goes with nature: so much depends on nurture. This wasn't the first time I'd executed a rescue. You should see my last rescues, guarding one side of our driveway—they had started out just as small and homely and pathetic as these guys. Though, being pre-virus, they were spared trial by disinfectant.

The open door invited in a cloud of blackflies. Swatting the air around his head, Jeffrey started the engine. He'd set the Lysol in my cupholder, preparing for our escape. I wondered if it killed flies too. The pesky things had swarmed me the entire time I'd been digging, though I'd been too focused to mind them. I was about to buckle up when another pitiful specimen beckoned from the ditch. It was taller and straighter than the others, a perfect mini-*Tannenbaum*. I just happened to have one more pot. Part of it was pinned under a stray chunk of asphalt, and for the sake of my back, I decided, best not be too ambitious.

"That'll do for now, hon," I said, climbing back in. I felt almost breathless, and barely had the seat belt buckled as Jeffrey pulled a fast U-ey. The potted kids in the back seat got jostled together and one toppled over—no biggie, though. Reaching around, I was able to stuff it back into its pail as Jeffrey gunned it past the medical supplier and the plumbing places.

I was just settling into my seat, when he let out a strangled "Oh shit."

I glanced around. If I had blinked, I'd have missed it, the little red-and-white sign fixed to the Honey Huts' fence: *This area is carefully monitored by* CCTV 24/7.

"'Carefully.'" I snorted. "In the middle of a pandemic? I don't think so, do you?" My laugh was scornful. "What would they be monitoring? Unlawful use of a porta-potty?"

"You'd be surprised." Jeffrey whistled slowly through his teeth, turned onto the main road.

We were home in fifteen minutes. As we pulled into the driveway, the neighbour across the street yelled, "Nice brood!" The rescues *did* resemble children sitting there, the tallest just above window level. Jeffrey helped unload and carry them down to the very back of the yard.

I went straight to work digging the holes. There was easily room for three or four more. Oh well, give these little guys time, I thought, and they'll be sufficient.

Should I rewind a bit, to the good old days BC, Before COVID?

The hurricane that previous September had done its worst, toppling trees, wrapping a crane around a construction site. It took out wharfs and boathouses, set yachts and fish shacks adrift. Fortunately, all Jeffrey and I had to deal with were a few fallen branches. In the yard behind ours, our other neighbour worked like a beaver piling downed limbs, twigs, and leaves into an ever-growing heap. I say "beaver" because he looked like one in his dark brown track suit, with his tawny, slicked-back hair. The heap made a ratty berm separating his yard from ours. I would even venture to say it crossed the property line.

We watched him work from our kitchen window. Jeffery and I have lived peacefully in our home for nine and a half years, though the neighbourhood is full of kids, and we are proudly child-free. Nine and a half years of digging, planting, mowing, mulching, and pruning—it has taken never-ending rounds of these to create and maintain the backyard of our dreams. Well, my dreams. You could say that in transforming a weedy dog-patch into a manicured sanctuary, I acted as project manager while Jeffrey did the heavy lifting.

Vlad, the berm-builder, was new to the 'hood, having arrived that summer. We'd heard from another neighbour he had a wife and daughter, though after ten months we had yet to see either. Generally speaking, ours is a friendly 'hood, if you disregard the kids and the chalk drawings of penises and chicken nuggets they leave on the street, the asphalt in front of our place their canvas. But generally people look out for each other, and in the summertime, before the pandemic, even circled lawn chairs for neighbourhood happy hours.

Maybe it was the language barrier that had kept us from getting to know Vlad?

From our window, Jeffrey and I would watch his fluffy calico kitty squeeze in and out of the cat door he installed in a basement window. Rain or shine, the cat would leap expertly from the cast-off bookcase positioned below it, appearing and disappearing as randomly as its owner seemed to.

In the months before social distancing and staying the blazes home, we suspected that Vlad's only living family was the cat. All winter the most reliable sightings of Vlad himself were of him pacing the length of his snowy deck in his slippers, otherwise dressed for a blizzard in parka and toque, while chain-smoking and drinking beer. (We keep the binoculars handy for birdwatching and spotting kids playing jailbreak in our yard.) His black late-model car rarely left his driveway. He seemed to come outside only to talk on the phone. Speaking in a heavy Slavic language, he had a voice that carried, booming *and* piercing—Jeffrey thought maybe he suffered from some sort of voice modulation disorder, or was hard of hearing.

His volume never varied. Even on frozen January nights with our doors and triple-paned windows locked up tight, we could hear him from our kitchen. Stepping outside to empty the compost, I'd catch the replies of whoever was on the receiving end of the call. They too spoke in a Slavic tongue. Its cadences made me think of Siberia or the Kamchatka Peninsula, somewhere cold and inhospitable.

Sometimes I would pause under the stars and listen, as long as I could stand being out there without a coat, and wonder what they were talking about. Vlad's inflections were morose and corrective, almost fatherly, as if he was warning his listener not to do something crazy or illegal, something they would both regret. His back-and-forth pacing added to the terseness. Sometimes he paced with beer in hand; now and then he'd set the bottle atop the barbecue, which, I might add, he rarely if ever used for cooking. By the end of the phone call there might be three or four bottles lined up, all whisked out of sight by morning.

Was Vlad giving advice? Was he threatening the person, or offering a lifeline of hope to a detainee in some Russian gulag? I imagined a friend or relative stuck in some cramped, post-Soviet apartment with acid-green walls and faulty plumbing. Maybe he was filling them in on the price of real estate in Nova Scotia. Maybe he was comparing the price of milk, or vodka. Maybe he was telling them not to drink so much. Maybe his name wasn't Vlad.

I don't know for certain that it was, to be honest. Jeffrey and I had only heard our other neighbour, the "Nice!" guy, refer to the fellow as Vlad. By the time these weekly phone calls took place, the man and his cat and his invisible family had been living there seven or eight months. Fall had given way to winter and the pandemic. By then, it was too late for us to casually amble over and introduce ourselves. It would have been weird, okay? Jeffrey was all about respecting other people's privacy. He developed a sudden migraine when I suggested he might just wander over and mention that all that piled deadwood might be a fire hazard. Fire hazard or not, the debris became the focal point from our window, never mind my carefully tended plantings of shrubs and perennials (Jeffrey jokingly calls them "perineals"). The eyesore interrupted what in summer had been a clean, lush sweep of lawn.

"Have you spoken to him?" the first neighbour wondered, calling to me from the street one day as I weeded a curbside bed.

I let out a sigh, imagining the deafening pitch of Vlad's voice amped up with anger. "I don't like to say anything." Though I refrained from saying so, if Vlad's language had been English I might have broached the subject. I might have somehow breached or sidestepped the offending barricade and knocked on his door.

A moot point, of course, once the pandemic hit.

As March waned, I noticed Vlad's nighttime calls grew less frequent. Perhaps he got tired of talking outside in the cold? As spring slowly dawned, and patches of snow and ice yielded to pea soup–coloured grass, I told myself to get a grip, to focus on priorities: love the one you're with, we were all learning. What was a pile of biodegradable debris?

Millions were sick, thousands were dying. People's finances were swirling down the toilet, legions of folks were out of work (though, fortunately, Jeffrey and I kept our jobs in insurance, working from home).

The grass greened from pea soup to emerald. I wanted to kick myself. "Welcome to the 'hood," I should have said back in the summer, and taken over a plate of fresh-baked muffins, even some store-bought cookies. After all this time, such a gesture would be glaringly odd, bizarre, and un-kosher with social-distancing rules. What would Vlad have made of someone, us, appearing at his door? The time for speaking out, as you must understand, was long past.

When he wasn't Zooming clients, Jeffrey lay on the couch reading *The Gulag Archipelago*. When I wasn't emailing clients, I raked and tended the yard, re-seeding patches of lawn that a team of grub-eating crows had ravaged. At night I had what people on Facebook called Covid dreams and shared in lurid detail. I refrained from sharing mine—they featured barbed wire, electric fencing, the Berlin Wall. I knew but couldn't fully accept that Vlad's barricade paled in comparison to these. Drinking my morning coffee at the kitchen window, I felt my blood pressure rise.

Maybe it sounds like I'm making excuses for my smallness of heart. What I am trying to do is explain the motive for the rescue.

Forming a tidy row on our side of Vlad's heaped branches, the "kids" took to their new home. They would need plenty of sun and water to grow tall enough to block the berm from view, but eventually, I felt, they would. At least I hoped so.

In a matter of weeks they put out a tender show of green buds, a sign of contentment. Who wouldn't prefer a leafy yard in suburbia to a trash-choked ditch on the fringes of an industrial park?

One afternoon, I had just finished giving them each a drink when the mail arrived. Something addressed to me from the municipality. A tax assessment? No, a notice, issued two weeks prior, of a "violation" that had taken place on a date in May, "contravening Bylaw # T-600," whatever that was. The rest of the notice was no more illuminating, filled with words like "provisions," "conditions," "permit," and "failing to comply." My eyes were playing tricks—I was due for new glasses but the pandemic had shuttered my optometrist's office. "Every person who violates...," I read, "guilty of an offence...liable on summary conviction to a penalty..." I had mindlessly grabbed a handful of chocolate-covered raisins, was chewing and about to swallow a mouthful of grainy sweetness as I took this in. "Not exceeding $5,000.00," the notice informed me, "or in default of payment, imprisonment for a term not exceeding six months."

It was a mistake, of course, it had to be, addressed to the wrong person. Good thing, I told myself, glimpsing the remittance form at the bottom. The guilty party must have done something pretty despicable, I thought. There was a warning, which I imagined being voiced in a thick Slavic accent, that if payment wasn't made in full "within fourteen days following the day on which the alleged violation was committed," further penalties and imprisonment could be incurred. Then, as I read, "Each day the offence continues constitutes a fresh offence," the possibility, the *indignity* of the possibility of guilt, dawned on me. I started coughing sugary spit, narrowly avoided choking.

There was a toll-free number to call to inquire "about the right to appeal." My first impulse was, get Jeffrey to call—if he had been home and not out for a walk. Navigating menus, listening as the warning about a high volume of calls looped endlessly, I was ready to hang up when a human finally came on the line. The man's voice had a slight Spryfield twang. By that I mean I could picture him outdoors in his sock feet, his shirt off, having a few rum and Cokes, catching a few rays.

He didn't give his name, but he sure was interested in knowing mine. His phone manner was all about turning the tables, I could tell. "Is this Giselle Hambly?" His tone was petulant: I had disturbed his fun. "Are you the co-owner of an orange Subaru, a 2016 model, plate number GDT392?"

Masticated raisin stuck in my teeth. "Um, yeeess?"

"Were you on or in the vicinity of Evergreen Place, Halifax Regional Municipality, on May 17th, a Sunday afternoon if I'm not mistaken, at 15:25 hours? You wouldn't happen to be the lady in a purple jacket, removing trees."

"Who is this?" Forget his banal accent, my first, crazy thought was, are you a friend of Vlad's?

"We've got you on tape, Giselle. Contravening bylaw—"

"Excuse me?" I'm sure he heard my gasp. I felt the blood rush to my face, a hot throb in my neck. "I haven't got the foggiest idea what you're talking about."

"Oh? What seems to be the problem? The info's there on the notice, you received it, right? Payment's due on receipt. You are entitled to appeal." He sounded doubtful.

"Right," I breathed, tongue-tied. Training my eyes on

the kitchen window, Vlad's deck beyond it. It was a sunny Wednesday, smoke curled from the barbecue but the man himself was nowhere in sight. "Payment?" I repeated, my voice a squeak. This couldn't be right, it couldn't be, it was so unfair. "I think there's been a mistake."

His impatient inhale curdled the air on the line. "You can google the bylaw. The deets are on the notice, ma'am." He paused, then began reciting about penalties "in default of payment," including "imprisonment for a term not exceeding six months. Each day that the offence continues constitutes a fresh—"

"Yes, yes, I know, but—"

"We have no record of your permit respecting the removal of trees on public lands."

"Trees! But this is nuts. Look, it was a rescue operation, that's all. I had no intention of, of—" I listened for Jeffrey. The very last thing I needed, suddenly, was him arriving and hearing all this. "Honestly, see, I was *reclaiming* them. It was an act of...reclamation. I had *no* intention of damaging..."

"I suggest you pay the fine promptly. Unless you can prove to a judge that the offence isn't ongoing..."

"Does this mean that as the trees grow so does the penalty?" I gasped out the question, threw up the hand not gripping the phone.

"Can I ask what you did with them?" Now he sounded amused. "Hon," he interrupted himself, "just think if everyone helped themselves, there wouldn't be a tree left in Nova Scotia, now would there."

Well that's just stupid, I wanted to say, because it was. But then I thought of Vlad and how he might respond, his answer unintelligible but his tone corrosive.

The man on the phone took my silence as acquiescence. "Giselle. We accept e-transfers or Visa, no cheques at this time." There was a pause and a gulp—I imagined the man in an office now, taking a swig of undrinkable coffee from a disposable cup. I imagined his breath fogging up a Plexiglas shield as he held the cup in a hand gloved in latex. Gloves like the blue ones in the ditch.

"Would it make any difference if I told you it happened because of a neighbour?" I hoped it didn't sound like I was begging. But I was afraid of Jeffrey stumbling in and overhearing, and I needed this resolved ASAP.

"Ma'am," the voice was weary, miffed if undefeated—here was a person as sick of isolation as the rest of us. "Tick the box if you want the option to appeal. Have a nice day."

"Fine. You have a nice day too." I was just hanging up when Jeffrey appeared. I grabbed the notice before he could see it and jammed it into my purse. I could just imagine his voice: *You broke the law for the sake of the yard? And you implicated me?*

Five thousand dollars. I felt like throwing up. Jeffrey would have too, if he'd known. He would have freaked.

I guess there was no return policy, I couldn't have taken the trees back. Even if there was, I couldn't have done it. They had taken root, they were thriving. They were exactly where they deserved to be—in an ideal spot, save for Vlad's berm. I put the fine on my Visa, money I'd have certainly rather put toward a privacy fence. Though what would have been the point of that? A fence would need to be as tall as a house and as thick as a highway sound barrier to block Vlad's drifting voice. Jeffrey was none the wiser.

I told myself, what price, five living things? A mere thousand dollars apiece.

Jeffrey and I were on our deck barbecuing chicken one hot Saturday in July, admiring how the maples' leafing out acted like a muffler dampening sounds slightly. Or maybe the sounds themselves had gone away—*pinch me, am I dreaming?* I asked myself, tossing the salad. But no, it had been a few weeks since we'd last seen Vlad on his deck, shouting into his phone. Not shouting so much as projecting, I suppose, like an actor ensuring his audience hears each and every syllable. The grass in his yard had grown knee-high and the dandelions gone to seed were like a soft grey smoke hovering above its green.

Jeffrey had just opened a bottle of rosé, and I was taking my first sip when a different sort of voice pierced the air beyond our yard. Voices, I should say. Female ones. Higher, brighter, a woman's and a girl's. Through a leafy web of branches, we glimpsed the woman playing chase with the child, their legs scissoring through the weeds. The small, thin woman had her dark brown hair pulled back in a French braid and was wearing jeans and a red sweater unsuitably heavy for the weather, though she didn't appear to mind. The girl was spinning around like a little cyclone, she was wearing pink leggings and sneakers and a shiny purple top and gold tulle skirt like an oversized tutu. She shrieked with delight as the woman reached to catch her in her arms and she streaked away. The woman's laugh was a soft, light-hearted gurgle, and the child's was shrill and delicate—if you could compare their laughter to anything, I'd have to say it was like the forget-me-nots growing under the lilac bush by our deck: light in volume and pale-blue and pink in tone. When the mother finally caught the child, they collapsed in giggles in a dandelion haze.

Though I felt sure they had been transplanted, it was as if they'd always been here, like my trees. By now the weeds had pretty much overtaken Vlad's berm, and much as I willed the woman to come to the edge of the yard and inspect it, she didn't notice it—if she did, she paid it no mind. I guess as far as she was concerned, that deadwood had always been there.

This is how everything begins, I told myself, how new stuff grows from old stuff.

I don't know where Vlad was. The car was there, he must have been nearby. A whiff of burning steak wafted over, gusts of smoke rising from his barbecue. Jeffrey took it as a cue to turn the chicken.

Picking up my wineglass, telling Jeffrey to turn down the heat, I made my way casually down to the back. I raised my glass and called out, "Hello? We haven't met. I'm Giselle. Welcome."

Faith Healer

YOU HAD TO HAND IT TO THE GUY, HE KNEW HOW TO hold a person's attention—if not for the man's performance, Carlisle would've had trouble keeping his eyes open. But dude was a magnet up there, skipping across the stage in his suit. Ma was right, the Reverend Percy J. Seawald was no average preacher. From what Carlisle knew of preachers. Not a lot, other than seeing them in collars like the one Jas put on her cat to kill fleas.

If not for Jas, he wouldn't be at Ma's. And if not for Ma, he'd have avoided this faith healing revival roadshow like the plague. All that stuff you heard about fast-talking preachers bagging people's money. But Ma'd heard this fella had the touch, and she was sick of fighting to catch her breath. A major production dragging her arse up and down the steps whenever she left the house.

He'd offered to drive her, never mind the Vineyard Assembly was just four or five doors down the street from her place. Pull the truck right up onto the sidewalk, help her inside with her "buddy" on its dolly, then disappear. The place had a ramp, he'd noticed since moving in. She was always saying how lucky they were having everything right there in the neighbourhood. What difference, though, something being next door or all the way across town if you could not take ten steps without keeling over?

"And what if I run into trouble while I'm there, Carl?" She didn't have a phone.

At least when the time came, the assisted-living place was right across the street, at the top of the hill. Ma's apartment house overlooked the port. If not for the high-rise next door, they'd have had a decent view of the cruise ships.

"Least you can do is be there for your mother, Carl. A real live faith healer! You don't run into one of them every day."

Like this would impress him.

He had tried to weasel out of it. "You've got that friend to go with, don't you Ma?"

"God love her, Carl. Noreen's in the home, for cripe's sake!"

So long as you are living under my roof, watching my TV, it's my house, my rules, she did not need to say. The price of a place to crash since the split, well, since Jas threw him out.

"And what else you got going on, hmm?"

So he was between jobs. A rainy Wednesday afternoon. At such times when things got to be too much he'd sit in the truck listening to Today's Country 101.9 FM. But even the truck didn't feel like his, belonging mostly to the bank. The custom decal he'd gotten on the tailgate—*Mullet Mafia*—only rubbed this in.

Now, here he was surrounded by little old ladies murmuring "Amen" into Kleenexes while this crazy-ass reverend ranted and raved. It was all end times, last days, second comings. No word (yet) on what might free Ma from the tank that accompanied her everywhere. He listened for the faint hiss of oxygen from the tube's prongs in her nostrils. It was quite the rig. Tubing snaked from the cylinder, forked under her chin, then a separate length looped over each ear—kind of like the ties of a mask. When they'd first rigged Ma up, Jas said it looked like face jewellery. At least it exempted her from masking up.

"Lord, I'd suffocate with one of them things on, it's the truth!"

Not an issue here. He glanced around. Only the odd one was wearing a mask; his was balled-up in his pocket. Nobody mentioned vaccinations—nice to see the rules relaxed, he thought. Nothing wrong with fighting the fear-mongering. Which the Reverend Seawald seemed to get, power to him. So maybe he was worth listening to?

Prancing back and forth, the preacher even hopped up and down, dancing a kind of jig to make his point. Whatever his point was, besides sin and hellfire. Spit flew as Seawald shouted into the mic, wagged his head side to side, gazing at everyone. Making sure no one felt left out? You could see the little drops flying out over the front row, lit by stage lights. If not for these, the dark panelled walls made the place dingy as hell, what little daylight came in dimmed by the windows' pebbled glass.

Or the drops were dust motes. At least buddy was entertaining. Parked at the end of the pew, cylinder hogging the aisle beside her, Ma could've been watching *The X-Files*. Her expression was a mix of terror and rapture, that word thundering from the reverend's mouth. It drowned out the whistle from her nosepiece, her canola, she called it.

Now Seawald was raving about a holy parakeet. Carlisle had heard of doves flying around in the Bible, nothing about tropical birds though. Ma mentioned this when he aimed his pellet gun at pigeons roosting outside her window.

The cylinder and its dolly were more concerning. A fuller house and the fire marshal would have been on their asses. But the odd seat was empty, go figure. People with better stuff to do. *Fawk.* What would Jas think? And who organized something like this on a weekday?

"If the guy's legit, wouldn't he wait till Sunday?" he'd said, hoping Ma would back down.

Nope.

Now, he shifted on the scuffed seat. Swivelled his head, arms pinned to avoid nudging Ma or the old doll in a droopy knitted hat on his other side. A friend of a friend of hers, possibly. The woman must've been from the assisted-living place; half the folks looked to be. Just mobile enough to go out on their own, they probably didn't venture out after dark—like he was one to talk. Pushing forty-seven, hands down the youngest here and definitely the only dude besides the preacher, he wasn't exactly a party animal. Not since Jas's ultimatum.

He leaned in, spoke up so Ma could hear. "What's wrong with Noreen? How come she's not here?"

She sank her elbow in his side, turning his way. "Now aren't you glad you came, Carl?" Her cheek had a waxy sheen, eyes the same. The whistling in her nose was a wheeze.

"Glad isn't the word. But I guess it's free entertainment."

And Seawald's sideshow *was*, until the collection plate began circulating. Carlisle jerked his gaze toward the stage. Even sitting three rows from the back, you could see the spit gathered in the corners of the preacher's mouth, white as cotton swabs.

Seawald blinked, gazed upward at the ceiling fan's regular chop-chop-chop. "Verily, *verily*," he spoke with a hush. As if any second the water-stained ceiling tiles would lift off and, *oh look!* a humungous hand would come punching down, and then snatch everyone up.

Saved.

Well wouldn't that give these old gals something to crow about, after sitting through Sodom and Gomorrah, Ma included. Something guaranteed to spring leaks in a few Depends, he thought cruelly. The reverend's promise of their being Raptured, beamed up out of this world and into Heaven. When a few missed pills were bound to do the trick, he reckoned as the plate landed.

Ma rummaged in her raincoat. He felt equal doses of pity and grief watching her knobbed fingers lay a curled-up five atop a scattering of loonies. Aging wasn't pretty. Not that Ma was there yet; he wished he hadn't thought of old folks in diapers. All the more reason they should be spared getting trussed up at the breathing and speechifying end, the business end, Reverend Seawald had called it, mocking the need for masks at the start of his show. Though the odd one *was* masked, sort of, wearing the thing like a neck warmer or chin sling. Like missus with the knitted hat.

The thought of being stifled, or stifling, brought back Jas's words. How she would *not* grow old with him, they couldn't pay her enough. Whoever "they" were.

The reverend was shouting now about signs. Carlisle's mind drifted to the *Blind Crest* sign opposite Ma's, the *No Left Turn* at the foot of the hill, those routing transport trucks to the container pier.

"The mountains are crumbling. Rivers overflowing their banks. Hell, look at BC," he dragged out the e-sounds, "farmland becoming lakes, folks. Before ya'll know it, your harbour right here will run red, people. With someone's blood. Verily I say unto you—just cuz it ain't happening today don't mean it ain't happening tomorrow."

Seawald scanned the hall, cricked his neck, loosened his tie. A smile haunted his eyes. "Hell, the man in the moon will wanna take a hi-a-tus, in't the truth."

A croaking laugh or two rose up.

"Sure, and I'm taking all this with a spreader truck of road salt." Carlisle's whisper was just loud enough for Ma to hear. He nudged her, winked. "Just making sure you're alive."

Should've known better.

The reverend quit talking. Like a rough-legged hawk, frozen, he zeroed in. Eyebrows raised, brows you could've taken garden shears to. Seawald's eyes glittered so Carlisle felt a little jab of shame. His stare alone could have reduced some of the gathered to tears.

Carlisle fixed his gaze on the whirring fan. Its hum weighed the silence with an awful expectancy. Then the preacher cleared his throat and in a low, steady voice spoke of plagues.

"In case you haven't noticed, folks, we got one of them too. Don't we. DON'T WE. Amen. Do I hear AMEN? For I am here to remind you, people. I am here to remind *you*, Do not fear! Nor should you run from the sickness. This vi-rus. For it is the Lord's will," Seawald barked out the words, fists shaking, "His will when innocent folks sicken and die. It is not up to the gubbermint now is it? To dictate who shalt live and who shalt die. Mark my words, friends, the gubbermint is Satan in a spiffy suit and tie waitin' behind your computer screen. Doing all he can to drive a wedge—a WEDGE, I say—between you and the Almighty."

Booming through the mic, his voice was a tornado tagged with squealing feedback.

"Look at me, folks—behold your brother before you. Your humble brother who loves and wants what's right by each and every one of you. Do I look scared? Do I look scared to meet my Maker? Tell me—peeeeople—does yours very truly, the Reverend Percy J. Seawald, look afraid? No fear of a vi-rus is gonna separate me from the Almighty. Do I hear a A-men?" A host of timid yeses wafted upward.

The preacher looked around, wiped away spit with his thumbs. Then he breathed into the mic, "So I commend you for bein' here today. For heeding the call, right here in Haleefax, Nova Scotia, so we can be free, free I said, to worship and praise. Never mind if you don't got an itty bitty piece of cardboard or plastic or whatever the gubbermint says you need to come and worship together. What I am telling you is, the Lord don't discriminate. He don't answer to no yes-man, no-man, no wham-bam thank-you-man. So I applaud you folks for joining with me today in hearing the real news, not the news on your CNN but the news we gotta heed. That our days are numbered. Truly and finally numbered, folks. These days are fewer than the hairs on your chin, ma'am, you don't mind me saying."

A single stunned giggle rose up, then was whisked away by the fan's whirring and the hush that swept the hall. *Don't all breathe at once,* Carlisle sighed under his breath.

Seawald did not miss a beat. "Hell, folks. We are like the birds of the air—here today, gone tomorrow." The preacher's voice became a murmur, then, with eyes closed, he crooned into the mic. The swirling murk of his words thinned to a mist. Impossible to tell what exactly he was saying.

Could the folks up front feel the mist settle on them, like salt fog or drizzle?

Seawald slipped behind the podium, leaned against it. In the orangey light, trickles of sweat shone from his temples. He looked too old to have hair so dark, worn spiked like that. Age aside, the guy was tired—boy, was he tired—Carlisle could hear it in Seawald's voice. *He* knew that weariness. The same kind of weariness he had felt loading his backpack and tool belt into the truck after Jas announced she was changing the locks.

"So won't you come, people. Come! All's we have left is measured in seconds, folks—this world as we know it. So yuz best be ready. The Lord is coming. And if He doesn't come right now, right this second, you had best go home when you leave this place today and pack a bag. You hear what I'm saying? Pack your troubles into that little ole kit bag or suitcase or whatever you tote your life around in. That money you never give to the poor, keep under your mattress or in the bank, whatever. I don't give a hoot where you been keeping it—you lay it down and someone'll be here to take it off your hands, and if not right here right now, just leave us your name and number. We'll take it off your hands so you'll be ready. For it is easier for a camel to pass through the eye of a needle, friends, than for a rich man, or, heck, a rich woman, to enter the Kingdom." Seawald's gaze was raw and pleading.

Ma shuffled in her seat. She'd left her purse home—good thing, since that's where she kept her chequebook and zippered change purse with her bank card inside.

"So are yuz ready? People! ARE YOU READY?"

The silence that fell could have lasted a week as easily as it lasted five seconds. People wiped their eyes with tissues. Ma dabbed at her face under and around the tubing, mopped a tear from under her chin. Lipstick pinkened the wrinkles around her mouth. When she spoke, though, her voice was filled with dismay, no, disbelief.

"Well I never," she hissed. But then the preacher started in again.

This time his voice was gentle, soft and coaxing. "Folks. If you are ready to meet the Lord, let it be said. He don't want cripples, He don't want no sick people in Paradise. Does He. No sirree, He wants ya'll to be whole. Free and heathy and whole."

Carlisle's thoughts strayed to the nearby Tim's and its showcase filled with donut holes rolled in sugar. The last time he had seen Jas was for coffee, before he'd loaded up his tools into his truck, when she had broken it to him that she was seeing someone. A friend of his—an ex-friend—who had bad hair too but a heart of gold, she pointed out, plus a regular job that paid above the table, and would no more joke about the Mafia or gangstas or crips than take advantage of an old lady, especially his mother.

"That is below the belt," he'd said, standing up. Leaving behind a full double-double and most of an apple fritter.

And it was. Completely uncalled for. But somehow now it felt forgivable. Compared to Seawald's droning on, completely forgivable.

"Now there is one thing you have got to do—just one thing. All you who are sick, all you who are infirm of body. I am asking you to come. Come to me so I can lay hands on you. Sister, brother, be healed! No more sickness now, and no more death, people, after the Rapture. What are you waiting for? I *ast* you. What's holding you back? Come on up and be healed, won't you?"

To Carlisle's amazement, people actually rose and a tiny queue snaked toward the front. Ma stirred, her sleeve brushed his. Before he could put out his hand to stop her, she'd gotten to her feet. He tried to grab for her hood, too late. Teetering from the pew, she pushed against her buddy, tried to slip ahead of it. As he lunged to help, the tubing snagged and pulled from her nose. Oxygen escaped in a loud, breezy hiss. Still standing, she fingered the nosepiece back into place just as someone butted in ahead of him.

Moving on her own steam, Ma pressed toward the stage, more stubborn and determined than Carlisle had ever seen her. All he could do was tag behind at a distance, hoping—all right, praying—she wouldn't trip or suddenly sag to the floor like a pillow, get trampled by the small herd muscling to the stage.

Kneeling at its edge, the reverend was muttering prayers. Reaching down, clamping both hands to heads bowed before him, one after the other. Weeping and some loud Amens echoed back, and the thud of something hitting wood. Some old doll had fainted.

Not soon enough Carlisle shoved past the lady blocking him from Ma.

He'd just managed to grab hold of her hood's slippery nylon when a loud, official-sounding shout came from behind.

"Police!"

"We're here to break it up, folks—illegal gathering. Public health orders. We'll be issuing tickets to anyone not in compliance. The fine starts at two thousand dollars, just to warn you."

The two officers, armed, vested, and wearing masks, pushed their way to the front.

Reverend Seawald had vanished. Besides the doors at the back, the only exit was behind the stage, half-hidden by a dusty curtain. Quick on his feet—raptured up and out?—the preacher could only have escaped through it.

But Carlisle's concern was graver. The shock of seeing police made Ma stumble. Barely catching herself, she slipped into a pew heaped with coats. He slid in after her. Eyes pinched shut, she was sprawled there, one hand pinned to her chest. The other fumbled with her nosepiece.

For one bad moment, Seawald's rant lingering in his head, he imagined the unthinkable. Entertained the ridiculous. Ma's coat lying flat atop the others, left behind, her cylinder tipped over, also abandoned, clear plastic tubing uncoiled like a snake. Ma herself vaporized. Raptured up and out of the world, his world, and Jas's world. Their world.

But she was still here, of course, and she opened her eyes and smiled weakly. "You're a good son, Carl. Don't know what got into me marching up here—like I was gonna get my five dollars' worth of fixing, healing, if it killed me." That sad laugh of hers threatened to once more pop loose her cannula.

Standing before the stage, the cop was taking notes. Seawald's followers had scattered like mice.

"Looks like someone gave you the slip." Carlisle's voice echoed in the emptiness. He was the only person able and willing to step up and volunteer information. Like he had any to give, beyond the obvious. Who could have imagined, when he'd parked the truck and helped Ma manoeuvre herself up the ramp, he would be a prime witness at a crime scene, required to give a statement?

"Preaching brotherly love, was he?" The officer chortled. He was a ripped young guy with neck tattoos. "How to be a super-spreader, share what you've got. Sharing and caring."

Carlisle smirked, despite the sick feeling that had dawned and was swelling inside him. The what-ifs beyond the obvious ones if Ma'd had her purse. If Seawald had laid hands on her and she'd fallen, cracked her head or broken a hip.

"Where's your mask, bud?" The cop gestured at his face.

He dug the thing out and slapped it on.

"That's better. This your mother? You know I can charge you and her both, don't you?"

"Whoa, wait a sec. Don't you think this is a little—I'm only here because she is. And she's exempt, right?"

The cop shrugged, then turned and began herding a couple of stragglers outside. There were tears of anger, outrage, and disappointment. Mutters of "Least they could've done was waited and let the reverend do his thing, eh?" and, "Sat here all afternoon and for what?" and, "I'm not ready to call the reverend a crook though, not yet. Even though I didn't get what I come for."

The other cop, who looked more as you'd expect, stared Carlisle down. "I'm guessing that's your truck out there? It's in a no parking zone, bud." Then, glancing at Ma, he told Carlisle to get a move on: "You'd best get her home."

Which he wanted to do almost more than anything in the world.

Sweet compliance. "Yessir." Sweet mercy.

And more than enough excitement for a year, let alone an afternoon.

To think he and Ma got out of there with no more than a warning. No wonder he felt lucky. That kind of fine would've killed him. He wished he could call up Jas and tell her. She might have been amused—who knows, even charmed?

His luck made him more optimistic, though not enough to hope for something so crazy as a second chance. A chance he probably didn't deserve. Still, he made a mental note to get his hair cut, a step in the right direction? Sooner rather than later. Get his whole head buzzed, leave just half an inch all over.

Afterwards, the strangest part was helping Ma up the front steps and into the apartment like nothing had happened. He put on her TV show and slipped to the kitchen. The breakfast sausages she'd taken out for supper were thawed, five little pink weinies on their Styrofoam tray.

In the apartment across the way—Ma's building was separated from the high-rise by a walkway wide enough to accommodate some green bins—a young woman was painting her nails. He'd glimpsed her now and then puttering around when her blinds were up, but was super careful not to watch her. Or get caught watching her. Out of respect, or something. Her hair was wrapped in a blue towel, phone shouldered to an ear.

For one very awkward second their eyes met.

He felt a terrible urge to call Jas—*don't do it, don't even think about it*—as the woman rose from her couch, frowned. Even separated by eight feet and the windows' rain-streaked glass, the look on her face made him want to dive under the table, and when it was safe, duck from the room and disappear forever.

But he was caught, until the woman held up her hand, blew on her nails, and waved. Was it the comfort of seeing someone else living a fishbowl life that made him wave back? He turned to the stove. His hand shook, grabbing the frying pan. *Forget it. Don't even think about calling.* He had his pride. Still he reached for the ancient beige wall phone. *Do not call Jas.* As he picked up the receiver, started to punch in the number, Ma yelled for a cup of tea.

He hung up, replacing the receiver as quietly as possible.

"Carl?" Ma had incredibly selective hearing, could hear whispers through a wall if she wanted to. "Who're you calling, son? I wouldn't mind having a gab with Noreen if you'd help me to the phone."

From what he caught of their conversation, Ma downplayed what she called her afternoon's "disappointment."

"I'm over it," she told him during supper, though she couldn't hide her embarrassment. "Good thing you were with me. Not that I'd have fallen for that fella's scheme. Imagine, playing on people's fears like that, fears that we're all going to hell in a handbasket. Fear. What does that have to do with love? Which is the whole point, isn't it, of religion? Loving your neighbour and all that—like that teenager cop said. I don't know what got into me, Carl." She hung her head, picked at her food. "I guess I was just greedy, for a cure. I suppose for a minute there I thought I could strike a deal."

"A bargain, you mean—with the Almighty?" He laughed into his plate. His sausages were getting cold.

"Of course not. With that damn Seawald. Guess I should count myself lucky all it cost me was five bucks."

He didn't remind her it was an afternoon neither of them would get back, or how lucky it was they weren't ticketed. Now *that* would have made her mistake expensive.

It was probably in his head, but was that a tickle he felt in his nose, a tickle that moved from his throat to his chest? The start of a cold, or—?

Ma's friend Noreen called three days later to say it was there, at the assisted living. An outbreak. The Covid. Ma happened to have the phone's volume cranked—the better to listen in on his calls?—so Carlisle heard every word. "You're lucky you've got that son of yours with you and don't have to be in here." There was an awful pause, the only sound the whistling from Ma's cannula. "Nettie was there, wasn't she? At that thing you were at the other day? With that healer? I had my suspicions about that man. Well, she come down with it first—the virus."

Ma let out a gasp. "Why, Nettie was sitting right beside Carl." Her eyes locked on his. "Wasn't she, son?"

"Well. That virus don't pick favourites. They took her up the hospital. She's in the intensive care, I heard the nurses and them whispering about it. They say it spreads like wildfire, and I believe it."

That evening Ma started getting the sniffles, just a cold, sure. But by bedtime she said her throat hurt, and in the night she called out that she couldn't breathe—not even with her buddy right there breathing for her.

Carlisle slid off the couch and out of his sleeping bag and was at her bedside in a nanosecond.

There was a button he could press to increase the oxygen level. When that didn't help, he phoned 911.

While they waited for the ambulance, he prayed to God—certainly not the God the Reverend Seawald heralded but the one he thought was up there somewhere in the ozone, where money and viruses didn't count for much if they counted for anything—or, for all he knew, was hovering around them in the close, steamy air of the apartment, maybe just above their heads. The one that was in Ma's reddened eyes and the little tears leaking from them, too…and even the one that he figured, hoped, might be alive someplace as distant as Jas's heart.

Love, he supposed it was, the God or whatever he prayed to.

Just as the paramedics arrived, wouldn't you know, his cell buzzed—vibrated in his jeans pocket—which he had been thinking of cancelling, since the only person who'd ever called him on it was Jas.

"Leave a message," he heard that voice like Siri's say, as the medics were hooking Ma up to a machine, preparing to load her on a stretcher.

A click as the caller, likely a scammer, hung up.

In the waiting room—Emergency a war zone from what he glimpsed through its swinging doors, everyone in puffy yellow gowns, plastic face shields, masks, and what looked like deep-sea diving equipment rigged up—he stared at his phone. For hours and hours. It was better than staring at the news looping silently over the TV screen above people's heads.

Finally they told him to go home. They would do the best they could to save her.

He was brushing his teeth that night when his phone rang. He was so unused to its ring tone, he wondered whether the sound was coming from the apartment below. He froze. Was it the hospital calling about Ma? She was gone—had she been taken? All his fault for going with her to the fucking meeting.

But the voice on the line was buttery-warm saying his name, drawing out the *-isle* the way he hadn't heard in what seemed an eternity.

"It's Jasmine." As if the voice could belong to anyone else in this world.

Swallowing minty spit, he could not believe it, tried to keep the surprise, the hope inside him, from spilling out, spilling over.

"I've been thinking. I miss you," she said. "Maybe we

could...should try again? That bullshit about the mob, the hair, I don't even care, babe—it doesn't matter. Nothing matters but..."

Ma's words came to him from months ago, when he'd first landed at her door. "More fish in the sea, Carl. Don't be selling yourself short."

But he imagined her now hooked up to machines, and what he guessed Ma would say if she could: "It's a gift being alive, son—don't take it for granted. No matter what, our days are short even when they feel darned long. Be patient, just not a doormat. Things work out. For the best, usually. Like when the Fella Upstairs closes a door, he opens a window, right? We live in hope."

Jas had the nerve to spell out her conditions—a steady job, better attention to grooming, and the removal of that asinine decal from the truck—but he heard Ma's voice give blessing.

It was exactly as if she was floating over his head, just below the stained ceiling, her spirit like a helium balloon slowly leaking gas.

"You'll be okay, son. You've got to let go of me now, Carl."

He waited for more, words like the ones you might expect from a preacher, though not a preacher like Reverend Seawald: the Lord will deliver, maybe not this week, maybe not next week, but sometime. His ways are not ours to question.

Didn't Ma once say you had to wait in quiet expectation?

Then he imagined her climbing stairs, stairs leading high above him. Clinging to the railings, each step trembling under her weight, Ma huffing and puffing but slowly gaining momentum.

And he imagined the Reverend Seawald smoking a cigarette under the fire escape behind the assembly, then climbing into a long black car and being spirited off to the airport or across some border—into New Brunswick or Maine, and from there? Christ only knew.

There was the soft sound of breathing, so close to his ear he could almost feel it. He could almost smell it too, redolent with cigarettes and Tic Tacs and something else: coffee with cream and sugar.

"Carlisle. You there? Talk to me, hon. Talk to me, okay?" A pause. "Okay. Maybe I've been a bit of a bitch—I don't know why. I'm just asking you to be patient. Like, love me, okay, I don't expect you to get me. You think we could…"

Carlisle breathed in, and when he finally spoke, though it was his voice all right, the words came as if from somewhere beyond the window. As much as he wanted to melt inside Jas's plea—even with Ma's blessing—he didn't. Something out there would not let him. Besides, he would soon have the place to himself, he sensed it, a place of his own, as soon as Ma let go of him.

"Hey, Jas. You don't know the half of what I been through. And I reckon it's too late to explain anyways. Sayonara, eh. Isn't that how it goes?" He paused, to let the finality settle. "Listen. I'm done."

The Spectre of Unknown Roads

HE WOKE IN A TOTAL PANIC—JUST AS A DISEASED PAIR of hands closed around his throat, tried to pull him into a bottomless sea. Heart pounding, skin crawling with the sensation, he sat up. Grabbed his phone, scrolled back to reality. Let the screen's glow chase away the aura of plague ships, quarantine islands.

The dream had less to do with sidelined travels, he decided, and more to do with his real-time nightmare of needing a place to live. Needing it *yesterday*, ever since government calls to come home had wrecked his trip, and just as he and this woman he had met were about to catch a boat to Lampedusa. The beaches there were fucking amazing, he'd heard.

When the airlines started cancelling flights, his folks had texted *Our door's always open, Josh*. Nice, but cold comfort. Who'd have guessed he would still be under their roof one hundred and thirty days later?

Earlier that night, before the dream, he'd cabbed home from pub crawling to find his mom waiting up. She was making toast, her voice could have sliced it. Seriously.

"Your father and I want to know your plans. I'm asking you, Joshua. You're thirty-four years old, son." She didn't say, *You can't keep living off your parents.* But he felt it. Like he was a tapeworm and they were the host. Forget how he had missed them on his travels—a few select times, when he remembered to. On taking the ferry to Messina, feeling alone. Drinking to his birthday in Agrigento, until he hooked up with the Sicilian one. Grabbing the last flight home from Frankfurt. He had missed them but not home or their house with its new kitchen reno, his room with shit from his childhood no one could throw out.

Teenage Mutant Ninja Turtles—really? But there they were on the shelf above his bed.

Shaking off a bad dream, being stranded here, six thousand miles from Sicily, felt vaguely mortifying. And it wasn't like he hadn't been working. For the past few months he'd been doing online sales. Swimming pools. Business had surged, at first, with everyone planning staycations—surged so dramatically that now, midway through July, the supply chain had dried up and, just his luck, so had commissions.

At least with the bars having been closed until summer, he'd saved a bundle.

In the dark of his room he scrolled Kijiji for rentals. But the thought of forking out a shitload of money for some rathole made him queasy. Especially when he should invest money in his future, like the old man kept saying.

A future that was, okay, a bit fuzzy.

Fine then. Scrolling places for sale he almost missed

it—the ad was buried under condo listings but could not have popped up at a better moment. *Home away from home, $8000 obo.* The photo showed a floating box: flat roof, beige siding, door, and picture window. A motel unit cut adrift? It was definitely no match for his parents' place on its South End lot—even better. A deck ran along the front and a ladder reached the roofline strung with signal or maybe prayer flags—hard to tell from the picture, either way a hopeful touch. No mention of kitchen or bathroom facilities. Incidentals, he decided, sitting up and planting his feet on refinished hardwood.

No, the floor wasn't swimming, it was his head. Until lately he had avoided the Liquor Dome, its younger crowd. But lockdown—the *end* of lockdown—had turned everyone into a kid again. He'd met a nursing student and her friends celebrating graduation. "Sharla," she had shouted her name in his ear, above Drake's mono-drone. The non-option of inviting her back to his place automatically cancelled any progress.

Add to this his mother's ambush: "Your father and I would *really* like to downsize. There's those condos our friends moved to, you remember the Creightons?"

He'd waited for it: Next stop, a nursing home. With no room for y-o-u.

Eight grand—the price was right, not to mention the added charm of no fixed address. And a floating office might accommodate the job his father wanted for him: with his partners, Josh's butt in his chair. It could work. He had a decent data plan and the cash in his account.

The ad had been posted eight hours earlier. This deal was too good to last. But at 2:30 A.M. the "Blair" named in it wasn't taking calls. He left a message and lay back, still wearing the clothes he'd worn downtown.

The AC's gentle chill swooshed away the dream's sweaty remnants. But who could sleep? He checked the weather in Siracusa, read about Venice's canals growing murky again with the tourists' return.

Clicking on the ad once more, he scrutinized the photo. In the background was the condo development where his folks' friends lived, sky-high waterfront value a ten-minute walk from here.

Even if the place had already sold, it was worth a peek. He grabbed a sweatshirt, slipped outdoors, and headed down Jubilee Road past its solid, stately houses. He could've walked the route in his sleep; it was the one he had taken to his parents' club as a kid, to tennis and sailing lessons. Not that the sailing lessons had gone anywhere, his parents not being boaty. Real sailors learned to sail at the yacht club across the Arm.

At this hour the stroll was peaceful, the air filled with the smells of flowers and trees and salt from the harbour. The soft hiss of the odd passing car. If he tried really hard, he could almost pretend he was somewhere exotic. He walked faster. There were still six weeks of summer, prime for living on the Arm. Halifax wasn't Sorrento and the Arm was not the Bay of Naples, but it was a lot more sheltered. Before climate change, anyway, the worst storm barely caused a ripple.

In no time he was standing on the tiny gravel beach beside the condos.

The houseboat was maybe twenty metres offshore, amid a flotilla of masts. The wooded hills on the opposite shore loomed dark, treed slopes dotted with monster houses, the gleam of an occasional light. In his mind's eye he pictured Cefalù's towering Rocca, little fishing boats bobbing below on its azure bay. Their bright reds, blues, yellows, and greens easily filled in the greyish outlines before him. He checked his phone, checked it again. Coached himself: *Chill, bud.* Who answers calls at 3:00 A.M.?

The houseboat swung lazily on the outgoing tide. It had a picture window not just at the front but on two other sides. Not like a motel unit but an aquarium, with a panoramic view!

The nursing student had a pink camo-patterned mask that made her dark eyes pop. Those eyes made him keen to see the rest of her. Still, he was spooked when she took off her mask to talk, though he'd kept his dangling from one ear. Hey, so quickly? Aggressively? Then he saw that she had removed it to stress a point. To shout around him, actually, when some Black men were turned away at the door: "But they *are* wearing masks!"

"Not the right kind," the bouncer had shouted back.

"Asshole," Josh had mouthed.

He liked the fierce way she tilted her chin. Her hair was a mass of springy reddish curls, her skin flawless. She had perfect teeth. A trace of lipstick smeared on them was like cherry Popsicle.

He guessed this was her first night out in, what, a hundred or more days? "So how did you pass the time avoiding the world?" Epic fail of a hook-up line, he knew as soon as he said it. But it was bound to be awkward seeing people in real life instead of on Zoom. He tried again. "From around here, Sharla? Okay, stupid question. Like planes haven't been invented or something." (Never mind the skies were still pretty much empty.)

He offered to spring for her martini too.

"Sure, why not?" She fired a smile at her friends, obviously in party mode making up for lost time.

When the drinks arrived, she took wipes from her purse and cleaned off both their glasses.

She reminded him, he said, of someone he'd met in Sicily. (*Too brown to be Caucasian, too white to be African*, he was careful not to say.)

"Oh yeah?" She'd just gotten on at the hospital, she said.

"Tell me something. How did you learn giving needles without actual people to stick them into?" (Would that Drake loop never end?)

She sipped her drink. "Josh? That's your name, right? Sorry, but that is *so* old school."

She brushed curls from her forehead, touched her eye by accident. Blinked at the ceiling, flashed a parting smile, and rejoined her bubble.

He chased his drink with a double vodka soda and a few beers. Felt like he'd fallen into a goldfish bowl, doomed for the rest of his life to swim around in circles.

He was heading up from the shore when the seller phoned. "Meet you in ten? Eight grand, firm, and she's yours. I'll throw in the tender." Twenty minutes later Blair roared up in a pickup truck, left it running outside the condos.

He was a string bean of a guy—late forties, smelled like weed, hadn't shaved in a while. On the beach he lit a smoke and waved it at a rowboat half-hidden in some bushes.

"There you go, man, all you need."

Faint notes of gasoline and sewage rode the incoming fog. The two of them dragged the boat out and Josh climbed in. He fitted the oars into the oarlocks, hauled back on them, felt the keel's wallow nudging deeper water. A street light's gleam buffed the surface. He dodged a Laser, thought of the hydrofoil he'd ridden across the Tyrrhenian Sea. A volcanic island, glittering black sand, sea spray. Man, he'd been pumped to walk Lampedusa's fine white sands, forget what his hook-up had said about refugees held there.

The tide helped his progress. Soon the floating box was right there, white trim around the door and windows a cheery note in the grey. Manoeuvring alongside, he tossed the rope, lassoed a capstan. The houseboat listed and heaved as he climbed aboard and he swallowed a shiver. The Arm was beautiful, but you didn't want to fall in, even if the sewage it carried was treated.

The door was unlocked, the room inside tall enough to stand up in, just. It wasn't light enough to see much more than shapes—but there were matches and a candle that he lit. A bed took up the full back wall. In daylight the view from it would be incredible. A corner cupboard had a sink fitted into it; a medicine cabinet hung over it. In the opposite corner was a large white bucket, like for making beer. In the middle of the room a patio table and two plastic-webbed folding chairs were arranged. In the candlelight a skinny poster featured pasta shapes—no, knots. Sailors' knots that mimicked the grain of naked plywood.

So much naked plywood, but easily brightened up with paint.

Naturally it smelled damp. But the only sticking point was the bucket, which hummed faintly of piss. He peered out at the fog. Shit—but, eight grand?! Throw in another two or three for solar panels, composting toilet, rain barrel, and he'd be laughing. He pictured himself sunbathing on the roof, reading books he'd meant to read since university. Sharla the nurse lying beside him on a towel, sipping Aperol. Okay, so this was a stretch, but he could fantasize, couldn't he? It didn't hurt to imagine.

The fog lifted as he rowed ashore. Everything gleamed a pale pearly blue, a just-waking-up blue. Only, a memory of seeing migrants camped out in Palermo decided just then to surface and take momentary hold. Dark-skinned people lying on scorched grass, huddling in dusty olive groves along the road to Mondello Beach. A scary sight but preparation, he had decided, for Lampedusa's grim side—a way of getting his feet wet, so to speak. Though home to Italy's finest beaches, it was also where refugees rescued from sinking death ships were herded into camps.

The houseboat wasn't *exactly* what he wanted. What he wanted was a villa on the Amalfi coast, less remote than Sicily. In the meantime, the Arm fit the bill, and just like the fog, any wisps of disappointment dissipated.

Blair was waiting. He held out a joint. Josh did the e-transfer on the spot.

"Enjoy, man." No receipt but a fist bump before the guy roared off in his pickup.

A few days later, Josh was all moved in, taking selfies from the roof, the Arm's blue glitter and woodsy shore behind him. He posted them on all his socials, hoped his Sicilian friend might see and like them.

He was enjoying a beer on the roof when a string of emails pinged. His mom inviting him to dinner. PoolsRMe promising that by autumn the supply chain should be restored. A customer wondering where his order was.

Check back in September, he fired off.

It was a gorgeous afternoon, too gorgeous to be interrupted. The Arm was jammed with traffic—sailboats, Jet Skis, motorboats, kayaks, canoes—some might say an accident waiting to happen. Just a few metres off his port-facing deck kids were taking sailing lessons. Their little Flying Juniors spun around in circles, tipped. He watched their skippers frantically bailing, jumping ship.

At least the kid sailors barely made waves. A group of kayakers glided past. He raised his beer in a becalmed salute. Minutes later, though, the wake from a huge motor launch rocked the place so violently the bottle almost shot from his grasp. Queasiness tightened his throat. The truth was, he had never really been that much of a sailor.

But, after being so adrift he felt he was where he should be, where he belonged, on the right track. The eight grand had taken a bite out of his savings. But, on the bright side, now that he had a home—a party shack, the old man called it—he'd quit blowing money downtown.

That evening he lit the hibachi, grilled a steak, had just cut into it when Facebook pinged. The first name was familiar if the last one wasn't. Sharla Williams—Williams? Then his memory of her face rushed back, her eyes, her skin, her mask the colours of Neapolitan ice cream. (He'd have killed for some Häagen-Dazs, killed.)

Hey, bet u don't remember me, the message said. *Just wondering if you wanna hook-up. For coffee.*

Hey. Swallowing, he messaged back. Held his breath, typed: *Did u mean, like, tonite?*

The miracle of FB! He could not believe his luck, sent directions. He left his steak on the roof and, still adjusting to his proximity to land, was waiting ashore twenty minutes early. After what felt like an age she came strolling toward him. Sharla. Stunning in a turquoise dress and sneakers, an orange backpack over her shoulder. As she approached she slipped on a mask printed with sunflowers. He helped her into the boat. Her eyes danced with the dark gold sun bouncing off the water. Rowing, he felt tongue-tied.

After a little while she stuffed her mask in her backpack. "Wow, you really live out here?"

"You got it."

"You know they had quarantine ships out here, right? A couple hundred years ago? Typhoid, smallpox, diphtheria, yellow fever, bugs they didn't want entering the city. Floating coffins, really. Full of refugees, immigrants, prisoners." She pointed to the far shore, to the yacht club for hard-core sailors nestled in a tiny cove at the foot of the hills. "There was this prison there—see? People who made it to shore were kept there, also Mi'kmaw folks."

Of course he knew about the prison. You couldn't grow up here without knowing about it. The building was still there; the club used it for storage—not that he had been inside or seen it first-hand.

The setting sun warmed his face, his ears. "You like history? I got a BA in history. So, there, we've got this common interest."

"Learned about it in public health unit."

"Well. Glad that shit was then and not now." His laugh wasn't meant to be ironic.

"And from my fam. Our ancestors—like, the Williamses have this book, right? My grandma got it handed down to her. It's crazy. Has all the birth dates and death dates of everybody written down, you know, after they came up from the States. Two hundred years ago."

Local history. The War of 1812 and afterwards. He knew about this too, sort of—anyway, it rang a bell from class. "Slaves fleeing America. For something better."

"Folks fleeing enslavement." Her eyes fixed on him. "Like they escaped that shit, coming here."

He cast the rope, knotted it like an old salt. This wasn't exactly his idea of first-date conversation, at least not so early on. But she was amazing. Drop-dead amazing. He wasn't sure what to say besides "Yeah." He steadied the boat for her to climb out. Shit, he thought. There'd been no time to stock the cooler. Forget the steak on the roof. What if she expected dinner, a nice dinner, special snacks? He did a mental inventory. Coffee, the end of a loaf of artisanal bread, the crumbs at the bottom of a bag of Doritos. Salad-in-a-bag past its best-before date, two or three beers. A couple of eggs, bacon—supplies for breakfast, that was good. If all went well.

The houseboat bobbed and shimmied under his feet. She was already halfway up the ladder.

"Hey. Just one thing. Ballast?"

She didn't seem to hear. Ignoring himself, he followed close at her heels. Focused on the thin gold chain around one lovely ankle. Once they both made it to the roof, the rocking eased. A bit. There was no sign of his steak. A marauding seagull's supper?

"Depressing, isn't it, the thought of quarantine ships. Disgusting." She couldn't seem to give it up. "Imagine folks stuck on board, bodies being thrown over. Not just the dead, I'll bet. No vax in those days."

"Like now." (She's a nurse, he reminded himself. This talk must just be her thing.) "Well, until now. You know what I mean—"

She raised an eyebrow, eyed his shirt's team logo: *SSC Napoli, Società Sportiva Calcio Napoli*. Smiled. "That some kind of cult?"

He laughed, waved it off. Heard himself babble, "For sure, shit happened. It happens, it's happening." He imagined her giving a needle. "The great thing about living out here? You can forget COVID exists."

The sun hovered at the Arm's mouth, cast its gleam the length of the long, fairly straight channel.

"Nice view. You must go through some pile of sunblock."

He turned to the hibachi, poked at dead coals. Wished there was something to grill. She stood too close to the edge, peering at the far shore. "Check out the little Versailles over there," he said to break the silence. "Someone's idea of glam. Hey. You might, um, want to step back a bit. Beer? Give me two secs and I'll find a glass."

His fast descent set them swaying.

"Is this thing actually safe?" Her voice filtered down, a mermaid singsong above the sloshing. "I'm no Olympic swimmer. Are you?"

"No worries," he hollered back. Rummaging. The cooler was awash in greasy water. He mopped off two beers in cans as best he could and while he was at it, smoothed the sleeping bag over the bed, kicked a stray pair of Jockeys underneath it. He dribbled water from the clumsy refillable bottle over dishes in the sink, pulled out two glasses, dried them. Double-checked the bucket, which he'd emptied after the kid sailors finished lessons.

Her shape in the doorway startled him. Wearing her mask again, somehow she had descended without causing a ripple. His eyes adjusted to the purply light around her in time to catch hers as she peered around. A nurse was guaranteed to obsess about hygiene. With any luck his quick rinse of the bucket had killed any smell.

"Nice digs." She eyed the beer he held out. "Thanks but no thanks. Not my thing. Plus I'm feeling a little..." She fluttered her hand, fanning away queasiness?

"You okay? You want me to take you back?"

"Uh-uh."

On the roof once more, she sat swinging her legs over the edge, studied the wooded drumlin that sheltered the yacht club's marina. He considered sitting beside her, knew it wasn't wise. Ballast. Assuming the same position on the opposite edge, his back to her, would have been weird. So he compromised, sitting there cross-legged, his back to the condos. Watching her, or pretending not to, as he sipped his beer. Finally, she turned to him.

"You know about the graves over there? On Deadmans Island? There's supposed to be, like, hundreds of bodies buried there. Folks from the ships, from the prison." She gazed at the dark outline of a massive house nested in trees. "Does nobody live there? Bodies practically in their backyard." She watched him inch toward the middle. He wished she would do the same, help combine their weight.

She glanced away. "Imagine, fleeing slavery to end up in the ground."

He wished his beer had a label he could pick off.

"Some of your people, I mean, your ancestors might be buried there, you think?"

"Um, like, probably."

"Have you been over there? To check it out?"

"Why? Nothing anybody can do is gonna raise them."

The sun was setting fast. A final burst of orange lit the treetops, then faded.

"Well, I just thought—"

"Won't bring no one back, will it?" There was a loud pause measured by lapping.

"Where do you really live, dude?" Another pause, more lapping. "Great view you've got. But I prefer dry land."

"Some do." His disappointment had been simmering. Now it began a sad, hard boil. "It's the freedom I like. Calling my own shots."

"Oh yeah, I get that." She pulled a sweater out of her backpack, stood up. He stood up too. In spite of the way things had gone he wanted to step close enough to slide an arm around her. She was taller than he'd thought. Their lips would have lined up perfectly—the vicinity of her lips under her mask. "Guess you people don't have cabs out here. Tomorrow's an early shift, you'd best take me back."

Let down, he felt his mouth slacken. Dug for his mask, remembered it was by the bed. "Sure thing. No worries." When was the last time he'd auditioned for something, anything, and flunked it?

Getting into the boat, she thanked him for "the house tour." A fingernail moon guided them to shore, where she pulled on her backpack and headed off without glancing back.

He was home and in bed, alone, by ten o'clock.

To think that in university, friends had razzed him for being born with horseshoes up his ass! The same friends who now had high-power jobs in Toronto.

But, maybe there was something to it—the thing about horseshoes.

A week or two later, someone else he'd met downtown texted. She had split up with her husband. They'd casually exchanged numbers. Now she wanted to have drinks—at his place, she agreed, enticed.

Jaime was short and round and wore her long reddish hair with a floral headband that matched her mask. Meeting her ashore, he whipped his off (recently retrieved from a garbage bag of laundry) as she stood, masked and on tiptoe, to air kiss both his cheeks. A faux pas on his part already? But during the row, they were like old friends catching up. She talked about taking gondolas in Venice. Skiing in the French Alps. Dodging tourists in the Alhambra.

"You sail, Jaime?" Much as he welcomed a yes, he secretly hoped not.

The sun made her squint, gave what he could see of her face a glowing warmth, though the onshore breeze was chilly. "No. But I've always loved the water. And you?"

"No place I'd rather be."

This time the cooler was well stocked, but it was too windy to sit up above. He set the chilled Prosecco and two clean glasses on the white plastic table, pulled out the webbed chairs. But the bed was more comfy, and a few sips in he could not believe his luck. Their masks askew, she was all over him—just like that.

"I guess technically we should be wearing them."

"You don't mind. If we. Keep them on."

They stayed masked the whole time. It made it a bit hard to breathe, but what the hell. The sun was like an orange highlighter decorating their bodies. Its flare seemed to last and last. He barely felt the tide turn. Afterwards, as they lay sprawled on top of the sleeping bag, the sun washed their nakedness hot pink.

"Maybe I should buy blinds."

"Why? Who's gonna see in?" She grabbed his Ray-Bans, tried them on. Between these and the mask her face was practically swallowed up. "Believe it or not"—a muffled laugh—"I've never done it at sea before." The sun's last traces of rose were so strong he squinted, kissing her boobs.

Way too soon darkness fell, and she groped for her clothes. The only light came from the condos, their huge waterside windows. Reflections skittered over the surface.

"Stay over? It's pretty sweet getting rocked to sleep."

"No offence, but I'm not good without, um, a flush."

He got it. Still, he couldn't help feeling offended and needing, somehow, to deflect it. "You're chicken of the sea, is that the problem? Creeped out by what's down *there*. God only knows what might be on the bottom." He walked his fingers down her leg, gave her foot a playful tug. At the same time something tugged at the back of his mind. Hard to put a finger on what, exactly. Regret that things with Sharla hadn't worked out?

"So, you'll be my gondolier?"

"No problem. Unless you're scared of the gondola sinking."

The next two nights, Jaime texted, he picked her up, and things unfolded exactly the same way. The sunsets made the sex pure gold. Afterwards, he lit candles, made the room bright enough they could have read to each other naked, if that had been a thing.

"Maybe curtains *would* be good. It's hard to sleep in when the sun comes up."

"Whatever." Crawling under the sleeping bag, she drew its zippered edge up to her chin. "You think some giant squid is going to peek in?" Her laughter was a snuffling sound. Three dates, and they still hadn't lost the masks.

"Don't you find it strange that we haven't actually mouth-to-mouth kissed?"

Before she could answer, a text pinged.

His mother. *Need to talk.*

If I can bring a guest, he typed.

Not a good idea.

Already Jaime had started to dress. He turned off his phone, jumped up and put his arms around her. The sudden move sent them rocking. He lurched to undo a button.

She seized his hand, held it. "How is this thing even anchored?" In the dimness her eyes actually looked scared, as if the mooring might let go, and next they would find themselves out at sea. Drifting.

He shared the cab with her as far as his parents' place. Before sliding out, he took his time kissing her good night. Luckily, she didn't ask to come in and meet them.

They were waiting for him, seated at the granite-topped island. His dad was staring at golf scores on his iPad. His mom looked unhinged.

"I'll let you tell him, shall I, Gerald?" Her voice was a cudgel.

His father lowered his device but not his shoulders, kept them hunched. "You remember the Creightons—they're in those condos? The ones your mother and I wanted to look into."

His mother started to cry. "Seems they don't need TV, for all the free entertainment. Out on the water, I mean."

"Your love nest." His father let out an agitated breath, fixed weary eyes on him. (So the party shack had morphed into…?) "Could you just for one second show respect? For other people, since you have none for yourself. This might shock you. But not everyone feels like watching a live sex show every night. You and your—" His dad shot an appealing look toward his mom. "Imagine *that* view from your two-point-eight million-dollar living room. There are laws against indecency. Nancy Creighton thought we should know. You're lucky no one's called the police."

What could he say? How was he supposed to respond?

No words. He had no words. He shoved back his upholstered stool and stalked out.

The next day, he was on the roof answering emails, when the Arm patrol roared up. The guy in uniform didn't look old enough to operate something with an engine. "This is a warning. You might want to clean up your act, bud." If not for his smirk, the cop could have meant dumping waste. He waved his arm, gesturing at the far shore. "Tie up over there, give yourselves some privacy. Guess it's too late to tell you to get a room." The bastard's laughter overshot the outboard's burbling.

Indignation burned from Josh's cheeks straight down into his gut. As the boat roared off, part of him, a big part of him, wanted to shock the Creightons so badly they'd curl up on their living-room floor and maybe not get up again. He trained his gaze on the wake's weakening swells, their calming motion. The farther shore, much of it parkland, *would* be more secluded. He could do without the kid sailors and their shrieking. He remembered what the nurse had said about disease-ridden ships anchoring there—many years ago, though. He pushed the thought away and googled marine towing. In all the excitement he forgot to notice that Jaime hadn't texted.

By the next weekend he was relocated, lounging happily in the woods' shadow. The only downside was the lengthened row to the civilized shore. He texted Jaime, got no response. Had her phone died, or what? He read Dostoevsky on the roof, then at dusk warmed up soup on his new Coleman stove. He slurped it down, watching the moon rise and spill its light over the water.

The end of August was creeping up fast. Already the houseboat had been home for six weeks. The evenings had grown suddenly shorter; it was only nine o'clock but felt later. He Messengered Jaime. Hopeless.

A dank chill seeped through the floor, and he crawled inside the sleeping bag to read.

His sleep that night was dreamless. He woke to a dense fog, the distant drone of ships' horns in the harbour the only reminder that the world—the world beyond his deck—existed. He stood over the bucket, emptied it over the side. Ate cereal from the box, googled composting toilets, tried Jaime again.

With any luck the weather would hold for another month or so, then he would need to find a place for fall with its neap tides and the coming of winter. He was trying not to think about it when his mother texted. For once her message didn't ask what he planned to do with his life. Instead, she gushed, *U'll have a front-row seat for Venetian Night!!* It was the first he had heard from her since The Confrontation.

Amused, cheered, he went online and made a sale, the first in months, an order for a small above-ground. On a high, he texted Jaime.

This time she answered almost instantly. *Back with hubby.* It was punctuated with an emoji rose, a smiley face, a blue heart.

Wearing jeans for the first time all summer, he was up above, eating Doritos as, one by one, boats moored near and far weighed anchor and headed to sea. They disappeared into the dusk, then, as sharply as Jaime's truth had kicked his ass, a blaze of lights appeared. A procession of boats had formed, was moving closer. Hulls and spars twinkled with holiday lights, reflections sparkled on a surface black as volcanic glass. Venetian Night! It came back to him, the event that happened each year before Labour Day. When he was small, his dad had taken him and his mom to watch the spectacle from a client's terraced lawn.

An infill, the property offered the best view. Perched on an Adirondack chair, he'd gobbled Bits & Bites, watching fireworks streak the night. Red, green, blue, and gold starbursts had lit up the yachts gliding by, the sound of their engines drowned out by loud booms and the squealing "oohs" and "aahhs" of party voices. Ghost ships. The boats had been ghost ships, the scene ten times more magical than the Disney castle under shooting stars.

Making its way up the Arm now, the formation swelled into a feverish display of light as it approached. He pictured the Creightons glued to their view. The burble and thrum of outboards and laughter echoed closer, and the ear-cracking blasts before cartwheels and starbursts flared and fell in streams of glitter.

He chased one beer with another, watching until the parade broke up. A few boats passed him, heading to the yacht club. Others anchored farther up along the more populous shore. A few metres from his door, three cabin cruisers dropped anchor and tied up together. The partiers aboard leapt back and forth from one deck to another, drinks in hand. He waved. A couple of people waved back but no one invited him over—because of social distancing?

As he went inside and tried to sleep, he could not help feeling excluded.

The partying continued deep into the night.

Impossible to say what time the sound woke him—it was dark, the sloshing was louder than usual. Closer to his ear. A rhythmic lapping very near the bed. A hollow, thumping sound. He opened his eyes to see both chairs flipped over, floating. The door was open and the sea was ghosting in. Flood tide. Wavelets spilled and broke over the floor. The thumping was the cooler knocking against the wall.

He was dreaming, he had to be. But, reaching out, his fingers closed around his phone. Real enough.

His toothbrush drifted past the bobbing bucket. An empty chip bag floated alongside. This desperate, crazy urge to take a leak seized him. His phone was at one percent—his solar-powered charger buried somewhere—but, standing up, water swirling now to his knees, he punched in 9-1-1. Just as the call connected, a thigh-high wave slammed the table into him. The phone shot from his grip and sank.

He was lucky to make it out the door. But his feet skidded, then lost contact with the deck. A chunk of it broke off and slid away. Sinking, it took the rowboat with it.

He managed to hit the water swimming. Its iciness stole his breath; its swirl froze in his ears. He swam fast, muscles taking over where his brain flagged. He treaded water as the whole thing flipped—the houseboat, his home, a sucking, glugging box—then disappeared.

The party boats were too far away to swim to. Bobbing, choking, he yelled for help. But everyone aboard must have been passed out.

In the blackness he felt an iron weight close around each ankle, the Arm dragging on his pant legs. As he moved in a thrashing crawl toward shore, he half-visualized a rope, a vine, a tree root—something, anything, being thrown by a rescuer, something to cling to.

But there was no rope, no vine, no root, and no one, only the solid darkness of the rocks and sloping trees ahead. He kicked, imagined shackles of iron cutting into his flesh, tried as he swam to fight off the feeling. He pictured a clanking chain settling in the muck far, far below. Fingers closing around its length, hauling downwards—a gangrenous hand attached to a gangrenous arm buoyed by salt water.

You've got three minutes to make it to shore, bud. Three minutes: a watery cooking-show voice sloshed in his head. The sound of the tide starting to ebb? *Can you die of hypothermia in late August?* the voice teased as his knees suddenly tagged bottom, hands grasped at seaweed, the slime of wet, rusty ironstone.

He hauled himself out and up over the rocks onto the dirt at the cliff's base.

He could feel and yet not feel its crumbling tree roots and stones and the razor-sharp edges of shells bashed by gulls. Dust in his nostrils, muck under his nails, a sour stink like leaf mould, rot, was everywhere. Crawling upward, clinging to nothing, he scaled the steepness. Twisted around just once to glimpse the water below.

Its oily, opaque black gleamed like a freshly paved parking lot. Not so much as the glint of a beer can hinted at where his home had been.

Everything he owned in the world, save some books and other stuff stored at his parents' house, was company for sea urchins, crabs, starfish.

Gone.

Reaching the top, he forced his way through pitch-black brambles. Dry, snapping bushes, branches. In places the earth under his bare soles was spongey-soft, carpeted here by moss, there by pine needles. Lulled, comforted, he tripped and stumbled, landed in a pit of mouldering leaves and dirt—dirt laced with jagged bits of glass. He clawed at the pit's edges to climb free. Leaf mould as papery-dry as rotted cloth disintegrated in his fingers. The rags worn by long-lost people?

His fingers grazed feathers. A putridness rose up. The rotted remains of a crow. Stones sharp as flint were bone, bone that hadn't become dust. Broken bottles glinted in the striped moonlight. The shards were eyes, defiant but dulled with suffering. The suffering of every injustice, every unfairness he was able to imagine, suffering through the ages.

The wind rose off the Arm, became the soft, low sound of singing, a whole raft of people singing. Had salt water short-circuited certain brain cells, replaced good sense with an echoing dream? Voices singing for survival, mercy.

Go toward the light, one of them called. A voice like his mother's?

No, like Sharla's, the nurse's. *What don't you get, Josh? You going to smarten up your ass any time soon?*

Blood warmed his palms and feet. Its stickiness had a piercing sting. His lungs shivered with it. His pulse thumped with it, thumped louder than any numbness.

The sting of being alive.

Between the pines' boughs, from a dip in the hill a sharp white light trembled, probably from someone's starter castle. A motion-detector light above a four- or five-car garage? Pushing his way through foliage, he stumbled toward its aching brightness. Instead of Sharla he thought, only for a second, of Jaime: of his wound, however fleeting, the feeling of being used.

He thought too of sea roads and their travellers.

The history of the world was the history of users—users

and the used, it struck him, grotesque as it was. Traders, traffickers, and the abused: Sharla's ancestors and those people fleeing God knows what, who were lucky if they made it to Lampedusa.

The history of the world. Fuck.

But, with any luck, he thought, somebody would be there, where the light was.

This Talk of Trees

Wild speech is...a language furred with moss, netted with lichen.

—Anne Simpson,
"A Hundred and Fifty Psalms at Twilight"

WE WERE JUST STANDING THERE, YOU KNOW, DOING what we do. Taking a breather after a quietly busy day, a regular day. Reaching upward. Breathing in, breathing out. Growing, taking things as they come. Hoping to catch a few winks. Sitting ducks, maybe that's what we were?

But how could we have known what would happen, after a day like all the rest? Starting with mist at dawn, dew lifting from lawns and flowerbeds. The silk of a salt summer breeze winding through us. None of us talking, holding the silence that people, some people, listen for. The odd bird tap-tap-tapping for a snack. The traffic's rumble setting in. Kids running about, playing hide-and-seek behind our trunks as the sun arced and slowly sank. Folks resting on benches under our shade, a few reading books and old-fashioned newspapers (the sort that cost our kind dearly).

The point of this recap? Just to emphasize: it was a normal day chased by a normal peak-of-summer evening, then dusk. The gates safeguarding us were locked. No security cameras, but in the velvety darkness we were safe. So we believed.

A normal night, until it wasn't.

How things change in a brutal instant, eh?

Guys, you have no idea.

Melissa sat with her notebook lying idle in her lap; I shuddered to think of the garbage she'd no doubt been scribbling before snapping it shut. Next she'd be writing "poetry"—spare me, dear listener. It was after work; in our garden behind the house, we were supposed to be relaxing. Lounging in her Adirondack chair, the one I'd painted purple just for her, she was fixated on the hummers dive-bombing the bee balm. She had this strange, set look on her face—no care for me, whose plantings attracted them. It was disheartening, if I may be frank? The way Mel loved nature more than people, definitely more than she loved me, for fuck's sake. Distressing, the way someone's love of nature can turn on someone else—her attention to it the very thing that made me fall for her in the first place.

If I had seen it coming, trust me, I might have walked the other way when she first introduced herself, before she sank her hooks in. But that, my friend, is another story—or is it?

For nature lovers everything is connected. Like Mel was connected watching those shimmery emerald, ruby-throated birds buzz up and down, tiny B-52s darting in and out of ragged red blooms. Her gaze ping-ponging. Tea going cold on an armrest, the tea I had dutifully steeped and brought outside, and her sandwich, cucumber and plant-based cream cheese, her favourite, mouldering in the sun.

Thrrripp, thrrripp, thrrripp went the birds, wings beating a thousand miles a minute. When one dive-bombed her and I yelped, "Babe! Watch out!" she gave no response. No gratitude, just the silent treatment. The equivalent of shouting, "You don't deserve the pleasure of my company. You are lamer than I imagined if you think you do."

I felt the burn of tears—not, I must admit, very manly. That's when I rose from my knee pad, quit weeding the dahlias, and went inside. Through the kitchen window I watched her get up and wander to the trees at the edge of the backyard. She touched each trunk like it was a child—the children we didn't have—these trees I had planted so long ago that all but the *Sorbus decora* were tall, thick, and straight, perfectly spaced for privacy. No thanks to Mel. Who of course has her own version. The truth being a slippery thing, wouldn't you agree?

Whatever my partner may think, in my heart it's words that keep me going—my love of words—though people, some people, question how I apply them. Early on, before he started calling journalists *news weasels*, my mister once asked, "Why not be a reporter?" The fact of the matter is I'm shy, uncomfortable with phoning strangers, asking difficult questions. Since the mass murders that happened two years ago, I have pretty much stopped watching the news.

Who wants to pollinate grief?

I'm happy enough doing Sales and Advertising at the paper—not that I have found my niche, as they say. But more than once I've won Sales of the Month for my custom content. One spring I got a slew of garden centres and nurseries on board—a coup for me—and along with a plaque, received a gift certificate for a farm-to-table brunch. Unfortunately, it barely covered my eggs Benny, and mister complained about the grit in his eggs Florentine.

Once we're all eating Soylent, the world will be a better place, he had said, and maybe people will learn to rinse spinach properly when they offer it.

I find it hard to know sometimes when he's kidding and when he's not. But it's this air of mystery that made my guy attractive. Also, I dislike cooking and since food is his thing, I hang in.

As my friend Jenna at work says, "You know what I'd give to have a dude who cooks *and* waits on me hand and foot?" When Jenna said this, I was on deadline with an ad feature on a sanitation service and didn't flinch.

Granted, some of my partner's experiments—"bacon"-flavoured oats, coconut-based "cheese" curds, and peameal "fish"—are less successful than others. Though as long as I get to come home to a tiny bit of calm after a day of cranking out copy that doesn't rate bylines, I am, or try to be, a happy camper. Besides, not only does he make food, he knows his way around a flower bed (if not to such reliable effect in a *bed* bed). It's amazing how he performs in the yard.

As you would see on a walkabout of our yard, it's with good reason that even Melissa praises my expertise choosing species for optimal results. There's no sense having a property unless it's a sanctuary where you can embrace solitude, watch the birds and butterflies do their thing. As Mel had been doing, sure, until coddling, no, fondling the *Sorbus*, *Acer saccharum*, *Betula alleghaniensis*, and *Populus tremuloides*. In other words, giving tree-hugging a whole new meaning.

Though, possibly, I was overreacting. Hyperbolizing, she would say. But I did not appreciate the way she ran her hands over the bark like it was someone's skin, and she was seeing, feeling, it for the first GD time.

This aside, parallel to my planting strategies is a deep commitment to native species, which you will appreciate. No exotics on *this* property, thank you very much. No *ginkgo biloba*, no wych elm cultivar *Ulmus glabra*, no *Fagus sylvatica 'Pendula,'* no London *Platanus*, or any other offshore hybrids. Just look at the fiasco created by the *Acer platanoides*, Norway maples, the city has planted with such gusto on every block, like growing sea monkeys. Add water, see them grow, an instant urban forest host to disease. One gust of wind and down they come!

No, I had seen to it. No foreign cultivars in our small neck of paradise, the paradise I created without help. Yes, Mel would hold the stepladder, rest a hand on my ankle as I climbed it to do the pruning. More like she was directing—a "little more off that branch," or, "eek, not so much off there, boss"—like I hadn't a clue. The last time pruning the aspen (the procedure like microsurgery), I swear she ticked me off so badly I felt like going to the shed, getting Jarnbjorn and handing it to her: "Here, chop the thing down, then. Spare us both the debate."

You know, there are times I wonder about being half of a couple, truly. Though every life has its ups and downs, I'm sure.

They keep me hopping at the paper, the never-ending pressure to attract ad revenue. The silver lining, the true bonus? Phoning strangers, convincing them I can grow their business has turned out to be the best thing for my shyness. Dealing with folks whose bark is worse than their bite has thickened my skin. Of course, it's nowhere *near* as thick as it would be calling a mom who's lost a child to a bad drug deal, or someone scammed out of their entire life savings.

Custom content is unfailingly, predictably, comfortingly upbeat. Which is what I enjoy about it.

And I need upbeat, as things have occasionally grown less than blossomy between mister and me. Isn't it strange how you can have the most show-stopping, curb-appealing sidewalk-facing beds and borders that passersby gush over, when the light that brightens the home behind these flickers and goes out?

Not a light you can switch on or off. It's not like you can sleep with Nova Scotia Power.

If you must know, Melissa and I met at forestry school, of all places. She dropped out; I should have walked when she proved more interested in *Jeopardy!* than forest management. While I applied myself to tree farming, then, following grad work at agricultural college, branched into lab-based food production, Mel took what little we'd learned in a communications bird course and finagled a job amongst humanity's worst: those who write about things they are too undisciplined, too lazy, too ill-equipped to actually do. She turned the rest of what we covered that first semester (plants and fungi, forest animals, etc.) into a vague, baseless hobby.

This mostly meant staring into space, like she was doing now. Pretending to care when I said the bee balm would need dividing if she hoped to see those hummingbirds return year after year. The stuff dies out faster than stink if you don't transplant it to different spots, keep it from depleting the soil of its favourite nutrients.

That stare of hers, so maddening! And it wasn't simply over garden matters, or only just now, but as if I'd done something horrible every time I asked her to wipe up after herself when she spilled a drink and her glass left a ring on the furniture.

The problem, good listener, our problem, I have come to realize, was that Melissa simply didn't give a crap. Not about yours truly, certainly. Only the trees and those birds she waited all year for until they returned each May. And with the news about monarch butterflies being endangered, she was showing signs of going OC over them as well. Her eyes following their mad flitting around the swamp milkweed I had planted.

"Some help would be appreciated," I'd said one fall, raking leaves. She had turned around and marched inside, and when I followed, there she was on the sofa watching TV. It was November, and she had the fireplace channel on. Kind of redundant, as the screen was right above our fireplace, and with the chill in the air I'd have gladly put on a real fire. Gone out to the carport with its hardwood that Jarnbjorn and I had carefully split and I'd stacked, junk by junk, and dried for this purpose.

When I suggested it, though, she got up and went into the bedroom and did her nails. "You're the one who wanted this place, with all its maintenance," she said. "Its endless yardwork. Fill your boots," she had the actual gall to mock me.

But, in all relationships, between life partners and work partners, friends and colleagues, a person picks his battles, am I right? The same goes for my relationship with trees, broad- and needle-leaf species alike. Defending native ones from foreign invaders.

Even if the light had gone out of our home, I believed mister would never hurt me. So I did what a person does, channelled my energy into my job, into earning bonuses.

Definitely, a child or two would have made a difference. But you can't have a show-stopping property and children. My partner would have had a conniption fit at the moulded plastic and trampolines that fill some people's yards. And I'm not kidding. I'm not sure I could have handled it.

Besides, he loves me, there's that. Of course he loves me.

Where would I be without knowing this?

So I've tried, for the longest time, to cultivate, maintain, an interest in things that interest him. And there *are* the trees. I've taken pleasure in memorizing the names of their parts, deciduous trees and conifers alike. Observing their growth, year by year, I pictured what was happening like time-lapsed segments on *The Nature of Things*. The bark cracking as the cambium under it expanded. The xylem and phloem, tiny pipes carrying the sap—water and minerals—from the tiniest root hairs, *up up up* into each leaf and bud. The trees taking in carbon dioxide. Chloroplasts converting sunlight, water, and nutrients into growth and greenness, or something like that. The trees exhaling, gifting us with oxygen.

Intoxicating when you pictured it. Miraculous.

Somewhat more miraculous than the conversion of palm oil into mister's version of cream cheese. His passion for synthetic flavourings.

It was late afternoon, a Sunday, much too hot to spend any longer in the kitchen than necessary, especially after weeding and fertilizing all day. So I prepared a cold supper of sandwiches and iced tea for us, took them outside and consumed mine hungrily before going in to tidy up. When at last Mel came inside, she tipped her sandwich, completely untouched, into the compost, and, honestly, something in me snapped. You could say it was like a gale-force gust meeting a cable tethering a tender sapling to a stake.

"I'm going out," she announced, and hurried outdoors. I watched her get into the Mazda. What can I say, I was maddened by this point—wouldn't you be?—and I followed her in the Tesla. I made sure to keep a city block between us, almost lost her in traffic on Quinpool and again on Summer. But then I spotted her parking outside the Public Gardens. The north side of the park, on the south side of Sackville Street. I was able to score a spot five or six cars behind, pure luck when someone in an SUV pulled away—a gift. You know what parking is like downtown.

I was in a sweat and admit I must have looked like a nobody from the 'burbs in my grass-stained khakis. Halifax has gotten rather snooty of late with its new development, businessmen from somewhere else descending to make it a glass-and-concrete copy of Toronto. When Melissa and I first met, the city was all historic wooden houses and everyone wore grubby jeans. Invaders, come-from-away invaders, a foreign species—that is what these developers are—and you can see what they have done. Made the city into a place its sons no longer recognize.

But I am straying from the point, perhaps. You might think so.

I followed Mel and, sure enough, spotted her entering the gate across from what my entire life had been the CBC building (an infestation if ever there was), but was now a condo development with a sushi bar downstairs (those reporter types having scuttled off elsewhere). I slipped through the gate, already knowing exactly where she was headed, to one of the benches under the depressing sprawl of the two-hundred-year-old *Fagus sylvatica 'Pendula'*—the

European weeping beech that was, God knows why, her favourite.

I've lost count of how many times we had sat there, making up after a spat. Eating ice cream, holding hands. She would laugh at how incongruous it was, the "peace" beneath this enormous, drooping, tent-like cultivar planted beside a fountain featuring a soldier from the Boer War, the statue aiming his antique rifle. The dense, deep cool of the *Fagus*'s shade was barely broken by the water's sunny gurgle. Mel would lean her head on my shoulder and ask questions. Ridiculous questions. How and why the hybrid had originated, and wasn't it a good thing the "built" environment featured such cultivars, and couldn't we get one for our yard?

"Not enough space," was my reply. The easy way of saying no. The thing would have crowded out everything else, the hardiest grasses unable to survive beneath it. I didn't mention its reproduction, done through grafting—let's not even go there. Its origins only slightly less dodgy than those of the twin Camperdown elms just across the path, if I may say so. The Camperdown a Scottish aberration of grafting and not-so-natural selection, crossing a perfectly normal elm with a mutant to create a hybrid whose branches grew downward not upward—like some biblical outcast doomed to creep low to the ground and eat dust all its days, and could, guess what, only be reproduced by further grafting.

The *Fagus sylvatica 'Pendula'* was no better. Oblivious, Mel had licked her ice cream and gazed up into its fat, serpentine branches, its foliage that curled as if blighted. "You can be so touchy," she had said. "If you weren't so good in the kitchen I would...I would..." Then she'd grabbed my cone and bitten the end so ice cream drizzled out, drawn her wrist over her mouth to catch the dribble. Dairy-free blueberry cheesecake vanilla.

Now, as I crept nonchalantly toward her, some jackass loitering on a bench was practising notes on a saxophone, a mournful bleating that did nothing to enhance my mood. Keeping to the curving path between two gloriously monochromatic perennial beds, I spied her seated on our bench under that sprawling, monstrous tree. Its canopy was too dense to allow the tiniest birds to flit through it, let alone admit sunlight. Mel was on her phone, probably texting work—some pushy colleague—or, it struck me like a thunderclap, scrolling through Tinder or one of those other sites. These days there was a site for every perversion and predilection. Why not Hook-ups for Birders? For Tree-Huggers? For Custom Content Creators? I'm sure those existed too.

When I saw her smile, something sliced through me. A feeling like hot metal severing things inside, looping tissue cut asunder, cut adrift.

I knew then I was being made a fool of, you will understand. And I had no recourse but to do the very least that my abilities warranted.

I don't think I can do this anymore, I texted.

Jenna responded pretty much instantly with a string of teary emojis.

I aimed my phone up at the heavy-laden branches overhead, took a picture, sent it to her. It was meant to depict my feelings.

My friend texted back. *Stop with the trees! Maybe change focus? How 'bout going for the birds & the bees?* LOL.

Overrated, I typed, then added the emoji for laughing hysterically. Of course I hadn't always felt this way about sex. My partner used to be quite the maniac—in a good way—when we were younger and our relationship was long-distance.

I don't really know what happened between us. Maybe it's the chemicals in the food he creates, using us both as guinea pigs. Or this powerful urge of his to lead, to have our property—at least at the front, never mind the back with its privacy—be a sign to all that he isn't just keeping up with the Joneses, he's outdoing them. Perhaps we can chalk up the brand-new Tesla to this? Although until lately I hadn't pegged him as someone overly concerned with what others think.

O-kay (?!) Jenna texted after a minute or two. *So. You're not thinking about leaving?*

The way she put it set my mind leaping straight to lawyers and that very scary scenario. I'd once done a full-page ad feature on a firm specializing in divorce.

"Why don't you write something we could both be half proud of?" mister had actually said, then caught himself. "Oh right," he'd sneered, "something a journo would write: 'he said,' 'she said,' 'it was reported.' *That* crowd. Worse than lawyers digging into other people's business, so self-righteous, like the sun shines out their asses. Like they're so perfect. No, stay where you are, babe. The news would eat you for breakfast. Though I don't know how you can stand working in the same building."

It took the rest of that night and the next day and evening to get up the nerve, you should know—it is rather discombobulating, after all, to turn one's hand to such purpose. I waited until Mel was sprawled across her side of the bed, asleep, the rest of the city asleep too, barring the odd drunk staggering home after the bars closed. The dead zone at 4:00 A.M. on a Monday, when even in the new glam-jam Halifax the streets are mostly deserted.

I loaded the Tesla's trunk with the little stepladder I used for trimming shrubs, Jarnbjorn in its sheath. Yes, *yes*, the accomplice that had helped chop and split that cord of wood awaiting winter. I had a plan, you see, no research required. What lay ahead simply meant tapping into my early knowledge, the field I might have stayed with (who knows?) if I had not met Melissa, if she hadn't complicated things. The long, solo stretches I'd spent tending the backwoods and clear-cuts of New Brunswick had grown impossible when I could not stand to have her out of my sight.

I know you will think it's a little touched for someone to be jealous of a tree, jealous of someone else's admiration for it. Perhaps it will seem less touched, less crazy, if I admit that, yes, in addition to favouring native species, I enjoy taming, *trying* to tame, nature. Manipulating it to my needs. What human doesn't?

Of course, all of this had less to do with Mel's fascination with hummingbirds than it did with my disappointment. Once, can you believe it, longing to make the world more beautiful—a place that deserved a Melissa enthralled by birds and insects, forget the stupid articles she wrote—I had briefly considered a career here, in the Gardens. Though it isn't what you're thinking. I'd suffered no thwarted designs on climbing *that* ladder; my lack of experience with tropicals had kept me from applying—as if tropicals count in a Maritime garden or Halifax could ever be considered an exotic clime. Obviously, I had moved on.

The way I hope Mel and I can too, once the bee balm goes to seed and the hummingbirds leave. Cultivate the quiet, contained life that suits me and would suit her too, she would come to realize, surely. If she had any sense.

We shall see.

As I scaled the fence it was plain a taller ladder would've helped. One false move and those wrought iron pickets would have sealed it: definitely no future progeny for this guy! A disappointment for Mel, perhaps, but not so great as to be insurmountable.

Far, far worse were aberrations left unchecked.

Best practice had taught me the surest way to rid a stand of its woody pests was to let nature itself turn on them. Besides, simply chopping the bastards down would have taken an army of arborists swinging from branches like Cirque du Soleil show-offs wielding chainsaws, working days on end. Imagine the spectacle, the racket of felling so many trees, mature ones, just like that! The worst offender, Melissa's favourite, was the oldest of them all, but the others? A hundred, a hundred and fifty years old at the very least, by my seasoned estimate.

Deep inside the Gardens, the *Fagus*'s foliage gleamed dully in the faint, distant glow of street lights. Beneath it, I was instantly engulfed in tomb-like darkness, taunted by a funereal air made worse by the Camperdowns watching. (No coincidence that others of their kind taint the cemetery nearby.)

At the first *snick* of Jarnbjorn's trusty blade, my purpose gripped then held me captive. Girdling is like paring the peel from an apple's girth—I will not concede to the comparison some of you may be drawing: like cutting the skin from a person or the pelt from an animal. The bleeding hearts out there are no doubt already imagining the invader crying out, actually weeping.

The only sounds were the slow, steady *snick snick snick* as Jarnbjorn did its work, the soft, repeated thuds of bark hitting the ground.

The effort to achieve permanent results seldom unfolds so easily. One little axe, a hatchet really, going scrape, scrape, scrape, hack, hack, hack...

So easily I made sure the offender would have plenty of company as it died its sure, wearisome death.

The news staff was going ballistic when I got to work: the CBC had broken a story first. Not the kind of scenario I liked to be around, so much yelling. Then Jenna texted from her cubicle: *Are you sitting down?* She couldn't believe I hadn't heard—I'd missed it driving in, listening only to the weather, then turning the radio off.

I was apoplectic. I slipped from my office into the newsroom—the place was on fire. An editor actually slid over to let me read the comments on his screen, under the CBC story. *A desecration. An assault on our city, on our entire community. What sort of monster? What sick f*ck? To think there's someone out there who would do this!*

All of us—Jenna, me, and the news staff, who hardly ever spoke to us—could not stop asking why.

Distraught, I asked Jenna to cover for me, and left early.

At home, beside myself, I went and stood under the aspen, rock maple, golden birch, and mountain ash, and one after the other, pressed my palm to their healthy bark seeking consolation. The berries on the ash had ripened. The branches thrashed with robins and starlings.

Retreating to my chair, I collapsed there. Held up my phone and tried to photograph a hummer as it zipped close and hovered. But my hand was too shaky, and I honestly cursed, begging the bird to keep still.

"Good luck with that," my partner said, appearing with two frothy beers. He was smiling.

Then, I couldn't help it, I started crying. I put down my phone, stared at him. The hummer could have landed on my arm and I would not have noticed. I saw only him, asked, "What are you so smug about?"

He grinned, shook his head. "Smug?"

His grin gave off a sick satisfaction, mixed though it was with outrage. Everyone was outraged. The whole city, the whole country if you believe social media, and I do. I picked up my phone and scrolled, like you do when you are lost. Photos had been posted of children's letters taped to the Gardens' gates: *We ♥ trees, how could anyone hurt them?* More comments, quoted in the story the paper finally posted: *Stripping a tree of its bark in a swath around its circumference causes it to die a slow but certain death of starvation and dehydration.* The source continued, *Whoever did this knows trees, knew what they were doing.*

"The gender-neutral they," I knew he would say, rolling his eyes if I were to read it out.

Already readers had responded: *If they'd stopped with*

the weeping beech it would be criminal enough—the weeping beech that was here before the Gardens existed—but the Maidenhair, two weeping elms, the Singleseed Hawthorn, the plane that was a gift from the city of London during Victoria's reign. The list goes on…

Thirty trees in all?!

"Oh look. Someone's posting a reward," I said through tears, desperate for a bright spot, trying so hard to smile. "A reward for information. A possible motive. Five hundred dollars, no questions asked."

"As if it was ever about the money, Mel." His voice was dead calm.

My throat went dry. I swallowed, almost choked. Flashed a photo someone posted of my best friend's trunk wrapped with burlap, a barricade of park benches and police tape encircling it, a sprinkler dousing the bandaged wound. A steady, hopeful stream of water.

I swatted a wasp hovering between us, then stopped. Just stopped and looked at him. Saw him as I never had before, ever.

"It wasn't you. It wasn't, was it? Please, *please* tell me it wasn't."

I thought for a full moment poor Mel would puke, her lips so pursed she seemed to be struggling not to. Then her jaw slackened and her eyes filled with something—hate? disgust?—that was, somehow, quite a lot better than the look I had grown used to, no look at all.

And what are you going to do about it? What, Melissa? I longed to say but instead grabbed her phone, caught a hummer in mid-buzz. A GD great shot, if I do say so. "There, babe.

There you go." As she looked at it, I wrapped my hand around her wrist, gripped it. Felt her pulse under my thumb, blood moving like sap. She got to her feet. Then I reached both arms around her waist—no mean feat after all those ice creams. Her ear was warm as I breathed into it. "What, or who, will be next, Melissa? Say one word and, not to anthropomorphize, it could be you."

The only place I feel safe is around the newsroom, where I doubt people notice how I look a wreck. They're too busy chasing stories to notice, or hounding the police for updates, even though the search for a suspect keeps yielding nothing. I might be tempted to leave an anonymous tip, if I didn't have my own well-being—my survival—to consider. Which makes me grateful for the paper, the one place mister will never step foot.

It took some time to work up the nerve to visit my friend, the tree that suffered the worst. One morning before work—a drizzly day threatening a downpour, not too hot, when I figured the effects of the injuries mightn't be too pronounced—I steeled myself for a walk in the Gardens. I saved the weeping beech for last, naturally, first circling the pond at their centre, where, amazingly, most of the wounded trees still stood. People were laying hands on them, stroking their bandages, burlap wrappings like gauze to protect skin grafts. An older lady and man reached their arms around the trunk of a towering ginkgo and murmured hopeful words, a prayer. Filtered through the drizzle, from beyond the nearby dahlia beds, a saxophone trilled a lament *and* a lullaby, its player huddled under a dripping American elm. I imagined the trees listening and drinking it all in, the moisture rising up through their roots and trunks to the tips of their boughs, a healing remedy. Medicine.

It gave me courage to visit the beech.

The tree didn't look very happy but it was still there, and though its leaves had curled and yellowed, just a few had fallen. I guess only time will tell if it will make it or not.

We are all connected, a tangled web of branches, leaves, roots, especially roots—hairs, fingers, creeping under the dirt, reaching for one another. When one of us passes it's not exaggerating to say each of us dies a little at a time, losing heart. But, you know, we try our best to persevere. Winter is good practice in resilience, as is drought. Of course we've seen a lot over the years. Acts of nature and acts of man, major catastrophes: hurricanes and explosions—but, until that July night, none quite so nefarious.

Still, each day, the sun rises and we reach toward it, whether in rain, fog, fair weather or foul. We're intelligent that way. Even when attacked we know in our heartwood how to survive, or try our best to. So, we stand.

Burntcoat Head

THIS IS THE SITE OF THE WORLD'S HIGHEST RECORDED TIDES, says the plaque—something to read while I wait in line. The times are posted on a school cafeteria–style board: high tide, low tide. Other signs warn of falling trees, rocks, mud, and the mother of all dangers: *Death. Drowning.* An icon of a swimmer in distress.

I can hear Bradford laughing: People swim here? Oh my God, Jo, don't even think about it. Who'd haul you out?

The guide beams beneath her tartan visor, directs a steady stream of visitors. They troop up and down the steps—heavy concrete ones embedded in the cliff. Its curvy red sandstone reminds me of buildings Bradford and I saw in Barcelona, some special sort of art nouveau. No tides in the Mediterranean, though; none we noticed anyway.

Below, the view of the Bay of Fundy opens wide: red mud, distant blues, the opposite shore a hazy purple-green smudge. Families trudge upward, winded and muddy. Little kids whine and beg to be carried. A tourist again (after how long?), as I wait my turn to descend the lineup only grows. There's a frail-looking man behind me and just ahead, a boy buried in his phone. Orange shorts, Blundstones, skinny white hairless legs. He reminds me of a grade twelve student Bradford and I taught. His oblivion makes me sad.

Get over it, Jo. I imagine Bradford elbowing me. Kids'll be kids. And you're here, about to strike a major item off your bucket list.

I've flown in from Oshawa, not the easiest venture in a pandemic. The ad enticed me: *Experience the world's highest tides.* (No tides in Lake Ontario either, last time I checked.) *Walk, play, and then dine on the ocean floor. Come for the food,* it said, *stay for the memories.*

What took you so long to make the trip? I can just hear Bradford. My first and, if all goes accordingly, last visit to this part of the world.

"Watch it on those rocks! Enjoy!" The guide is so cheerful. Orange Shorts takes the steps at a sprint. I take my time, though I'm hardly geriatric. At the bottom, moulded concrete gives way to steps carved, apparently, by the sea. The tide reaches this high? Clinging to the metal railing, the fellow behind me ties up traffic.

The muddy plain extends as far as this eye can see. Straight across a narrow, empty channel a towering island floats on nothing. Beached, it casts its huge shadow over the seabed. A *flowerpot island*, as explained on a plaque near the park entrance: *land severed from the shore by the tides* in 1913.

They can put a date on that? Bradford's voice feels comfortingly close.

Sheer red cliffs, layered sandstone. Trees bristle from the island's crown. Late afternoon sun flickers through the branches. I imagine picnickers admiring the view from up there before the island got cut off. Country people in their Sunday best, and over the millennia as the bay was being formed, the Mi'kmaq.

Even from below, the vista steals my breath—slightly more inspiring than the one from my condo, though the far-off sound of surf could be cars on the 401. They say after losing a spouse you should wait a while before making a major move. I bought the place just months after Bradford passed. Our house, with his basement workshop and my studio, was only gathering dust. My painting was never more than a hobby; things always looked better in my head than I could make them look on canvas. You could say I simply lost interest—plus, there's no room in the condo for an easel. It isn't a home Bradford would have chosen, not after twenty-five years in our house.

In the island's deep shade I pick my way along the sea floor, slimy mud flecked with grey pebbles. My stomach growls—nothing to eat on the plane besides a packet or two of nuts. At home I'd be microwaving dinner right about now. Without Bradford, I don't think that much about food.

Believe it or not, I barely skimmed tonight's menu, posted online. Dinner's biggest draw? The time is set by the tide. If the times listed are correct the whole thing should be over by 8:00 P.M.

In the far distance red gives way to a frigid-looking

blue. The slowpoke of a man behind me is little more than a dot, recognizable by his green golf cap. "You'd make a better door than a window," I'd have said earlier to someone more hale, trying to read around him yet another plaque by the entrance—something about each tide moving the equivalent of a one hundred square kilometre chunk of seawater in or out of the bay, how many times a day? Imagining its swirling action like that of the circular saw Bradford taught kids to use in shop class.

I stop to get my bearings. Mr. Green Golf Cap is no longer in sight. *If you love something, set it free.* Bradford's goofy saying still makes me smile and roll my eyes. Imagine the waves saying this to the land. My decision to come here had everything to do with setting *something* in me free. Not that I was anxious to paint again, but the scenery in the ad struck me as a test. If the place is so beautiful, it might revive my interest? Then there's its name, Burntcoat Head, which reminds me of burnt sienna, a better descriptor for the mud, actually, than red.

And if seeing it didn't immediately start the juices flowing? Well, it would be a pretty good clue that my final decision was the right one.

Clarity. We all want clarity. Boredom, ennui—call it what you want—has a way of nudging a person toward this, don't you think?

Scoring a reservation was like winning a lottery—just one spot left when I finally got through on the phone. *Thank you, Bradford,* I'd breathed, hanging up. Of course I took my success as a sign.

As for clarity, not a cloud mars the sky overhead. Tidal pools dot the mud. They mirror bits of brilliant blue, make terra firma look holey as an old sweater. The slippery surface underfoot slants, dips, takes a dive. To think I'm scaling a gully gouged by the ocean; Bradford would be over the moon. Feathery fringes of lime-green eelgrass and algae are slick as greased steel. A walking disaster not just for someone as frail and fragile-looking as Golf Cap, but for anyone on two legs, I'm just saying.

Now wouldn't that be the cat's ass (another of Bradford's sayings): come all this way then break a hip? Take a pass on dinner after forking out a small fortune, lie here instead, and wait for the incoming tide to wash over me, wash me up, wash me out. That would be cutting to the chase, I guess—going out with a whimper, hardly a bang.

I won't say what this is costing. Happily, Bradford doesn't know.

Now, Jo, you're sure this is what you want? His voice pipes up again, closer this time. Well, it's cheaper than flying to Switzerland. And who says I'm miserable? I look around for Golf Cap, nowhere to be seen; of course I don't mean to be unsympathetic. There's relief in reaching a resolution, Bradford always said. Don't get me wrong, I am not ill. If it were possible to boil my feelings down to desperation, I might have come sooner. Much sooner.

But this walk is discombobulating. Like I'm defying gravity, walking upside down, sneakers squelching over the underside of a cloud. The tiniest imaginable hermit crabs scoot through pools, legs poking from minuscule shells—insects flitting through water instead of air?

Watch you don't tramp on the mud-piddocks, Jo. Bradford's voice is excruciatingly near: Check out these little critters lugging around their homes. Be glad you don't have to lug around that shoebox of a place you live in on your back.

My day pack's my only burden, ballast as I suck in my gut. Arms flung wide to keep myself from wiping out.

A human family scuttles past. Do I regret that Bradford and I didn't reproduce? I might not be here if we had. Bradford wouldn't have had time for coaching. Our students were all the kids we ever needed, wanted.

Again the vista sucks the wind out of me. Long grey ridges are shipwrecks? At the mudflats' furthest edge pinky-red turns purple-brown. The kid in orange shorts, the one still ahead, is barely a speck heading toward the water's changing colour. Dots I mistook for rocks are more people. Red as Mars, the terrain is a whole other planet, while the distant blue creased with whitecaps remains firmly, for now, part of Earth. Can the tide still be retreating? I check my phone: forty-five minutes to dinner. How soon before it turns? I've lost sight of Orange Shorts. A stone settles in my gut: the kid looked to be in a hurry. Wasn't going to keep walking, was he, out into the water, over his head? Play chicken with the tide, try beating it at its own game, even as it starts to race in?

Why would I even think it? The salty breeze whispers oblivion.

There's no way I could paint this scene and do it justice, not one iota of it. Ridiculously, my brain skips back to its old habit of worrying, which I thought I'd overcome. I feel around for my keys. The rented Corolla isn't the ride Bradford would've picked, that's for sure.

What *about* the rental—will it drive itself back to the airport?

Meanwhile, what a ton of work, I think, to throw an ocean-floor dinner! If Bradford were alive we might have enjoyed the event as a couple. Booking it, I felt like one of those warrior women you hear about on Facebook: no backing down.

Now, to be honest, I wouldn't mind company, seeing a familiar face. Not Bradford, that would be too complicated, but my condo gal pals. They like sharing occasions, though not so much occasions considered "passages." A term that reminds me of pin the tail on the donkey, that ancient game: wandering a strange hallway blindfolded, feeling for a paper ass to pin a paper tail to.

But I have promised myself not to think of the past, including the Past Before Bradford.

From out of nowhere Orange Shorts appears, comes striding along. Thick, curly hair framing eyes that don't see me. His clothes look dry, boots caked with mud. No expression on his smooth, narrow face. *Did you reach the water? How far is it?* I want to call out, as if I'd never left the classroom. Hadn't been set adrift with handshakes and a watercolour of the school building painted by a student.

Visual art was my specialty; industrial arts were Bradford's. I did my best to nurture a love of art in the kids, probably spent too much time prepping classes many of them skipped. "You try too hard," Bradford used to say. But he was the one who got roped into coaching softball. If not for softball, he very likely would still be here, might even be walking this very sea floor with me. Snapping photos, suggesting things I could paint.

This useless thought throws me off balance. One heel skids, the other leg shoots out so I swear I feel my hamstring's twang. By some miracle I avoid landing on my well-padded ass. *White linen tablecloths, casual chic*, the ad said. Now that would be cute, yellow jeans slathered in mud, bad enough my sneakers are white. I glance around as if this burnt sienna plain is the staff room. Why didn't I dress up? Put on makeup? Because I never wear makeup; why start now.

Besides, look at the world, the state it's in. Bradford, you have no idea, I tell him—tell the wind, I mean. Sometimes I think you're lucky that kid cracked the ball across the field exactly when and where he did—not that his aim was intended or necessarily true.

Boarding the plane, I'd had the idea that experiencing one of the world's top wonders would rinse away such randomness, the feeling of doom that has followed me since. That it would fan the hope that bucket-list beauty *could* give me over to painting again. A way to outrun dread.

But even as Orange Shorts makes for the steps, I imagine him falling under a wave, hearing his screams for help—then what? Would I dive in and try to save him?

A freak accident, the principal called what happened. Who knows what you'd have called it, Bradford. If in those last, dreadful moments you had been able to speak.

The artist's job is to reflect the world, I wrote on the whiteboard, just back from bereavement. Sneaking in art theory while the kids painted papier mâché heads. They barely glanced up. It was definitely a low point, when I most needed their engagement to keep me afloat. After class, flipping through an art book in the library, *Drowning Girl* or *I Don't Care! I'd Rather Sink than call Brad for Help!* caught my eye. I've never been a Lichtenstein fan, don't enjoy comic book–style art, but this one made me laugh, might have even planted a seed: I would rather sink.

Don't be an ass, Bradford's voice had whispered. The first time I heard it loud and clear after he died. As if he were right there in the stacks.

The sun perches above the trees at a pinkish slant. Before all this happened, seeing such a sight I might've grabbed my paintbox, laid out the tubes of oils, chosen the colours to replicate it. The light of happy hour.

Beyond shelves of compressed mud, a flock of penguins troops past the island's shadow. Yellow boots, white shirts, black pants and aprons. I pick up my pace, not easy negotiating the muck. The penguins carry portfolios that magically unfold into tables. Shake out white sails, tablecloths. Some distance behind, a mismatched queue tramps after them. Panama hats, baseball caps, flowing dresses, Bermuda shorts, sweaters worn like shrunken capes.

Don't know why, but the sight inspires near-panic—there's something so easy and earnest about their procession. I fight the urge to escape up the stairs and into the car, and hurry back to the airport.

So the bucket-list dinner appears set to begin. Better not be a letdown, I can just hear Bradford, who always warned against having inflated expectations. Expectations are different from plans. I am pretty certain I won't pick up a paintbrush again, ever. All this time I've blamed my surroundings for my lack of inspiration, when my limitations are responsible, bogged down by the notion that things must be perfect, exactly as hoped or imagined—as if things ever pan out that way!

The dinner is sure to be a test of this. Stumbling toward the queue, I stop to glance over my shoulder. The tide is a faint pink-and-blue line. I still can't tell if it's coming in or going out. Shouldn't there be a whistle to alert people? A man in a Tilley hat and a woman in a flowy fuchsia dress wave to me. So I've been spotted. Do I know them? Of course not.

You don't have to go through with it, I hear Bradford say. The penguins are struggling to set the tables, arranged end to end in a row. Three tables, each with four folding chairs. The breeze is no help. Tilley Hat and Fuchsia pin things down with stones. At my feet a tiny creature inhabiting another's shell scoots to safety.

It's too late to do the same. "Jo-ann?" a voice, a real voice, calls out. "Jo-ann Laramee? Thanks for coming this evening. What can we get you to drink?"

"Champagne?"

The sparkling wine, I'm told, is being saved for the seafood course.

A double vodka martini? Bradford snickers.

"Sorry. Red or white?"

The wind rat-nests my hair. For what this is costing, I'd be within my rights to demand a full bar. Never mind.

"Sit wherever you like." The young thing in charge is perky and brusque, everything I wasn't at her age, reed-slim, glossy-haired. In another life she's a lawyer, a dancer? Or, this is her life, as a restaurateur.

Tilley Hat and Fuchsia join me at the table furthest from the steps. The steps are distant enough that I can't begin to fathom (sorry) how deep the water gets when it covers this stretch of sea floor. Soon all the places at the tables are taken, except the one opposite mine. It's a party of grey-hairs. Like you're one to talk, I anticipate Bradford's teasing, his reality check. The woman beside me at the adjoining table is cheerfully loud.

It's their second time, says the wiry, polo-shirted man beside her: "She loved it so much, here we are."

The plastic seats are a little hard on the butt, we agree. *Small-term pain for long-term gain*, I imagine Bradford snorting, though I am a little distracted. I picture Hokusai's famous print, *The Great Wave of Kanagawa*, coming to life, a red tsunami sweeping us off our chairs. People chit-chat. The wine could be colder; is there a drug added to it to make us feel we've all known each other longer?

A lanky young man hurries toward us, a late arrival. The gal in charge mutters under her breath, "Finally." I recognize his face, his lack of expression. His bright shorts have been replaced by wrinkled black jeans. He's our missing table mate? No, the evening's busboy.

A stooped, balding man limps slowly closer over the mud, eventually takes the seat across from mine. He has left his green cap behind.

Wasting no time, the head penguin announces the first course. A seafood terrine, handmade crackers. The crackers taste no different from store-bought, but that's Bradford talking. The terrine is delicious but comes from a single dish being passed around—not exactly pandemic protocol. I would prefer it was served individually, more work for the servers though. And this is like camping, sort of, Bradford reminds me.

Tilley Hat keeps digging in. The crackers soon run out.

The expressionless young man whisks away dish and plates. A junior penguin is already refilling wineglasses; it's as if everyone has known each other forever as we laugh and raise toasts.

Salads appear on small white plates, skimpy but delicious, each decorated with a flower.

Laughter blurs the sound of Hokusai's wave cresting in my head.

The main server, the brusque young woman, has set a huge stainless steel pot on a flaming gas burner. The next course is mussels. I'm not the biggest fan of mussels, they give me bad dreams. *But, when in Rome*, I tell myself, and scoop out the slimy orange bits of one using the shell of another, and so on and so on, until my bowl is empty.

Look at you, chain-mussel-eating—in lieu of chain-smoking? Bradford whispers.

Someone coughs. Next up, seafood croquettes. I have never eaten tastier food, flavours sharpened by salt air. Course after course, the man sitting across from me barely picks at his, though. After a little nibble, he pushes each plate away. He looks worse than sickly, I can't help noticing. Or perhaps his complexion is greyed by clouds scudding across the lowering sun. Behind him the bay glints, white-capped blue rimmed with pink. He catches me looking and smiles. His eyes are hollow, his lips bluish, though the sun stays strong enough to ward off evening's chill.

"Fred Baird," he says, extending a frail hand over the basin heaped with mussel shells. "And you are?" Hesitating but anxious not to be rude, I reach out and grip his hand lightly. It feels cold and bony—the way Bradford's would, I imagine, if he had lived to develop a terminal illness.

We're ordered to drink up, unnecessarily in my case since I've twice drained my glass. Next, the sparkling wine is popped and poured, to accompany miniature quiches served with lobster. Fred takes just one small bite, that's it.

He gestures toward the sea—"Isn't it marvellous?"—which has moved somewhat closer, perhaps, but not so the others notice, or appear to. "So does dinner live up to the buzz?" He fixes his eyes on me. The hint of a grin warms their greyness, something of Bradford's grin there, I think.

Before I can reply, our plates disappear, and tiny cups of something yellow and frothy replace them.

A lemon/vodka palate cleanser, the dark-haired woman announces over our heads. Her eyes are on the bay. A final touch before dessert, strawberry rhubarb cobbler served in little ramekins by her helpers while she consults her phone.

Already the busboy and servers are gathering things up, piling dishes into baskets and bins and plastic totes. My companion folds his hands, his dessert untouched. He peers at the incoming blue, still a distance off. "We'd better get a move on," he says, "it could be they've misjudged the time?"

Hurry up and wait, I think. The cobbler's so good I would kill for a second helping. Fred Baird nudges his dish toward me, lifts an eyebrow encouragingly.

The far-off rushing sound is closer, louder than before: the steady sweep of waves, not only wind.

Polishing off their desserts, Tilley Hat and Fuchsia Dress move from the table. They're tipsy and trill about the hot chocolate to be served, next up, around a blazing bonfire on the clifftop.

"A bonfire of the vanities." Baird laughs, then looks worried.

The other guests and most of the servers, lugging their assorted burdens, have moved off too and hurry toward the steps.

There's just the two of us left, and the busboy and gal in charge. They race around bundling up tablecloths, snapping lids on totes. The sound punctuates the meal's end with an awful finality. Indigo shadows bathe the mud, rocks, and shelves of stone. The rushing mimics the roar inside a shell held tightly to an ear. Baird's panicked joke weaves through it.

"What would a dying Innu guy do? Sit tight and wait, or walk out to meet it? Kidding, kidding—I'm not there yet." He's having trouble getting up off his chair, appears stuck there. "Well, Jo-ann, looks like we're being kicked out."

The busboy is folding our table. "Dude. Twenty minutes and she comes in like a f—freight train. I'd move my ass if I were you guys." He practically tips me from my chair and folds it, slings it under his arm. Baird's sigh is like Bradford's, when I would swing by the bleachers to say supper was getting cold.

"Hate to be a pain, Jo-ann, but I wouldn't mind a hand—if you could just help me up to the stairs, I'll stay out of your hair. I promise. Unless you want company."

In his look is a loneliness worse than mine could ever be, a determination that matches the determination I've harboured and worn and feel being pulled over my head like a skin. His is emboldened by sickness, I realize. I feel its strength like a burn, taking his arm, helping him to his feet.

A slow, steady burn as we stumble and stagger, an awkward four-legged creature, dance partners, to the stairs. Already the sun has begun to set, tinting everything a gilded orange.

"Beauty before age, or age before beauty?" he jokes. His laugh is an exhausted wheeze as he stops and insists I go ahead.

His gesture could be from another era, a gesture I could get steamed about feeling the light, self-satisfied touch of his hand on my back, just for a second, before he grips the railing. But as I climb, pausing on each step to make sure he's behind me and is okay, I feel my resolve lift and fly away. Off it flaps into the wind that's pushing whitecaps and swirling waters closer. There's a roar like a subway train nearing the station.

Above the trees on the clifftop a pale full moon has begun to rise, the body in charge of all this movement, the mysteries of currents and tides.

Each drop of numbness—my taxing, accumulating grief?—ebbs as surely as I had hoarded it.

The party is waiting in the picnic area past the top of the stairs. Guests murmur with contentment, circling the firepit in plastic chairs that gleam in the fading orangey light. I help Baird into his seat, take the only one left, next to him. Mugs are passed around, hot chocolate as thick and silky as mousse. Happy to have made it up here, Baird gets a second wind. Nudges me, grinning.

"See? Looks to me like you'll be a return guest, maybe even a lifer? Here's to years more ocean-floor dinners, Jo-ann, you don't mind me saying. Sure she'll be back, won't she—how could she not?" He raises his mug to everyone. "I'm willing to bet, anyway, even if I'm not a betting man. Some of us can't get enough ebb and flow." As he speaks, the moon peeks from behind pink strings of cloud. His voice is thin and reedy, no competition for the wind and surf but keen as a blade slicing soft stone. In his words it's Bradford's voice I hear, louder than a whisper in the library or adrift on the breeze above the ballfield. I would know it anywhere; I was married to it for twenty-eight years.

The busboy lights the fire, an artful arrangement of driftwood and logs. The leaping flames illuminate the dusk, and all I see is the circle of familiar faces, and beyond the circle, the fence guarding us from the cliff edge and the flood tide below. The tide's indigo glimmer and the island float there, float, yes, surrounded and buoyed by its flow. The boy's smile could be a pyromaniac's—no, it's the smile of a kid nearing the end of a shift, a summer job, the best of his life ahead of him, as far as he can see or any of us imagine.

Threshold

SHE WOKE TO A SCRATCHING SOUND. WAS IT A RACCOON at the door, snuffling around the doorstep, ready to pick a hole in the screen? Or some church person nosing around out there, trying not to rouse her? These folks came at the weirdest times to leave stuff. Timmie's, mostly. Coffees and donuts, sometimes sandwiches.

All around her was pitch black. Next, a burst of loud, fast knocking.

"Hey, April. April, girl. Wake up!"

In the darkness, seconds before she remembered where she was, it was easy to think she'd fallen down a hole someplace, was in a cave back in the woods by the lake. Or lost at sea, adrift. But, nope, she was here, in her tiny container. Cocooned in her sleeping bag, toasty warm.

"April, you comin' or not, girl? Gotta get out there. Said you'd be ready."

Bits of shredded dreams flitted. Memories—okay, nightmares. Snowy woods, wet sidewalks, dead cars, pills. Picking through these, she hit on it: Jacky's birdwatching thing. She blew out a breath, let its warmth envelop her for one long second. Rescue her from everything that had happened ages before the shit about sickness and masks, that pandemic bull that she and pretty much everyone seemed like they were soooo over.

Jacky's voice pressed in, pushy as the draft around the door. "April. You never seen owls, sistah. This your chance." He called her "baby" sometimes too, but never perv-like, never as if, like, wanting to do her. The way Ty had been, back in the day, and the guy in the next apartment.

She sloughed off the sleeping bag, still half asleep. Yelled so he'd wait. "Yeah, yeah. Hold your shit, man. I'm up." Wriggling free, she squirmed to her feet. Didn't bother putting on the light; brightness killed when you first woke, especially if it was still night. All she wanted was to dive back inside her flannel cocoon and sleep, sleep forever, and why not? She could hear him out there kicking something, a can, an empty cup?

She'd only said she wanted to see owls to be nice.

Plus it was *years* since she'd gone near those woods, literally years. Even if she had stuck pretty close by all this time, barely leaving the 'hood, she'd been careful to avoid them. Never mind the mall where the Frenchys used to be. It closed even before the Covid hit, due to thefts and too-high overhead—that's what the lady who'd worked there said, when she'd come around the other day offering a ratty sweatshirt, a hand-me-down times ten. As for the woods, they were never far enough away but, as it happened, way too close: a straight line through a land of beige to the end of the street, a jog past some boulders and the car graveyard and in toward the lake.

"You coming or not? You don't move your ass, we gon' miss them."

"Give me a sec, okay. Okay?" She hollered to make sure he heard. At least she was dressed. Flannel pj pants, hoodie—pretty much her day/night uniform. "Just gotta put on shoes, 'kay, dude?"

First stop, the Honey Hut, she didn't add.

She shoved on her sneakers, threw on her parka, stepped over the threshold onto the concrete slab. Standing there, Jacky grinned, eyes black as pond water in the hazy light that spilled from the church entrance. He had on his orange toque, a big thick scarf coiled around his neck.

"We gon' miss them waking up, you don't hustle."

He had the kind of smile that could talk anyone into doing crazy shit. Well, good crazy shit. She felt his smile warm her as she locked up. The blind in the window was down, no worries about folks peeking in—all good—even if it was the middle of the night. You never knew who might be hanging around. Kind of funny to think how, sharing a tent, she hadn't worried about this kind of thing, not so much.

"Don't wan' miss them waking, Grey. Whatever yo' name is now. Come on. It the best part."

"Yeah, yeah." She hurried to the porta-potty across the lane, the shortcut the Sunday people took to the parking lot. A white painted gate blocked it the other days.

Make a splash, the porta-potty had in big letters on the side. Even under a street light's distant beams the thing glowed bee-loud yellow, HONEY HUTS with a phone number on the door.

"It's some friggin' cold," she called from inside. Washed her hands, dried them on her pants.

"For April, ha ha. Your birth mama have some brain cramp giving you that name." Jacky nudged her when she came out, joked, "It the cruellest month, man."

But he didn't mind the cold, wasn't he always saying so, and he gave her his scarf. She thought of the first time they'd met, really met, just after Christmas, once she was moved in. Waiting outside the hut for her turn, she'd figured it was a dude living next door, the seat always up. Jacky had taken for-freaking-ever in there.

It wasn't the greatest using a porta-potty all winter, especially at night, but better than pissing behind some bush. The other day the priest had come by to say he was looking for "a facility in better taste," after a parishioner complained about the "make a splash" bit. The words' rudeness, maybe? Which April found funny, though she guessed she could see where the hater, probably some ancient old lady, might be coming from.

"Hoot-hoot-hooot!" She let her breath steam the air around Jacky's face. It was the sound she would hear coming from his unit at all hours, when he wasn't working.

"So, you're wit' me, right? If you're not wit' me, girl, go on back, you are against me." He patted her shoulder and laughed. Then, going totally silent, he led the way through the parking lot and down St. Jude's Avenue. The street was dark and empty, a total bland-land of cookie-cutter houses done in beige siding. Their fronts gleamed dully in the street lights' greyish yellow. The light was almost the colour of Jacky's dreads.

It was actually pretty embarrassing having a church for an address. But, at least having an address she got her cheques, eligible, finally. Though it never stopped feeling weird writing it down: Unit B, St. Jude's Catholic Church. Like she was a nun or something. And Jacky, in Unit A, was some sort of crazy old monk. Which he kind of was, in her opinion. A loner. Though the both of them were. Loners. Which explained why they were friends.

Except, while Jacky sorted bottles at the Enviro-Depot she kept her loner-weirdness to herself, contained inside her unit. A square metal box like a miniature shipping container, tinier than those tiny homes for rich hipsters you heard about. But hey, it was warm. A roof over her head that didn't leak. A place she could call her own, with a door that locked, a place to charge her phone, have heat and an actual light. A bed, off the ground.

Nothing to complain about, like Jacky said. "We have fuck-all to complain about, April Grey," he was always saying. Which reminded her to be grateful, as grateful as could be for finally having an address. Even if it was behind a church and wasn't a forever home, like the SPCA sought for pets.

At the end of the pavement Jacky turned and looked all around a bunch of times. "Not like I'm paranoid or nothing. But, man, you know they are everywhere, the cops."

Right here and at 4:00 in the morning? But he had reason to watch out, she knew. One day the cops had come knocking on Jacky's door. The Enviro-Depot must've sent them, because he wasn't working that day. April raised up the window in her door even though it let the rain in, just so she could hear what was happening.

It was a bullshit story only the cops could make up. The same cops, probably, that had tried to kick everyone out of People's Park in the middle of a snowstorm, which was how she and Jacky ended up being neighbours.

Some kids playing in the woods had found a cave and in the cave was a shitload of shoes. Random shoes, ladies', women's, girls'—mostly with high heels. The kind April imagined she would wear someday if she got a job, a real job, in an office somewhere or maybe in a store.

Someone must've told the cops Jacky spent a lot of time back there in the woods.

The priest must have seen the cruiser, because he came out too and stood by while Jacky explained what happened.

"It was a fox. I kid you not, sirs. A thiefing fox. Seen him with my own eyes—I swear to God, Father, I did. He was running with a shoe in his mouth from over there." Through the driving rain Jacky had pointed at a house with a dumpster in the front yard. "Followed him myself, and seen this mess of ladies' fancy shoes. Nothing a dude could or would wear, make no mistake, buds."

She must've laughed because the priest glanced up and spotted her, and kind of shook his head, and said unless the cops had hard evidence they shouldn't be coming around bothering a man at home, accusing him of some vague thing he hadn't, or probably hadn't, done.

When she'd first seen the cops out there, she was scared. But as soon as they all started talking she had decided Jacky might be crazy but was a good guy, more than all right, and maybe the priest wasn't so bad either.

Jacky was always looking out for her, even if it could get annoying. He kept saying he'd get her a job counting bottles. "Easy-easy like that, April. Count 'em up for the ladies and gentlemen, give 'em they cash. Ten cents a bottle. Thirteen thirty-five an hour, man—how about it?"

So far the job hadn't happened, but now the owl trip seemed about to. For the longest time she'd figured she had a total looney tune living next door, hearing all the crazy sounds coming from Jacky's. The sounds that came from the church were one thing—singing and guitar-strumming and once in a while loud buzzing notes that rattled her window screen and made her bunk and the overhead light vibrate—though not enough to be a problem. But Jacky's bird sounds were something else. "Hoo-hooo-hoo-hooo-hoo-hooot-cook-cook-cook-you." "Plock-plock-plock-plock."

"Tu-whit tu-whoo, tu-whit-to-you-too, dude," she had yelled back a few times. Not that he'd heard. As far as she knew.

Standing there at the top of the path, Jacky peered at her from below his toque with his big, sorrowful, kind eyes, and she felt suddenly shy and undeserving. But not the sad, undeserving way she'd felt when the cops raided People's Park, a wedge of grass in the middle of town with benches and bushes and space enough for folks to set up tents. A pile of grocery store pallets to sit on and eat off of around the ten-gallon drum they used for campfires. The first couple of snows—big snows—had convinced her it might be time to move on. Not the snow itself, a clean white blanket over everything, but the wind that drove it.

The wind was the killer. It had flattened the tent she

was sharing with a couple of guys she knew off the street. That fall they had all got sick with the fucking plague and it *was* bad, but they got better. The week before Christmas, after the cops kept appearing in their masks, telling everyone to leave, she'd heard about the church program. Emergency units being installed on church grounds. She was totally skeptical, not down with it at all: why would anyone trust a church? But then she got to peek inside one of the boxes and, for what it was, it seemed ace. Especially the built-in bunk with a foamy under a brand-new sleeping bag, and electric heat you could turn on yourself. An outlet you could plug a phone charger into and an actual kettle. All of this just waiting, like someone had seen inside her head all those rainy, sleety, windy nights in the tent. Only, she wasn't so sure about having it all to herself, not sharing. She had never lived on her own, all alone that is, ever since her stepdad kicked her out. For a few years, she'd bounced from apartment to apartment, couch surfing with five or six or seven or eight other people. That got old.

A trap, she'd figured it was, at first. The church thing. What system let you use its stuff without demanding other stuff in return?

"It's all yours, April," the priest had said. Demonstrating how to flip on the light. "Let there be light," he'd said. Like she was a wild animal or something, didn't know how a switch worked. The only way she could tell he was a priest was the black shirt and stiff white collar he wore under his puffy down vest.

For the first few days, until she met Jacky, she had felt totally guilty. Unworthy. As if the Catholic guilt she'd heard of somewhere flowed like the juice that came through the wiring.

"Hey," Jacky had said, stepping out of the porta-potty. Letting the door flap behind him. An icy wind had whipped through the empty parking lot that afternoon. It was too cold to walk up to the McDonald's where they let you use the washroom if you bought a coffee. The sinks were better than the one in the Honey Hut. But it was a long way to go to wash your face, the tiny plastic sink okay in a pinch.

Jacky's eyes had looked right through her, at first. Then she couldn't resist. "What, you got a bunch of birds living in there with you?" She'd imagined a flock of feathery things with big hooked beaks and claws, pooping everywhere.

He had stopped abruptly, and warmed to her. "You like birds, man? You wanna see the birds sometime, hey?"

It was maybe the strangest invitation she'd ever had. Like there weren't birds in the trees around the parking lot, even in this insane cold. Like their singing didn't wake her when there was no reason to get up. When all she could imagine doing was lying there, warm in her sleeping bag, breathing in its dry, flannelly smell.

Jacky had stuck out his hand, fingers burning red from the cold. She didn't want to, but she had squeezed them. It was obvious he didn't remember her from the park. "It's better, being neighbours, hey. Us watching out for each other. Like, if crips come around wanting to fight or break in or hassle you or something, hey."

"But. That priest—" She didn't know what to make of him.

"'Ome sweet 'ome, girl. He is not a bad guy, once you know him." Jacky had a deep, hooty sort of laugh. "The places are ours till May. Then they go in storage till next winter. So I hear. Like it stops raining then, hey.

Hooty-hoo-hoot-hoooo." He rolled his eyes. "But. For now we are in the best place." He'd waved at the spruce trees past the end of the street. "It is paradise back there, man."

"I'll take your word for it."

Just then, the wind had bent the fur on her hood. Had whipped the ends of his scarf in his face.

"Wind, it blow where it will to. You hear the sound it make but do not know where it come from or go."

"Whatever." Then she'd spotted a church lady hurrying toward her, carrying something, and ducked inside quick.

A plate of little old lady sandwiches. Egg salad. Crusts cut off.

A couple months later, and still a few weeks before the owl thing, on the first official day of spring, freezing rain bashed and slashed outdoors. With the blind down and the light off, April had trembled inside her little home, half expected it to start drifting and bobbing toward the parking lot.

The lot, as it happened, was packed with cars so it must've been a Sunday, early. The church people kept some wicked hours. Jacky knocked on the door and invited her over to play cards. *Shove your cards*, she wanted to say.

"I've got cookies," he said.

Shove those too, she had to keep herself from snarling.

Nice as he was, Jacky was always going for the feels. Sometimes too much in your face. "You got something better to do, girl? I got soup, too."

"WTF," she'd said, hauling herself up. Dragging on her parka over the cozy plaid pants someone had left hanging on her doorknob. Gifts were okay, she decided, as long as the givers stayed away and she didn't have to talk to them. She felt shitty for taking their presents, shittier for *having* to take them. At least the pants fit okay.

"Hey, girl. Nice pants. Seriously."

It wasn't like Jacky could see her ass in them, with her parka down over it. The first new or new-to-her pants she'd had in as long as she could remember.

He had a tiny kettle with its own cup, plus a china mug with a church on it and a leaning tower for a handle. The whole mug was slanted and looked crazy to drink from, like, imagine sipping hot tea while you were shit-faced. The handle's tower had eight stories and was attached to the cup with a patch of "grass."

Jacky emptied a whole packet of Cup-a-Soup into it, added hot water and handed it to her. "Hey. A hot breakfast, if you please."

On the wall above his bed was a poster tacked up with safety pins. It showed a huge grey owl swooping in, its gaze like whoever was looking at it was prey. Eyes homed in. The bird fixing to take you out.

"You got a thing for them, or what?"

"Owls? Sure. Something wrong with that, girl?" He joked that he'd wanted to be an owl when he was a kid. "The way they know stuff. Fly toward the easiest opening, like they have got radar. Hey, you cannot fool an owl. They are not wise for nothing."

"I guess."

"So. You have been back there, where the owls live?

The woods down there, my paradise?"

"Naw," she lied. In high school she'd gone there lots to get high, back there by the lake. It was somewhere to drink and smoke and screw around where no one could hassle you. She'd scored and done friends a few times, not exactly the way it sounded, once or twice in the cave. The fox's cave. Then she'd gotten clean. Somehow. Had promised herself she wouldn't go there again, ever. The last time, she had almost died—or could have. She really could have.

"I miss the park," she said, for no real reason.

Jacky slurped the dregs of his soup and stood up. Her sign that the visit was over, time for her to go. She spotted the cookies on a paper plate under a shiny piece of plastic wrap. Oatmeal and raisin by the looks of them. A tiny trail of raisins on the floor, like deer poo.

"For the robins, man. They don't have nothing to eat till the ground unfreezes. Here, you take 'em, eat the rest." He shoved the plate at her. "I don't much care for sweets. I am sweet enough, ha ha. But let me ask you, Ms. April, what is it you are scared of? I see you're scared like a rabbit. There is nothing to fear. You know what I mean?"

"Not really."

She couldn't wait to get out of there and back into her sleeping bag. But the soup had warmed her insides. Warmed away the feeling she'd got remembering being back there by the lake, in the cold, in the wet. She got into her sleeping bag and ate the cookies one after another. Fuck knows what Jacky had against raisins. Then she felt sick from all the sugar and picked the last cookie apart. Set the raisins aside for the robins, like he had done.

With no cops in sight Jacky moved with a wiry lightness. Before climbing down the shoulder, he bent and tucked his pant legs into his work socks, pointed at her legs. "You don't wan be getting ticks on you, girl."

"Are you serious?" She had no socks.

"Naw, I am just makin' sure you awake. Now stick close, hush up yourself. You cannot make a peep or they will frighten. Quiet now. Be like them church folks say: I'ma speak now and forever hold ma peace."

"But how are we ever gonna see?" There was no moon or if there was, it was hidden by wispy clouds or fog, but the odd star blinked through. She followed Jacky, climbing over the rocks below the road and down onto a mud path into the woods.

The spruce trees surrounded and swallowed them up pretty much instantly, and soon there was only the path underfoot, then the grey of bare rock walled in by forest. It was different from the path she knew. There were no swampy parts, no wrecked cars nestled in weeds. Huge curbs and humps of sloping rock sprouted tiny spindly trees with prickly needles, so many pale skeletons dancing in the dark.

"Them are Jack pines." Jacky laughed his laugh, only quiet, quiet. "Mind you don't walk on the sweet little crowberries, hey, they are very, very rare, and if you want to know the truth, April, they grow no place but here."

It was so dark and silent, unfamiliar and perfectly still in the cold, she thought for sure she was dreaming this. Or had actually swallowed that pill, years ago, meant for a loser hook-up. Instead of all the shit that had gone down since, she had died, and this place, these woods, were what being dead was.

A scared, panicky feeling tickled then drilled inside her. Maybe she wasn't dead at all, and if she wasn't dead, what other creatures were alive, too, prowling then stalking her?

Jacky read her mind, he did. Forget how he'd said no talking, he named them in a sweet whisper. Coyotes, fox, white-tailed deer, porcupine, rabbits. "Hush now. There isn' nothing to be scared of, April." Then, like this would make her feel better, he pointed to a faint, steady glow way beyond the trees in one direction. "That be the Sobeys, girl—they got the lights on there 24/7." Then he pointed to a little red light high above the treetops in another direction. "That the cell tower we can see from our places. And over that way, far far off, you can't see it but you can believe me when I say it is there, that the 500 block."

How could it be she had lived by these woods practically all her life, and now they were another land, a different wilderness, on another planet, maybe in another universe?

Jacky waved at her not to speak and cut loose a string of eerie, alien whistles, clucks, and chirps. The sounds of fragile things that did not live in this world? Then, holding his finger to his lips, he pointed.

Over there, he mouthed. "A barred owl, hear him?"

And she did. A low, echoey "hoot-hoot-cook-cook-you."

Jacky answered with a matching string of "hoot-hoot-cook-cooks" and, like magic, came the response—an echo that hummed behind her eardrums and in her throat and made her swallow and swallow again.

"A family. Over there." He pointed once more, a sweep of his arm. "A mile away—I have seen where they nest. And over that way"—another sweep—"is a family of great horned owls."

He called again, more sounds she had never heard a human make. Never thought a human could make.

A full-on chorus answered, the sounds echoing over miles of nothing.

The cold from the rock crept through her sneakers, through her toes and into her ankles.

"But I want to see them." No wind, not a breath of wind. Her whisper pushed at the branches. "Why can't we see them?"

As she spoke, a fuzzy grey light started to melt and blot up the dark above the forest that, as far as she could see, had no human directions. No signs to say near or far, north, south, east, or west.

"April. But they are here." Jacky's voice was soft and patient but tired. "You heard them. With your own ears, girl. They are out there nesting. You do not need to see them to believe, aren't I right?"

All at once, as the sky brightened—its trembling light so slow but quick, so gradual but sudden her eyes were tricked!—the woods exploded into song. The trees pulsed with it. A wilderness planet's insane, free symphony of tu-whit tu-whoos, chuck-chuck-chucks, dee-dee-dees, and ca-na-da-ca-na-das, like every bird in the world was right here, hidden but calling, *Wake up Wake up Wake the fuck up.*

Somewhere in the distance a dog barked and another dog barked back, and from not too far away AC/DC played over a radio or stereo—from a beige house in another land of beige houses, up by Governor's Brook? Where, as far as she knew, her stepdad still lived.

"I've had enough all right of this kind of living," Jacky said soon after, "for a while anyways." On the night before what she guessed was Easter, a Saturday night, he finished packing.

He had a present for her, treasures from the depths of somebody's blue bag. "Imagine, throwing they out. Maybe these will make up a little, April? For your disappointment? Not the real thing. But, still. How foolish can some be, thinking every single thing recycle-able, hey."

The owls were the size of salt-and-pepper shakers—an almost-matching pair of ornaments made of shiny, moulded ceramic. One was a little taller than the other. Its feathered breast was the same mauve of the sky overhead just then, as April looked up. Looked away, looked anywhere but at him.

Its wings, talons, and beak were the same dusky gold, but its eyes were mismatched. Turquoise ringed the deep blue pupil of one, a pale, gentle green the pupil of the other. The owl's smaller, plainer mate was glazed in watery blue, brown, and greenish beige.

She couldn't help thinking they were like Jacky and her.

"I cannot take them with me, girlfriend. They cannot go rough. You'll cherish them, yes?"

It was an order, not an ask.

Jacky had a seagull feather in his toque and it tilted in the wind as he hoisted on his backpack. It was army green and had a rolled-up tarp attached. The grass and dirt in front of their units was soft and wet with spring melt.

"We've got another month, you don't have to be out. Not yet."

He was used to sleeping rough, had told her stories

since their night in the woods, about sleeping in graveyards and stairwells and sharing space with money machines in banks.

"Wait till it warms up a bit. I don't see why—"

"Aw, April. You don't see it? What man has not built in his own image, has not tot'lly fucked up, will save us. Not just me but you and all the people."

Orangey-pink light peeked through the trees by the parking lot, where cars sat row by row by row. The first signs of buds bristled red in the maples, like the ends of a zillion lit cigarettes.

"I will see you in Paradise, girl."

The priest must have spotted Jacky leaving. He appeared at her door out of breath. He was wearing his super-fancy church clothes, a white robe stitched with gold. The vigil was just about to start, he needed to hurry back upstairs, he said. But he wanted her to know there was news. Good news. The archdiocese might reconsider its plans for May. But even if it didn't, a parishioner had an apartment available. A really small one, but affordable. Very affordable, and the parishioner might even help with the rent.

"You'll miss your buddy, I know." The priest did a funny thing with his teeth, sucked them and bit his bottom lip. Said she was welcome to come inside, join in if she wanted. "It'll be warm, there'll be lots of candles." His voice was encouraging, like this would entice her.

She'd heard about Easter, this fairy tale about a dude who'd come back from the dead. Which maybe wasn't so totally out there, considering the same had kind of happened to her—well, if you thought about second chances, third, fourth, or maybe fifth ones.

"Naw, I'll pass." But she stood outside, watching as he raced up the front steps, his fancy swag billowing. He joined some people waiting out there coatless, shivering in shirts and dresses. Beneath grey stone arches, light quivered from behind blue, red, green, and yellow glass.

They had a portable fire pit set up outside the entrance, there on the concrete. She could smell the woodsmoke, see wisps of it rise before the wind flicked them away. The fire looked to be dope for cooking on, roasting hot dogs or whatever. She watched the priest light a honking big, tall candle off it. The candle was so huge it took him and a dude wearing what looked like a white housecoat to hold it steady.

Then someone lit a skinny white candle off it, and someone else lit another skinny white candle off it, and someone *else* lit *another* skinny white candle off it, the way you'd light smokes one off the other. On and on like that, until everyone had their candles lit and they disappeared through the opened doors and inside.

Twilight had quickly turned to night. Jacky would be way past the smaller rocks by now, hanging out on the big ones, waiting till it got good and late and quiet enough to call his friends, the owls.

Thinking of his sounds, she couldn't hold back a laugh.

Close by, the music started and in the plain arched windows right above her unit, candlelight glowed and trembled gold. So much trembling, quaking, aching light.

Miserere nobis, she heard a voice sing, in some strange other language. *Dona nobis pacem. Dona nobis pacem.* She didn't know what it could mean, but it sounded so beautiful it almost made her cry. The world was full of bullshit, but there was good in it too, she guessed. Funny stuff, surprising stuff. Maybe like the story the priest and his people, or someone, must believe in. Maybe it was even true?

Hey, anything was possible. She'd never thought her and Jacky would be friends. She'd never thought she'd hear an actual owl either. And look at her. She glanced down at her hands and sneakers, wiggled fingers and toes just for the joy of feeling them. She was still here, wasn't she.

Flight Paths

It's the evenings I find long—even late summer ones like this, the deep blue shadows creeping over the deck. The sinking sun makes monsters of the vines that hide me from the neighbours. Party sounds filter across the yard: ice clinking, booming laughter. It's been some time since Kirk and I lived it up like these people do, even before aging and the plague gave us an excuse not to. License for my husband to hole up downstairs with the news, its numbing loop—a hangover from the days of lockdowns, now, thank whomever, firmly behind us.

Oh, but he has his reasons not to sit outside with me. Too buggy. Too damp. Though I can guess why, presently, he favours the TV's company. It was an evening like this when things changed for us, when our son left us for good. It's something we hardly talk about, which doesn't mean we don't think about it. You never get over a child's absence, though if you are very lucky or very tough, maybe you grow used to it, like a grievous illness but worse, much worse.

Only slightly louder than the neighbours' voices, TV voices creep from the basement window. I don't want to hear about the royal family, the latest nut taking over the Conservative party. Drinking my nightly cup of tea (herbal) I sink deeper into my Adirondack chair (made of twenty thousand recycled bottle caps, our daughter's gift). Tilt my head back, watch the sky's periwinkle blue deepen.

A star appears, another and another. The dark's soaking up the shadows cannot happen soon enough. It's the light's slow fading that depresses me. Hearing from Meggie would help; nice if she would call. I could call her. But she'll be busy with the kids, getting tomorrow's gear together. Tennis, sailing: their last lessons before school starts.

Behind the shrubbery a cork pops. A fizzling burst. Toasts pierce the breeze. These neighbours are always celebrating, things Kirk and I would barely note. Purging the basement, offloading stuff to charity. The lawn being mowed, for Pete's sake. Chores Meg hires people to do; lucky her husband makes such good money. Unlike her dad, who sold insurance—and brought home a salary decent enough to keep us while she and Michael were growing up, and I "worked in the home." Not as glamorous as being a lawyer like her partner, as she calls David. Between this and her keeping her last name, how's anyone to know they're married?

The harvest moon rises through the trees, three-quarters full. Throws pinkish light over the garden gone to seed—it's too much for a pair of seniors to tend. Meggie says her father and I should sell the place, get a condo.

Who knows, maybe we will. Just not yet, not yet. This house is too packed with memories, memorabilia, to let it go that easily. And what would I do holed up in a glass cell with just a balcony to sit out on?

"But the view you could have!" Meggie casts possibilities like a big, shiny net. "A place on the thirtieth floor looking out to sea! Motherrr"—she makes that gagging sound with her voice, hoping to seem younger?—"you could watch the cruise and container ships coming into port."

As if this would make the evenings snappier. Lights twinkling on the horizon, hulking shapes acquiring details. As long as I'm on this side of the turf, I will live as close as possible to the ground, thank you.

But Meg is persistent: "You could get a place near the Gardens. Think of it, you two could walk there every day. See concerts in the bandstand. Enjoy the birds, the flowers—all that colour without planting a thing!"

When she pitches this angle, I picture the great blue heron that hung around the Gardens' pond one summer. He looked lost, a celebrity hermit perching on the tiny model *Titanic* anchored in the middle. The paper even had printed his photo.

"A condo would be easier for Dad," she says.

Well, yes, Kirk has never enjoyed home maintenance. At times I've wondered why he decided married life, family life, would suit him—all the responsibility. Yet he managed it nicely, until our boy went off the rails.

"Don't blame yourself," I had said.

Trying to get us to move, Meggie even broached it once: "If Michael was around, he would..."

"What, dear? Have us sell? Clear out his room, move

us and his belongings into a sterile little box like the kind you're so keen on?"

"He'd agree with me, Mum. That's all."

Then your brother's disappearance, his ghosting, would be complete? I thought, but would never say.

The moon hovers atop the pine tree, the section last fall's hurricane left behind. That tree was a seedling when Kirk and I moved in forty-four years ago. Before storms became major news events and veered quietly out to sea, stopped by the cold if they made it this far north. I swear the air was saltier then, too. As a child, Michael's favourite smell was in early spring, when, as we learned in school, the Labrador Current mixing with the Gulf Stream made the fog that covered the city like wet wool.

"The smell is like snorting seaweed," Michael said once, much later on.

But on those mornings when he and Meggie set off to school, the salty smell would remind me that each day was a gift. I still believe it is, bearing in mind that a gift can be a curse. Which is why the stubborn evening light wears on me, delaying night's coziness. Underscoring the emptiness where, once, the hours were packed, the days never long enough.

Finally, dusk falls. Time to retire indoors, to repair to bed, as they used to say in books. My relief equals the first sip of a bubbly cocktail, until the neighbours' chatter about cruises, causes, and poolside bars flattens it. The moon climbs higher, the sight, in spite of everything, an invitation to linger. From next door a woman's shrill laugh makes me wonder about Meggie. Where she'll be when her kids are grown and David's still too busy to keep her company. When life's fullness is behind her. Its letting go of things too numerous to count.

If we moved, I could ask, *how would Mikey know where to find us?*

Meg would no doubt shrug it off. Glued to her phone, she prides herself on keeping "connected."

Autumn's velvety cool tinges the air, a hint of when the sun and sky will feel more remote. Not that I'm one to wish away the days. But I wonder, obtusely, as I do every year, if winter's days being shorter might give them more fullness. The way the cold brings mergansers to otherwise empty inlets each January. Watching them and other winter birds brings a quiet joy that, briefly, brings Kirk and me together.

For now, in September, we await the herons—a non-event for many, I'm sure, but for us special. Before they leave for wherever they go to winter, a colony appears from wherever they summer, and congregates, not in the Public Gardens like that hermit, but in the wilderness park beside our neighbourhood. If you can still call it wilderness, apartment towers springing up around it.

Though I would never tell Meggie, the park and its birds are my truest reasons for staying here. It's a longer walk to the pond's wooded shores than a stroll to the Gardens from a nearby condo would be. Which is fine.

Given my penchant for early bedtimes you won't be surprised (or maybe you will be?) to learn I'm a crack-of-dawn riser. If long evenings are grating, mornings are a salve. A reminder that possibilities, however small, remain. Another day, another go-round under the sun that might be used to set some piddling thing right.

When this evening's damp sends me indoors, I slip downstairs to say good night. A nature show has replaced the news: whatever, Kirk is gazing at his device. His cheeks look shiny in the TV's flickering light. And I'd thought he had forgotten. It's the anniversary of the last time we saw Michael—though his withdrawal from our lives happened over years, I realize. Not a one-off event but an accumulation of events, moments, scenes, that Kirk goes to his iPad to forget.

He wipes his face with his palms.

"Oh, now, dear," I whisper. "Don't beat yourself up." I've said this so often these past two decades I could say it in my sleep. And in the same snoring breath, *What could we have done differently? Where did we go wrong?*

Unanswerable questions since Mikey was fifteen, sixteen—thirteen or fourteen? Smoking dope, stealing from the liquor cabinet, topping up his dad's rye with water as if Kirk wouldn't notice. The time Kirk went to pick him up, found him drunk out of his mind, wandering around the bus station. The calls from the police, once from a cop who didn't have to phone but was trying to keep our boy from harm—further harm.

Then the heavy—heavier—drugs. The time Kirk was out of town for work and Meggie away at university and Michael was, what else, at loose ends, living with us after being on his own. Whatever that meant, being on his own. That night, I awoke to noises in the kitchen, the back door banging open in the rain. A pot of cooking oil smoking on the stove, frozen fries dumped on the floor, and a phone—Michael's—under a chair, buzzing, buzzing. Beside it were pills. Bluish-grey ones I knew instinctively weren't prescription. Michael came staggering in, drenched, barely coherent. Cursing me, he slammed back outdoors yelling that his phone was gone, what had I done with it? He stayed away that time for two days. Came home looking like he'd slept in a car, or worse.

Kirk glances up from his tablet. "The heron's migration patterns, I've been googling them." Eyes meeting mine, he puts on a smile. Contrary to how special we find it, the great blue heron is as common as a jay. But knowing this makes the species no less magical. One thing we agree on.

When Kirk speaks again his voice is bitter. Bittern, I think: a bird not to be confused with the heron. "You could have done more, Margaret. You were here. You were home." These words come crashing out of the blue. "You should have—"

"Should have what?" My tongue feels dredged in sand. "Talked to teachers? The doctor? A counsellor? As if I didn't. You think I wasn't scared?"

"We both should've—"

"What could we have done, Kirk, locked him in his room?"

At fifteen Michael was a foot taller than his dad, stronger than the two of us put together. As burly as Meggie was stick-like.

What could we have done but wrap our arms around our boy, held him for the minutes, seconds, before he broke free? What could we have done besides love him? What can anyone do, besides that?

Kirk shrugs, his weariness hoarded there. "So many years, not knowing if our child is alive or—"

"Dead," I say. The scenarios leading up to this, the

possible scenarios, are too ugly, too horrific, to name. In the hours before sleep they eat at me.

"Stop, Margaret. *Stop.*"

The weight of it all is a plank—wedged behind my eyes, unwalkable, unnegotiable.

Kirk is right. It isn't and never has been useful to pick the wound. As if the wound has ever scabbed over.

"Well, good night."

"I'll be up in a bit. I'm just trying to find out if the moon affects their comings and goings. Maybe not much, if at all?" His laugh is scratchy, as if there's something stuck in his throat. I think of the word they use on the news, a stupid word: *closure.* As if there is such a thing.

Completely by surprise Kirk tugs at my hand, squeezes it. "We'll see if they're there in the morning, okay? The herons?"

I wake at five-thirty, shower, dress, apply lipstick. (Meggie would approve: "That shade's a superrr pick-me-up, Mum!") Kirk makes coffee, fills two travel mugs. On the way out the door I remember the binoculars on the landing.

Refreshed, more or less, we march quietly, stiffly at first through the subdivision's dim, slumbering streets. We could walk these streets blindfolded, following our route to a dead end, the park's entrance. In the dimness goutweed borders the path, a scourge that would overtake all the wood- and wetland plants. Eyes to the ground, we watch each step. Dawn has just begun to light the bottom of the sky.

Meggie would be aghast. *You guys! What if you fell? Think*

how long you'd lie there before someone found you. And, coyotes! Aren't you afraid?

Imagining this, I roll my eyes. *Yes, dear—and of skunks, squirrels, porcupines, deer, and snapping turtles. The animal threats never end, do they,* I would say, as though human ones do. *Don't be silly. Your father and I...*

But Meggie likes having the last word. *Like there being two of you makes a difference.*

Defending ourselves—*Of course it does!*—I would need to dig my heels in. Even if the rest of the time her dad and I keep each other at arm's length.

It was only after I noticed the herons during a solitary walk around the pond, Kirk agreed, grudgingly, to accompany me. That was our first time, after the parks reopened following lockdown. Oh, he fretted about the gutters needing cleaning, the hassle to find help, not to mention the walk itself. The pond is lake-size. But when he spotted the herons all was forgiven, if not forgotten.

Screened by marsh holly at the water's edge, Kirk and I stay stock-still. Binoculars were his idea. Out in the middle of the pond the herons congregate, like folks from another realm, old souls who don't much like or need each other's company. Reluctantly he hands over the glasses, my turn.

Viewed through their lenses, the birds make me think of pterodactyls, prehistoric visitors parachuted into now. Their presence almost suggests that whatever wiped out the dinosaurs didn't fully succeed: what once was could be again? (Or, like Meggie, I read too much into things?) Long-legged, wispy-feathered, bearded, they perch one to a rock, their feathers the same whitish grey as their roosts, half-submerged boulders anchored by lilies.

There isn't a breath of wind. The rising sun washes the

glassy surface orange. The birds—some of them tall and slender, others stocky—stand perfectly still, not a feather ruffled. They could be statues carved from their perches, although I can't imagine any sculptor carving those stick legs from granite. One, two, three…I count four birds, then scan the rocks closer to shore, spot two more, then a seventh. A cormorant perches nearby, a straggly hanger-on.

"Heron pairs mate for just one breeding season, you know," Kirk whispers. Nudges me to give back the binoculars. They find new *partners* each year, he says, the emphasis meant to amuse me. He explains to me what I've read: "By day mothers hunt for food while dads feed the young regurgitated goodies and guard the nest. At night the parents switch roles."

What youngster doesn't prefer having the mum there in the dark?

"The great blue heron is as common across Canada as—well, I was going to say flies." He sighs. "At this point, at least they're not endangered."

Handing back the binoculars, I marvel all the same: How magical to see them in numbers! Even small numbers. Each bird like a watchman guarding the edge of one world where it gives on to another, one humans can't enter—not in the bodily form that, especially on summer evenings, leaves me filled with an unbreachable longing, not for Michael's return, that would be too much, but just to know he is alive and, against all odds, okay. For him and Meg both to be—what, as I wish they could be? For Kirk and me to be what we haven't been for years, close? For the world to be one where goodness not awfulness prevails.

Meggie would hang up on me if I even mentioned this gloomy disposition, the disappointment that, who knows, plagues most mothers? The fact that we raise children to leave us, happily or aggrieved. To fledge their way into lives separate from ours, with other people, other bonds. Deeper bonds. Or no bonds at all.

Her kids, our grandkids, are too young for Meg to have more than the tiniest inkling of this.

Sharing his wisdom, Kirk tells me more of what I know. "Heron offspring leave after they fledge and disappear for nearly two years before they return and, if conditions are right, rejoin the colony."

Beside him, squinting, I fix a naked eye on the birds, a spy watching for movement. For one of them to bend and dart its bill below the surface to nab breakfast, for another to follow some urge to disappear. I imagine Meg coaxing nine-year-old Ava and seven-year-old Jonah from their beds, pouring almond milk, flinging toaster waffles on plates, drizzling on maple syrup, spreading plant-based butter, telling them to hurry because they can't be late *again*, and then, oh, telling me over the phone she has too much on her plate for any one person, what with kids and work and the house, while David's off on his daily jog before meeting clients.

In my imagination, I interrupt: *Tell me you're happy, Meggie*. The words would rush like hair gel from a tube squeezed too hard. Goop accomplishing no more than annoying her, delaying the start to her day.

So, forget words. Forget the speculations Kirk silenced before I could find the nerve to utter them. About Michael, of course, as lost to us, it's come to seem, as a fledgling scooped up by an eagle. Or trampled into the dirt of a beaten path by an unsuspecting hiker. The words that have never quit clamouring: *Suppose he's alive, where on Earth is he? Is he safe, fed, clothed, housed? Is he sick and suffering? On the street, or in jail?*

We raised him exactly the way we raised Meggie, the two just twenty months apart. How can the offspring of the same couple raised in the same nest turn out so differently?

We were too soft on him. Or too hard.

A heron flexes then lifts its wings. Its squawk volleys over the pond as it takes flight, a stiff grey arrow shooting toward the trees on the opposite shore, then gone. This leaves six great blues standing as still as can be, sleeping?

Is Michael asleep, wherever he might be?

On a trip to Vancouver before COVID, Meggie spotted a man who resembled him. He had Michael's build, Michael's slouch. The man was standing in the rain under an overpass, near some soggy tents and tarped shelters. There were needles on the muddy ground, people lying there. Some were shooting up, others looked unconscious, possibly not breathing. She looked the fellow in the eye, she told me, and he looked at her and, perhaps, in the wildest reaches of her imagination, there was recognition—a smile or a panicked look—before he turned to a woman in ripped jeans, then...

"No, *no*," Meggie had corrected herself, "Mum, it wasn't him. I would have known for sure if it was, he'd have spoken, I know it. A sister would know her big brother, right?"

I gaze out at the vacant rock, then turn away. Another squawk echoes and wings beat the air. The climbing sun pulls vapour from the pond, and I think, foolishly, *Where there is daylight, things lost should somehow resurface—shouldn't they?*

Kirk and I stumble back toward the path. Catch a parting glimpse through leafy boughs of the birds that have stayed put: the smaller ones, the females? But the exhilaration of our sighting has already begun to fade. Somewhere out in the harbour a horn blasts the *Love Boat* theme, one blared note at a time, a cruise ship signalling its departure, or so I've been told. Meggie knows these things. A good thing, I guess, having the cruise lines running again.

There's a story I recall from Sunday school a thousand years ago, about a woman who turns her house upside down looking for a lost coin, all the money she has to her name. How did she know it wasn't stolen? I used to wonder. How, in the first place, had she let it roll out of sight? Then there's the story of the profligate son whose father snubs, or seems to snub, the dutiful brother by welcoming home the ne'er-do-well with a feast of fatted calf the likes of which the good son would never dream of. Where's the fairness here? Beside the point, I guess.

Absence makes its own rules.

Kirk isn't a believer. I don't know if I am or not—even though the herons strike me as visitations from another, unearthly realm. Which I wouldn't dream of telling Meggie. She would drag me to the nearest dementia ward, have me assessed for whatever makes people lose their reason.

Motherrr, I can almost hear her, unable to keep a wistful envy from creeping into her voice. *Next you'll be naming one of them Mikey! Like he's morphed into a bird and if you wish hard enough, concentrate, there he'll be, perched on the deck or in the pine tree.*

There were times, I admit, Michael and his troubles soaked up attention better paid to his sister. All the same, correcting her, I would need to speak sharply, firmly. *Herons only gravitate to water, dear. Fresh or salt, as long as there's fish.*

End of discussion.

Except...did he look like he was eating? Was he dressed warmly? Was he sober? Did he seem all right? These are things I've longed to ask Meggie for four years and still haven't brought myself to. Because I know how she'd begin: *Mum, it's not like we chatted.* Because I'm afraid of her answers.

The last time we saw Michael, his dad yelled at him to shape up, get a job or get out: his choices. I cheered Kirk on, at least part of me did—the part that was sick of making excuses for Michael, of telling myself he just needed to "find himself," needed more time, etcetera, etcetera. The part that was tired of cleaning up after his messes in the kitchen, the squalor of his room, the angry chaos that seemed to trail him the way dust and dirt trailed Pigpen.

"This is how slums start!" I once shouted. As if I actually knew.

Gnawing disappointment, worry, a seedling grief—what I naively mistook for grief back then—these I knew, intimately, these feelings my close companions.

His final leaving was so quiet it caught us off guard, took several days, a week, to sink in, even though he took his backpack, his sleeping bag, his phone, and a few more clothes than what he was wearing.

"He's gone camping," Kirk said. "He'll be back."

After the third night, I wanted to call the police, report him missing. The dispatcher told me to phone around first, check with his friends, check the hospitals, make sure he wasn't admitted. I did. He hadn't been. By the fourth or fifth night I feared the worst.

"Don't worry," Kirk said. "When he wants money he'll be back."

It was true, Michael always wanted money. I was grateful when he asked instead of helping himself to my purse, his father's wallet, our dresser drawers.

On the sixth day, we filed a missing person report. A month or two later, the police confirmed they didn't know where he was. Imagine my relief when a few months after that we got a phone call: Michael saying he was in Alberta, wasn't coming home, and it would be better if we stopped hassling him, let him live his life.

"He's got some major growing up to do!" Kirk was right, of course. Except in my mind's eye I couldn't stop seeing the child Michael had been. Six years old, black-and-red rubber boots, yellow raincoat, a Ninja Turtles knapsack strapped to his back. The child whom I hadn't wanted to grow up, if I am being honest. Certainly not as he had.

The look in my boy's eyes still haunts me—a frozen, wounded look—before he hauled on his gear, headed out the front door, and disappeared for good.

You never know, do you? You just never know.

People say so all the time, but how intently do they mean it?

Meg's SUV IS in the driveway when Kirk and I turn up our street. Even loping along we're winded. She and the kids sit huddled on the front steps. Meggie's on her phone. The look on her face is fraught, more than just distracted. Has something happened? The kids refused to go to lessons? She and David had a fight? Oh, heavens, they're splitting up? When she sees us, she pockets the phone and dashes out to meet us. Her blond hair wisps out every which way from its large pink clasp, though she's dressed, I suppose, for work. It's hard to tell with those yoga pants and hoodie. ("Do you know how much these cost, Motherr?") She could as easily work part-time at a gym as in a dentist's office, where it seems every day is casual Friday. Receptionists come a dime a dozen, I gather: she's been let go? But then I see her nervous, flustered excitement.

"Maybe you guys should sit down. You're not going to believe it. Mum. Dad." She pulls in a large breath. Her hand flits to Jonah's shoulder, lights like a dragonfly. "He's contacted me. He's gotten in touch."

"Who, dear? Who?"

"Not Michael." Kirk's hand flutters to his chest.

"Yes, *yes*, Michael. It's true. Mikey. Our own."

I don't know if her tears are tears of joy or terror.

Kirk has his arms wrapped around both grandkids, crushing them in a hug.

I huddle on the bottom step, curl into myself. Breathe into my hands. I cannot move. My heart is in my feet, dragged to the tips of my toes by exhaustion, false hope, despair, and an old, old desperation—even as something inside me, something feathery, fragile, and unwilling, lifts.

Kirk reaches to pull me upward, to where he and the kids sit. Holding on to us, he buries his face in Ava's pink backpack. When he looks up I see a darkness in his eyes take flight.

"No, no," I keep saying. It's impossible. Questions enough for four lifetimes flood my head. But in my mind's eye—I have pictured this a thousand times—our boy approaches, getting closer and closer, lugging a grimy knapsack, a bedroll lashed to it. His face battered by weather, clothes ragged and filthy, and his heartbeat in my ear.

It's the sound of my own heart pounding, hedging disappointment, disbelief, the hope that hovers in between.

There's a soft, distant flapping, like sheets drying on a clothesline, and I look up, way up and away from Meggie and her liquid eyes, from her fledgling joy and dreadful fear, and though it is too far away to be certain, I'm pretty sure the grey shape winging its way over the house and treetops is a heron.

It's like seeing someone walk on water.

When? Where? How? The words are in my mouth but I cannot let them out.

"He's in town, Mum. He wants to come by. Asked if you guys are willing to see him."

We spare no expense, cannot include too many treats in our welcome-home feast. Meggie leaves the kids with us and goes to Costco, brings back lasagna (vegan and non-vegan), ribs, barbecue chicken, mac and cheese, tiramisu, non-alcoholic wine, chips, nuts, gummi worms and all kinds of stuff the kids love and, I'm guessing, she and David do too. She unloads everything while I race around the kitchen making a chocolate cake from scratch—Michael's favourite, the cake he always wanted on birthdays.

"You two are like chickens with their heads cut off," Kirk says. "You'll scare him off with all this stuff!"

Baking the cake calms me enough to set the table. Seven places. The good china, crystal water glasses. The silverware that hasn't been out of its chest since Meggie's wedding. Then I wonder, with a terrible pattering in my chest, if Kirk is right, if I'm jumping the gun, if the fuss—even just his sensing it—might drive Michael away from me, from us, once and for all. My nerves could be down feathers tickled by a breeze no one else feels, or feels as violently as I do, a breeze that would knock me down.

Meggie takes the children home to feed the dog, and then to pick up her brother—from where, she won't say. The bus station? The airport? A long-lost friend's? Kirk pours himself a drink, stiffer than usual. By now it's early evening; he's sipping it in the living room when the commotion starts out front. Meg and the kids pile out of her vehicle, just as David pulls up in his Audi. They've even brought the dog, who I hear before I see, a retriever that would lick you to death if you let it. Dogs make good buffers, Meggie believes. Byron bounds across the neighbour's lawn and squats.

David's busy unloading a case of something from the trunk of his car: champagne? The kids linger in the driveway, yelling to the dog. I don't see Michael—my boy is not to be seen; he's not here, at the last minute decided not to, refused, to come? Dismay, disappointment—closer to me than a twin sibling, it feels like—rush in, fill me with something murky as storm water. Meggie, meanwhile, digs around inside the car for a poo bag. Then, at last, she's opening the passenger door, the door opposite the one the kids hopped out of, holding out her hand.

The man who steps out is old—older than anything could have prepared me to expect. He's a little stooped and rugged-looking, but still tall and not badly dressed. He pauses there, looking down at the driveway's weedy interlocking brick, like someone who has landed in a foreign country, needs to figure out the terrain, find his bearings.

Meggie loops her arm through her brother's and rolls up on tiptoe to kiss his cheek.

No fatted calf. No slighted, righteous sibling, no fortune squandered—none that I am or have ever been aware of.

I'm stumbling down the steps, fumbling to take him into my arms.

Michael is thinner than I remembered. His grey suit smells of cigarettes and Value Village but fits him surprisingly well. He smells of hardship—and I think of the people I've seen outside the shelter where our neighbours, the ones who like to party, once invited me to help donate a meal. A huge casserole of hamburger meat, macaroni, frozen vegetables.

"Mom." His eyes warm to their old, soft hazel, the colour burned into my mind. His voice is the same, only—perhaps—a little rougher and yet gentler. Afraid?

When he speaks I see the gap where an upper molar is missing.

The kids hang back, hauling on Byron's collar, apt to strangle the poor dog with affection. Meggie pulls all three of them to her, crouching there, reining them in. David stands still, the carboard box in his arms.

Meggie shoots him a warning glance. "Mikey's been clean for, what, Michael, a couple of years now?"

Even standing on tiptoe I only come up to my son's chin but he bends into my arms and I hug him and hug him until our bones meld—that's how it feels, his an extension of mine: ribs, spine, shoulder blades under thin grey fabric, under the press of my hands. But only for a second, a long, fleeting second, before he pulls away from me and stalks slowly toward his father.

"Hey, Dad. What's goin' on? Don't look so worried. Think I'd come all this way after all this time to stir up shit?"

Inside the house everything is set. The food has been heated in the oven, is ready to be served. The cake is iced, the water poured. But something about the sun's angle, the evening with its soft yet fall-ish air keeps us there, suspended in this moment, each of us breathing it in.

Its shadowy light ripples over us, its blue the colour, I think, of mercy. Of second, third, fourth, and fifth chances—an untold, infinite number of chances, it has me believe.

Even when I imagine flight.

Acknowledgements

SEVERAL STORIES, OR EARLIER VERSIONS OF THEM, HAVE appeared previously: "Animal Kingdom" in *Understorey Magazine* (understoreymagazine.ca); "What a Friend We Have" in the *Coast* and in *Cape Breton's Christmas: An 8th Treasury of Stories and Memories;* "More Fish in the Sea," a response to Arthur Lismer's *Sackville River* in *The Group of Seven Reimagined: Contemporary Stories Inspired by Historic Canadian Paintings;* "Ripple" in The Scales Project (thescalesproject.com); "Scrub Land" in *Inside;* and "Flight Paths" in *The New Quarterly.* A much different, much earlier version of "Ship Time" appeared in *Aubade: Poetry and Prose from Nova Scotia Writers.* Thanks to their editors and publishers, respectively: Katherine Barrett, Stephanie Johns, Ronald Caplan and Breton Books, Karen Schauber and Heritage House, Bethany Gibson, Nevermore Press, Pamela Mulloy, Douglas Arthur Brown and E. Alex Pierce, Boularderie Island Press.

The epigraph to "This Talk of Trees" is from Anne Simpson's *The Marram Grass: Poetry & Otherness* and used with her permission. Information that appears in "Animal Kingdom" on the turtle's significance in Indigenous culture and spirituality is from online sources, including: "The Turtle teaches us TRUTH" (prevention.nd.gov/files/Seven_Sacred_Teachings.pdf); "Turtle Symbolism & Meaning" (whatismyspiritanimal.com/spirit-totem-power-animal-meanings/amphibians-reptiles/turtle-symbolism-meaning/); "Native American Animals: The Turtle (Keya) Symbolizes Grandmother Earth (Unci Maka)" (blog.nativehope.org/native-american-animals-turtle-k%C3%A9ya); "Snapping Turtles, Traditional Animal Foods of Indigenous Peoples of Northern North America" (traditionalanimalfoods.org), all accessed 11/10/2023. Additionally, the quote on page 30 is from Alan Syliboy's Daily Drum post on Twitter, now X, April 7, 2022, used with his permission. The term "thrival," on page 61 in "Alpha Frontier" and used with its wordsmith's permission, is from my friend, author, and poet Sheree Fitch. The information about Emily Jane Spicer Dewis in "Ship Time" is on display at the Age of Sail Museum, Port Greville, Nova Scotia; information about cruise ships and the *Mary Celeste* is from various online sources, including travlerz.com and smithsonianmag.com, respectively.

Thanks as always to my friends and family for love and support, a special shout-out to my PCSC bubble for camaraderie during and since the plague years, and to Lorri Neilsen Glenn, Ramona Lumpkin, and Binnie Brennan for their feedback on many of these stories as they took shape. Thanks beyond words to the crew at Vagrant, especially Whitney Moran, whose encouragement and vision mean the world, and my brilliant, wise beyond words editor, Paula Sarson. Thanks to Fulton Lavender, Martha Leary, and Kathleen Hall for the otherworldly Backlands birding experience, and thanks to Jeremy Vaughan for the use of his beautiful painting, *Herring Cove, Look-off Trail* (2019), a location close to my heart and the heart of these stories. And thanks to Bruce, my sweet travelling man. May we revisit all our favourite places.